Poppy's Dilemma

JB

Karly Lane lives on the mid north coast of New South Wales. Proud mum to four beautiful children and wife of one very patient mechanic, she is lucky enough to get to spend her day doing the two things she loves most—being a mum and writing stories set in beautiful rural Australia.

Also by Karly Lane
North Star
Morgan's Law
Bridie's Choice

Karly
LANE
Poppy's Dilemma

ARENA
ALLEN&UNWIN

First published in 2013

Arena Books, an imprint of
Allen & Unwin
83 Alexander Street
Crows Nest NSW 2065
Australia
Phone: (61 2) 8425 0100
Email: info@allenandunwin.com
Web: www.allenandunwin.com

Cataloguing-in-Publication details are available
from the National Library of Australia
www.trove.nla.gov.au

ISBN 978 1 74331 161 5

Set in 12.5/17 pt Sabon by Midland Typesetters, Australia
Printed and bound in Australia by Griffin Press

10 9 8 7 6 5 4 3 2

The paper in this book is FSC certified.
FSC promotes environmentally responsible,
socially beneficial and economically viable
management of the world's forests.

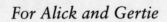

For Alick and Gertie

One

Poppy Abbott closed the door to her apartment and leaned against it wearily. Thank God it was Friday. She kicked off her heels and dropped her handbag on the hallway table, tugging her silk business shirt from the waistband of her grey pencil skirt on her way to the bedroom. She dropped the clothing into the laundry basket and pulled on her comfortable old yoga pants and T-shirt with a sigh of relief.

She poured herself a glass of wine and then sank down into her comfortable lounge, taking in the beauty of the Sydney skyline through her large glass windows. She had the life, she thought with a smile. People killed for a view like this, and it was all hers.

Her smile faded as she recalled the scene in the car park after work. Bloody Gill!

She hated that the job she loved so much was slowly

becoming a burden. It was getting harder each day to drag herself out of bed when she knew what, or more to the point, who, she was going to face when she got there.

Her phone buzzed on the kitchen bench and she didn't bother checking it. She could guess who it was.

Turning away from the twinkling lights of the city, Poppy looked over at the two boxes of photo albums she'd brought back from her grandmother's house in Warrial almost six months ago. She felt a twinge of guilt as she realised she hadn't even bothered to move the boxes from where she'd dumped them after the trip. She hadn't done a lot of things where Nan was concerned lately.

A few years ago, Nan had asked her advice—after all, having a granddaughter who was an accountant had to have its benefits. She wanted to borrow against the house to free up some cash and travel overseas. In order to save her grandmother taking out an equity loan and going through all the stress and worry that would have entailed, Poppy had bought her grandmother's house. It had solved a lot of problems. Nan had been able to live in the house indefinitely, without the worry of a loan hanging over her head, and it had provided Poppy with a decent investment.

However, *now*, six months after Nan's death, Poppy still couldn't face actually dealing with her grandmother's things. Each time she thought about it, she baulked. It still hurt to think about packing it all away. It was too final.

Nan had been such a huge part of her life. Poppy's father had died when she was seven and her only connection to him had been through his parents. Nan and Pop were the only set of grandparents she had, since her mother's parents had both passed away before Poppy had even been born. Her mother had remarried only a year later but she'd always been adamant that Poppy shouldn't lose touch with her father's side of the family.

Her stepfather hadn't wanted any more children—his were already teenagers when he'd married Poppy's mother. To her new half-sister and half-brother, Poppy, at eight, was too old to be cute and too young to be anything more than a pain, so she never quite felt as though she fitted in with her new family. Had it not been for her nan, and going back to Warrial, she wasn't sure she would have coped with feeling so much of an outsider at home.

Most school holidays and every Christmas break Poppy had spent at Warrial. Her nan had been part of every major event in her life.

Poppy didn't handle emotions too well, in fact she tried to avoid the more messy ones, like love and grief and rejection, wherever possible. She wasn't ready to face the finality of Nan's death just yet. It was too soon.

In her current mood tonight, though, she actually felt like a trip down memory lane. She needed something comforting and familiar to ward off the unpleasant events of her day.

She flipped through the brown-edged albums and smiled as she pored over the photos of her family. There were Christmas mornings when she was a toddler, everyone sitting around a small shabby Christmas tree, blurry-eyed, with bird-nest hair; her first day at school and school photos her mother had obviously sent so Nan could place them proudly into her albums. Poppy cringed at some of them, with the atrocious haircuts and missing teeth. She hoped Nan hadn't shown too many people these photos over the years—how embarrassing.

Poppy picked up the last album in the box and noticed something beneath it. She reached in and took it out. It was an old leather-bound book. Turning it over she saw gold-embossed initials sprawled across the front—*MA*.

Inside were folded pieces of paper which had yellowed with age. A large brass latch held everything securely inside. This was a diary. At first she thought it must have belonged to her grandmother, but the initials on the front were wrong.

The leather was well worn, as though this had once been someone's treasured possession. Poppy hesitated briefly as she released the clasp and opened the book. A diary was private. It was the place you could write your innermost secrets and dreams. But Poppy looked at the date scribbled on the inside cover and realised whoever this belonged to was well and truly gone, and she felt marginally better about intruding.

This diary belongs to Maggie Abbott.
February 1914

Poppy smiled at the youthful handwriting and tried to place the name. Obviously this Maggie, being an Abbott, was some kind of relative, although Poppy couldn't recall ever hearing of her. She did a quick calculation with the dates and realised Maggie would have been the generation before her grandparents, so it was going back quite a way.

The first year or so were girly ramblings that Poppy read through briefly, wondering at the innocence of the era. However, further on there were some neatly folded letters—*old letters*—in between some of the pages, scattered throughout the book. A quick examination of the date in the top corner of the first one made Poppy sit up straighter on the lounge. It appeared to have been written during the First World War. She began reading and was instantly captivated. This was a love letter. Written by someone who was pouring his heart out to Maggie.

She carefully refolded and placed the letter back where she'd found it. A brief glance at the dates on the top of the letters seemed to indicate that the placement of the letters may be important to the flow of the diary. She didn't want to read anything out of sequence, so she forced herself to go back to the start.

Two

9th June, 1914

How I hate winter!

I also hate cows! I will never grow up and marry a farmer. This morning there was a frost on the ground as we headed out to bring up the cattle for milking. I usually try to avoid the morning milking; I'd rather do anything but walk about outside in the cold and dark, chasing silly cows. Frank and Tom laugh at me hopping on the spot to keep warm—it's all right for them, they're boys and everyone knows boys can't feel the cold! Tom said I should go stand in a cow patty to keep my feet warm . . . I think Tom should go stick his head in one!

18th June, 1914

Bean harvesting has started.

I hate beans.

20th June, 1914
I saw Alex today, while I was picking beans. I was working close to the fence when he rode up. He was covered in dust and sweat but I thought he looked rather dashing—like a bushranger or something as he galloped up the driveway on his big brown horse. I almost fainted when he pulled to a stop beside me to say hello. Dulcie was across the paddock and had to spoil it by coming over to hog the conversation. Oh well, at least it brightened a dreary after-noon picking beans.

15th July, 1914
I'm tired of hearing about war. It's all Dad and the boys can talk about over dinner. The newspapers are full of horrible stories about Germans and the terrible things they're doing to people. Mum says it's nothing to do with us, that these things are happening in places on the other side of the world. I don't know what to think. I've always thought Germans were nice, like Mr Schulze and his wife who grow tomatoes a few miles out of town. They're German and it's hard to think of them as monsters, with their kindly smiles and cheerful 'gooday's' in their funny accent. Maybe it'll all blow over soon.

23rd July, 1914
I saw Alex today. I was delivering some beans (I'm so sick of looking at the darn things!) to his mum and he was home! Mrs Wilson made tea and we sat and chatted. It was nice not to have Dulcie there hogging the conversa-tion—although I always get so tongue-tied when Alex is around. Thankfully he didn't talk much and I was able to

answer most of his mother's questions without making a fool of myself.

His hand brushed against mine as he walked me to the front gate . . . I don't think it was an accident.

4th August, 1914
England has declared war. The news has sent everyone into a frenzy. Already men are talking about heading off to the city to sign up.

Mum and Dad are making Tom wait until they know more before he goes away to sign up. I think Tom wants to leave today, but he's said he'll stay and help Dad on the farm for a little while longer. I worry about him going, as does Mum, even though she tries to hide it. They all say this will be over before it even starts anyway. I hope they're right.

6th May, 1915
Tom has left for Newcastle today to sign up. He and Alex and three other boys from town took the train this morning. I'm not sure when we'll see them again.

7th August, 1915
Tom is home for a few days before he goes overseas. There's a strange mix of excitement and dread in the house. Tom can't wait to get over there and Dad is very proud of him. Frank's like a puppy bouncing around and wishing he was old enough to go with him. He looks very dashing in his uniform.

So does Alex.

12th August, 1915
The house is very quiet tonight. It's the last night before Tom leaves. Dad is very proud, of course ... and I think Mum is too, although I see her looking at Tom the same way she looks when she reads out the death and wounded notices in the paper. I know she's trying not to think about it as she packs his things, ready for the train tomorrow.

Frank is jealous—he's pouting because he can't join up yet. I don't know how I feel—scared mostly ... but then they say this war won't last too long ... I just pray Alex and Tom come back soon.

It was sad to wave them both off at the train station.

15th November, 1915
We heard today that Fred Barton was not allowed to enlist. When asked why, the recruitment officer told him that he already had four brothers enlisted and with his father having recently passed away, he should stay home and take care of his mother. The poor man obviously didn't know Fred's mother. Everybody calls Mrs Barton 'Granny'. I'm not sure why, she's hardly the soft, warm kind of woman you would think of as Granny. In fact she scares me a bit. I don't think I've ever seen the woman smile. Anyway, when Fred went home and told his mother what had happened, she marched back down to the hall and demanded that they sign him up. It caused quite a stir from all accounts, and after giving the recruitment officer a mouthful, Granny Barton announced that she would take her son down to Maitland and enlist him there!

I have to wonder why a mother would fight to send her son off to war ... maybe I'm just being silly, but I can't imagine why you would want all your sons sent to a far-off place like that.

20th October, 1915
It was a strange day. The boys marching from up north came through town today. Seventeen local boys signed up. There was much excitement and high spirits, mixed with a few tears. Mr Tobias Brown decided to make his opposition to the war known by following the procession with a pot on his head and marching in a goosestep fashion, just like the Germans! This didn't go down too well, of course. Granny Barton led the attack on poor Mr Brown, hitting him with her umbrella and calling him names (I told you she was scary!), then some of the boys from the march threw him in the river! It's not wise to openly oppose the war when so many of our boys are so keen to go and fight.

Poppy

Poppy found herself enthralled by the diary entries. Maggie was a spirited young thing and she clearly detested farm work. Each day there was something about the silly cows and all the extra work Maggie's family were doing to keep up with the demand of producing food not only for the local population but also for the war effort. Rations were getting tight, although at least Maggie and her family had plenty of fresh meat and dairy products, which was more than a lot of people must have had back then. Their farm was primarily a dairy farm but it seemed they also grew crops.

There was sprinklings of news about Tom through the next few years, and Maggie made mention of what she'd sent over to him in packages. Socks apparently were always welcomed, and Maggie wrote of how she, along with her sister and mother, would knit plenty of dark woollen socks to send in each parcel.

Maggie was a clever little thing, too, judging from the way she'd devised ways to save money and make a few small changes to the farm budget in order to send her brother a little extra money. Life it seemed was hard for a soldier on single man's pay.

It wasn't until she reached the entries from 1918 that she noticed there was a different tone to the diary; a maturity that had been slowly blossoming and was now unfolding between the pages.

> *12th January, 1918*
> *Tomorrow I start my very first paid job. I have been employed by Mr Fortescue at the bank and so I shall now, finally, be treated as a mature young woman!*

Maggie

Maggie stood patiently at the bank counter inside the solemn old building. She'd always loved the smell of this place. The rich, dark mahogany timber always felt cool to touch and the fixtures were so fancy and posh—nothing like the homey furnishings in the farmhouse, many of them made by her mother and grandmother over the years. The bustle of the street faded away once she walked through the heavy glass doors and into the sanctuary of the bank. Ever since she was a small child she'd loved everything about this building.

From the corner of her eye she watched Billy McCollum rub irritably at a bead of sweat that had been building on his forehead as he laboured over the sheet of numbers in front of him.

Mr Bruxton, the owner of Bruxton's Manchester store in town, tapped his podgy fingers against the counter as he waited for the daily takings to be deposited into his account. 'Hurry along, boy. I don't have all day,' he grumbled.

Maggie bit back the desire to reach over and correct the problem she could see from where she stood, at the counter next to him, chewing at her lip impatiently.

Arithmetic was her passion, always had been. From a young age she had helped her father keep the farm log, a journal that recorded everything from rainfall to the price paid and received from cattle and pigs sold at the markets. By the time she was eleven, it had become her job. It wasn't long before she was faster at calculating than her father and he was more than happy to hand over the financial side of the business, much preferring to work the land than spend his time adding up figures and paying bills.

However, her love of numbers was not something she would ever be allowed to indulge in outside of the basic accounting she did for her parents. She envied the employees who were able to come to work inside this majestic old building. What she'd give to be taken seriously enough to be given the opportunity to work here, to do what she was good at, but that was never likely to happen. Why was it men were the only ones deemed intelligent enough to hold important positions in the community?

School days were now over for the Abbott children. Frank had left school in order to help Dad, and Dulcie had been working as a maid at the hotel in town. Maggie was the only one of her siblings who had hated leaving school. Frank had let out a whoop of joy the day his father told him he was needed at home and would have to leave his schooling. Maggie, on the other hand, had cried and begged her parents to send her to the city so she could go on to study, but university was out of the question. There was no way her parents could afford to pay for further education when there was a war going on—even if her father had agreed—which he hadn't. At all. Maggie's future employment looked bleak indeed. A position was opening up as a trainee maid where Dulcie worked and she'd already put Maggie's name forward as a possible candidate. It was hard to look grateful when she couldn't think of anything worse than a life of drudgery, washing someone else's sheets and dusting their fine bone china.

With Tom away, life at home had become increasingly hard. Her father was one man short and it was now up to her younger brother, Frank, to do the majority of the work, with her mother, Dulcie and herself lending a hand whenever they could.

As usual, whenever she thought of Tom she felt a loneliness and a tight knot of worry as she wondered how he was, where he was, if he was all right.

'And just how do you expect me to continue to fund your little ventures when I keep losing employees to this damned war?'

The manager and his wife brushed past them, oblivious to Maggie and the other customer waiting at the front counter. Mr Fortescue was as loud as he was round. As the manager of the London Bank, he was the most respected man in town, along with the local doctor and the magistrate. However, it was Mrs Fortescue Maggie was most fascinated by and she stared from beneath lowered lashes at the woman as she followed her husband towards his office. She'd rarely seen her up close. Maggie recalled passing her once in the street; the smell of her perfume had lingered heavily in the air long after the petite woman had climbed into her fancy car and driven away.

Mrs Fortescue was what her mother would call a fish out of water. With her fashionable clothing and exotic, singsong accent, she seemed such an odd match for the portly Mr Fortescue.

The French woman's soft reply was lost as they disappeared through the door with the gold plaque inscribed with *Manager* across it.

Maggie turned her attention once more toward Billy and the tally sheet. When it became unbearable to wait a second longer, she leaned across the desk and took the pen from Billy's hand. 'You've miscounted up here. See? In this row.' Maggie quickly scribbled out the sum and added up the column with lighting speed, turning the sheet back toward Billy with a triumphant smile, which quickly fell away when she saw a furious Mr Fortescue, who had come out from his office unnoticed, glaring at her from behind his bank teller.

'What is going on here?' he demanded in a voice that seemed to echo around the chapel-like building.

Billy immediately began to stammer, 'S-s-sorry, Mr Fortescue . . . I-I-I was . . .'

Maggie cringed at Billy's stumbling attempts and stepped in quickly. 'I'm sorry to have been impertinent, but I really couldn't bear to stand here and watch Billy McCollum massacre that tally a second longer.'

For a moment she was met with shocked silence, then a small tinkle of laughter floated through the air from behind the manager.

'Oh Harold, I think you may have found a solution to your problem right here.'

'A solution? Are you insane, woman? Hire a *female* teller?'

Maggie's heart leapt into her throat. Surely she hadn't just heard what she thought she'd heard.

'Why not, *chérie?* You need another employee, and clearly this young woman has more than enough ability. Why would you turn such an opportunity away? Honestly, this country is so primitive in its thinking,' the woman scolded in her lilting French accent.

'I can't hire a female bank teller,' Mr Fortescue protested, although even to Maggie's ears his protest seemed weak.

'Of course you can. You are the manager. Who's going to stop you?'

This seemed to fluster the man even more, but his wife remained unflappable, standing her ground with a cool poise that Maggie found astounding. She wasn't used to seeing women stand up to men, and certainly not in public and with such self-assurance.

In fact Maggie was so caught up in her astonishment that she almost missed the announcement that she was to turn up the following day to begin her training. It seemed she had a job!

Her initial excitement soon vanished, however, once she informed her parents.

'Absolutely not! No daughter of mine is going to work in a bank.'

'You say that as though working in a bank is somehow immoral. It's a respectable job,' Maggie argued.

'It's not done. Women don't work in banks.'

'Well, that's just plain silly. If I can add up faster than Billy McCollum, why shouldn't I be allowed to work there?'

'Maybe we should think on it a little,' her mother cut in quietly, placing a hand on her husband's arm. 'I admit it's unusual . . . but what isn't these days? We're all doing things we wouldn't normally do . . . and we could certainly use the extra income.'

Maggie was certain that she had never loved her mother more than at that very moment.

She held her breath as she watched her father's frown slip a little, and when he threw his hands in the air and shook his head, she knew he'd given up the battle. 'The whole damn place is going crazy,' she heard him grumble.

'Language, dear,' her mother rebuked, but sent Maggie a small smile.

And with that, Maggie became the first female bank teller in Warrial.

Three

Poppy parked in her usual place the next morning and groaned when she saw that Gill was waiting for her by his car. Shutting her door a little firmer than was necessary, she pressed the lock button on her key and headed toward the elevator.

'Good morning, beautiful,' Gill said, falling in step with her.

'Morning, Gill.' *Just keep it professional,* she told herself.

'What's wrong? You seem uptight. I know how you could get rid of some of that tension,' he said, dropping his tone suggestively.

Poppy forced herself not to react, hitting the lift button and willing it to hurry.

Leaning against the wall, Gill reached out a finger and lightly traced it up her arm. 'I had a dream about us last night. Would you like to hear it?'

'Gill,' Poppy snatched her arm away, 'this isn't really the place for it.'

'Name the place, Poppy,' he said and there was a strange, almost urgent undercurrent in his tone. This was exactly the kind of thing that had been setting off her internal alarm bells for the last week or so.

'Gill, this has to—' she began, then stopped abruptly as the elevator doors opened and two men stepped out.

She stepped inside reluctantly as Gill held the doors open for her. Her hopes of someone rushing in at the last moment were dashed as the doors slid shut. 'I meant it, Poppy. Give me a time and a place to meet. We could go out to dinner . . . or something.'

'Gill, I can't.'

'It's because of Lynette, isn't it?'

'Your wife, yes,' she hissed. 'This *can't* happen.'

'Let me handle it, okay?'

Handle it? *Handle it!* Poppy shook her head in exasperation as the doors opened and they were in the foyer of their office. She didn't bother saying goodbye; she couldn't even look at the man. She hated that he was putting her in this position. In fact, she was certain he was deliberately playing dumb—no one could be that obtuse. For the last week she'd been avoiding him, ever since that one, *stupid* mistake. With a sigh, she collected her mail from the new receptionist, giving her a harried smile, then shut herself in her office, happy to escape Gill, hopefully for the rest of the day.

At lunch, Poppy made her way down the hallway, peeking around the corner to make sure Gill was busy in his office, and almost cheered when she saw he had a client in with him. Relieved, she slipped into the lift.

Not far from her office block was a quiet park. On days like this, she loved nothing better than to kick off her high heels and feel the grass between her toes. Finding a shady tree, she pulled out her packed lunch. Rummaging in the depths of her enormous handbag, she withdrew the diary she'd dropped in at the last minute on her way out the door and picked up where she left off the night before.

15th January, 1918

It's been a while since I've written. Although Dad isn't thrilled with my new job, he hasn't interfered, thank goodness. However, just because I now have a job doesn't mean I'm excused from helping around the farm. Bank duties are easy compared to farm work, but at least the work around the farm is tolerable now that I have some small escape when I go into work.

My presence at the front counter is certainly causing a bit of a stir with the customers. I've overheard more than a few complaints to Mr Fortescue since I've started. I'm not sure if he defends his decision to hire me because he actually likes my work, or because he doesn't want to look like he's admitting he's made a mistake by firing me. I try not to think too much about it—he's my employer and he scares me, so I just do my job and keep to myself.

28th February, 1918

I can't believe what happened today. I don't know how I will ever be able to show my face again! I acted like a complete numbskull! There I was, minding my own business. I'd just finished serving old Mr Coats, the grumpy old thing! When I looked up and smiled, ready to welcome my next customer, who should I find there grinning at me like an idiot? Alex Wilson! As large as life and cheeky as you please! My insides were jumping about like a cage of butterflies. I felt myself turning every shade of red imaginable and then stammered like a complete fool and I'm sure I made no sense whatsoever! Oh, I wish I had sounded grown-up and composed, instead of like a blubbering idiot!

Maggie

'I didn't believe Tom when he told me his baby sister was now a working woman.'

Maggie blushed deeply.

He was so . . . grown-up. A man. His dark hair clipped short, and his eyes, a deep mossy green colour that always made her think of the rocks down at the creek, sparkled back at her. He was as handsome as ever—maybe even more so in his uniform—and she struggled to compose herself.

'Hello, Alex. What a surprise to see you. Are you back . . . for good?'

'I'm afraid not. It's a working visit. I caught a bit of shrapnel from Fritz, so the army decided to put my down time to better use on a recruiting drive.'

'I wasn't aware you'd returned home.'

'No one was. I wanted it to be a surprise.'

'Not even your mum?' Maggie asked with a worried frown.

'Nope, not even Mum.'

Maggie stared at him in disbelief. Who did such a thing to their dear old mother? The poor woman had to be well into her sixties and not of the healthiest disposition. 'How did she take it?'

'She'll be right. Once she regains consciousness.'

Maggie's mouth dropped open in dismay, then abruptly closed as he laughed at her and she realised he'd been having her on. 'That was not nice, Alex Wilson. You should be ashamed of yourself, dropping by unannounced and then making fun of people like that.'

'You always were fun to have on. Come on, Maggie, don't be mad at me. I'm a returned hero, you know. You're supposed to treat me like a king,' he said with a grin.

'Did you come here for a reason today?'

'Yeah. To see you. But I s'pose now I'm here you'd better put this into my mum's account. She's a stubborn old goat sometimes, won't take the money I send back for her.'

Maggie stared at the money in Alex's big callused hand that rested on the counter and her heart melted just a little. Underneath that larrikin exterior was a gentle and caring man. For as long as she could remember, Alex had been part of her life—he was almost like an extra brother, only not quite. He and Tom had been inseparable ever since they were small boys. He seemed to enjoy spending time at their house, but Maggie had always thought it must be terribly lonely to not have any other brothers or sisters of his own . . . even if sometimes she wished she was an only child.

She could never explain it, but even as a young girl she'd known there was something special about Alex. He'd lost his father when he was young, and his mother, quite a strong-willed woman, had raised him on her own. And because of this, Alex had to take on the role of man of the house at a very early age. As she took care of his transaction Maggie felt tongue-tied and flustered. She was acutely conscious that he was looking at her, and he was leaning far too close across the counter for her peace of mind.

Her fingers seemed to fumble as she counted the money, and for the life of her she could barely manage the most basic of additions, but eventually the ordeal was over and she had locked the money in the drawer beneath the teller's counter.

'I'll be seeing you around then, Maggie.' He gave her a wink before putting his slouch hat back on his head and turning away.

All she could do was nod and summon up a weak smile of farewell. After watching him walk away, she found herself staring at the doorway for quite some time, jumping guiltily when her next customer cleared his throat to gain her attention.

Oh goodness, Alex Wilson was home.

Four

If there was one thing Poppy was most proud of, it was her professionalism and her dedication to her work. But that was before she'd discovered Maggie's diary. How such a seemingly innocent little object could weave itself into her life so quickly, she had no idea. She'd never been interested in history before, but there was something about this story that touched her.

She needed the distraction, too. Things at work couldn't continue as they were for much longer. She knew people were starting to gossip, and Gill wasn't helping by constantly hovering over her. She'd never had a particularly close relationship with any of her female colleagues, not that she didn't like any of them, but most of them were married and had children. She wasn't usually invited to any of the family-orientated gatherings outside work, and that was fine by her—there was only so much conversation she could take about the appropriate age to start potty training, or where to send your child to school. The funny looks she'd been getting lately, though, were beginning to annoy her. Maybe it was time to think about moving on.

Poppy put a frozen meal for one into the microwave and shut the door, setting the timer before she opened a bottle of wine and looked for a clean glass. She only had two. In fact, she only had two of pretty much everything. It made packing easier if you didn't have to waste time on a cupboard full of dinnerware you never used. She liked things simple. She suspected that was another reason she didn't quite fit in with the women at work—she wasn't interested in being set up with a boyfriend.

She preferred the no-strings-attached kind of involvement. It always amused her that it was completely acceptable for a man to have a different date each night—it meant he was some kind of stud—but if a woman did the same thing, she was labelled a slut. She didn't have a different guy each night of the week, of course; in fact she was extremely selective in her choice of men.

She didn't mind being on her own; she'd grown used to it. She liked not having ties to anyone; there was a certain freedom in the knowledge that she could just pick up and move whenever she felt like it.

She didn't see much of her stepfamily. She kept up with their whereabouts via her mother's weekly phone calls, but she had little in common with them, and she didn't feel any strong family connection to them. She'd left home as soon as she was old enough and she rarely went back to visit. She loved her mother, and they had an amicable enough relationship, although part of Poppy felt betrayed that she'd managed to move on after her father's death and been able to fit into a new family far more easily than she had. Admittedly it had been hard for any of them to get through to her—she'd been grieving the loss of everything that had been familiar to her and she hadn't been an easy child to love back then . . . She wasn't so sure she was any easier to love as an adult either. She liked people to keep their distance. It was always easier to push people away than get too close to them.

Taking her meal for one over to the lounge, she picked up the diary and settled in to read. Poppy didn't normally think of herself as a romantic, especially at the moment, but Maggie's budding romance was contagious, and Poppy found herself caught up in the thrill of Alex's return.

17th March, 1918

I've always thought myself a sensible, straightforward kind of girl. Dad's always telling me how dependable I am and people are often telling Mum how mature I am for my age, but ever since Alex Wilson has returned to Warrial I've found myself as breathless and giggly as those silly girls I detest who hang around town and bat their eyelashes at all the boys. I really don't know what to make of it. The moment I see him, I get the most dreadful attack of nerves and I can't for the life of me string together a complete sentence! Me, lost for words?

Maggie

Alex Wilson was not supposed to fall for her. It was supposed to be Dulcie, her older sister. That was what everyone had been expecting for years.

Maggie, though, had always thought about Alex. He was the hero she'd worshipped from afar. He'd been older, running wild with her brothers, while she'd been the annoying little sister her brothers had had to drag around with them and keep an eye on. But now they'd all grown up.

He was a man and she was almost nineteen.

He was the same age as her brother, Tom, but he seemed older somehow. Although no one really talked about it in front of her, she wasn't blind or deaf and she read the papers just like everyone else and she knew they would both have seen more of life and death in the last three years than anyone had a right to see in a lifetime. Looking into his world-weary eyes, Maggie could see that the experience had chased away all remnants of his youth and in its place was a wiser, quieter man. Was this what Tom was like now too? Had the war changed her carefree, handsome brother the way it had Alex? The thought saddened her.

She wasn't the only one who idolised Alex. Her younger brother, Frank, followed him around like an oversized pup and hung on his every word—constantly asking him questions about the war.

Dulcie thought Alex was boring. That brooding, lost look he sometimes got seemed to frustrate her and she'd stopped playing coy whenever he came around, fixing her attention instead on the other available men left in town. In small-town Warrial, 1918, there weren't many men left, available or otherwise. So many of the boys they'd grown up with had left for the war, seeing it as a grand adventure—a way to travel the world. Far too many of them would never be coming back.

At first Maggie had been envious of her older brother getting the chance to escape to foreign lands—what an opportunity! How else could anyone from a small rural town like Warrial ever hope to travel overseas? The war had been seen as a once-in-a-lifetime chance to travel to the other side of the world to places they'd never even heard of before—places *no one* in Australia had ever heard of before. The same places that were now being read about in the daily newspapers and bringing so much worry and grief for the families left behind. Maggie was no longer envious of her brother or the other boys who'd gone away. More and more of them were returning as the war dragged on and she could see they were shadows of the men they'd once been.

While Dulcie's infatuation with Alex had faded, Maggie's had flourished. During his recent visit to their home Maggie remained in the background—her usual place—while Frank and Dulcie dominated the conversation. However, Alex seemed to seek her out. He took a seat close to her and Maggie found it hard to concentrate on the conversation as she breathed in his scent of smoke, leather and soap and felt the warmth of his body radiating close beside her own. One look, one crooked little smile on his handsome face and she all but melted and went weak at the knees.

This was Alex, the same boy who had teased her mercilessly and taught her how to spit cherry seeds behind the chook pen. She couldn't explain these sudden new emotions, and they both thrilled her and scared her.

One afternoon as she prepared to leave work, Maggie tied the ribbons of her sunhat beneath her chin, gathered her long skirt in one hand and started to walk down the front steps of the bank. As she did so, a man detached himself from the front wall where he'd been leaning and Maggie caught her breath.

'Hello, Maggie.'

'Alex.' She sounded breathless and she fought to gain control over her senses before she made a fool of herself again. 'What are you doing here?'

'I thought I'd wait for you and walk you home.'

Her gaze ran up the length of him, dressed in the stiff woollen khaki uniform. When she reached his face, partially shaded by his slouch hat, she stared mutely. She was fairly sure she'd forgotten her own name. He was so handsome.

'Maggie?' he prompted, a small frown marring his forehead as he dipped his head to look into her eyes.

Embarrassed to be caught staring at him, Maggie felt the blush creeping up her neck and dropped her gaze. Before the war she could remember how she would look forward to seeing him when he came back from the bush after spending weeks hauling timber. Dressed in simple work clothing, he'd managed to make Maggie's heart flutter, but dressed in his army uniform, he looked like a different person—someone dashing and brave . . . someone who didn't belong here in Warrial's main street waiting to walk her home.

'You didn't have to wait for me,' she said, flustered.

She saw a slow smile spread across his face and she clenched her teeth against her body's treacherous reaction.

'I wanted to. Shall we?' he asked, putting out his arm for her.

'The army's turned you into a gentleman,' she said as she slipped her hand nervously into the crook of his arm.

'It's turned me into a lot of things—a gentleman is probably one of the better ones.'

Alex was stopped by quite a few people and he nodded his greeting to a lot more as they walked along the main street. Maggie tried to ignore the knowing looks and heads bent together in rapid whispers as they passed by. Part of her was embarrassed to find herself the subject of gossip, but another part beamed with quiet pride that Alex was quite openly showing his interest in her. Once they were out of town a silence stretched between them, but it wasn't uncomfortable. Maggie was enjoying the strong comfort of Alex's arm beneath her hand and his steady presence beside her.

'I hardly recognise you any more, Maggie,' Alex said after a while.

'Me? I haven't changed. Nothing changes in Warrial,' she added dryly.

'Some things do.' He went quiet for a while before adding, 'Tom showed me a photo your mum sent him—the one of you all at the show.'

Maggie knew the photo he was talking about—her mother had made them line up for hours to get it taken, to send to Tom.

'I stared at that photo for a long time.' He paused. 'I couldn't stop looking at you, Maggie,' he said finally. 'I couldn't stop thinking about you.'

'Oh,' she breathed.

Alex stopped and took his hat off his head, turning it around in his hands as they stood at the side of the road, facing each other.

'When I was told I was coming home I knew it wouldn't be for long and I knew that I couldn't waste the only opportunity I might get to tell you that,' he said in a rush, and Maggie glanced up at the uncharacteristic note of uncertainty in his voice.

'To tell me . . . what?' she asked quietly, holding her breath.

'That I can't stop thinking about you,' he said, sounding slightly exasperated. 'I've been pouring my guts out to you, Maggie, in case it escaped your notice,' he said with a soft chuckle and a shake of his dark head.

Maggie swallowed nervously. 'Oh,' she said again.

'Oh? That's it?' he asked.

'No,' she said with a slight stammer. 'I mean . . .' She searched her befuddled brain for something sensible and mature to say. 'Thank you,' she said weakly.

'You sure know how to humble a man, Maggie,' he said dryly.

'I'm sorry,' she said in a rush as she realised she'd hurt his feelings, reaching out to rest her hand on his arm. 'I'm just not sure what to say, Alex. I've always thought you were . . . I mean, to me you've always been . . .' She stopped and closed her eyes briefly, wishing she were as grown up and sophisticated as he somehow thought she was. Then she opened them and took a deep breath. 'I've been thinking about you too . . . I've never stopped, actually . . . since long before you went away.'

He searched her eyes for a moment before a slow grin spread across his face. 'Really?'

'Really,' she told him, trying to ignore the blush creeping across her cheeks.

Alex lifted a finger and moved aside a lock of hair that had come loose from her bun. His touch sent goosebumps across her skin and set off butterflies in her stomach. How long had she dreamed of Alex looking at her like this, as though she were the most precious thing on earth? Maybe it was a dream.

'What's wrong?' Alex asked, his finger dropping from her face uncertainly.

'I was just thinking . . . maybe this is all a dream,' she said.

He grinned again and took a step closer, his hands cupping her face gently as he lowered his head and kissed her. 'Does this feel like a dream to you?' he asked, his voice sounding husky.

'Yes,' she breathed. 'Only better than all the times I've dreamed of it.'

He chuckled softly and kissed her once more, longer and deeper, until Maggie thought she might self-combust at any moment. Over the next few weeks, Alex spent whatever free time there was back in Warrial between his recruitment commitments around the district. Maggie wasn't afraid of Alex's small lapses in conversation, or the way he startled at loud noises and sudden movement. She knew that it must be hard for him to suddenly find himself in a place where he no longer had to watch his every move. Something like that wouldn't be easy to turn off.

A gentle afternoon breeze blew up the creek where Maggie and Alex were resting after a lazy afternoon of swimming. For Maggie the day couldn't have turned out any more perfectly. She, Alex, Frank, Dulcie and her new beau, Gordon, had taken a picnic down to the creek, but the others were swimming further downstream, leaving Alex and Maggie alone.

'Do you get scared over there, Alex?' Maggie asked, breaking the peaceful quiet that had settled upon them as they listened to the others frolicking in the water.

'Yes,' he said simply.

Maggie turned her head to look at him. His strong jaw was set, but he seemed relaxed enough, resting on one elbow, and his expression didn't seem to be warning her to stop asking questions. 'I heard how you got your distinguished conduct medal,' she said quietly. 'That was a very brave thing you did.'

He looked away. 'I just did what had to be done. Someone had to get those guns up there, and I was in charge.'

'I think there might have been more to it than that.'

Alex shrugged nonchalantly but his face seemed guarded now. 'I just did what anyone else there would have done,' he said again, pulling at a blade of grass. 'Men are dying over there every day doing far more heroic things. I'm no hero, Maggie.'

'You are to me, Alex,' she said gently, and felt her cheeks darken as he lifted his gaze to hers and held it.

For a long moment, Maggie held her breath. She yearned to reach out and touch him to make sure he was real. How many years had she adored Alex Wilson from afar, dreaming of him noticing her. Why would he have? She was the younger sister of his best friend. The *plain* younger sister at that. Dulcie was the pretty one with, bouncy blonde curls and big blue eyes, not to mention curves in all the right places that seemed to draw boys to her like bees to honey. Doubt settled heavily inside her and Maggie chewed at the inside of her lip anxiously. What could someone like Alex possibly find attractive about a plain Jane like her?

A sudden shriek filled the air and drew their gazes towards the water, where a water fight had broken out between the others, and the tranquillity of the moment was broken as yells and screams echoed up the creek.

'I miss this,' Alex said after a few minutes. 'The sun on my back, people laughing, the *quiet*.'

Maggie wished she could think of something to say, but really, what could she say to make the reality of what he'd been through seem less horrifying? The fact that he was due to go back again just made it worse. 'Maybe it will end soon?'

She heard his bitter little chuckle and instantly felt depressed. How many more would have to die? How many more endless days of worrying and wondering were loved ones supposed to endure?

'Even if it does end soon, nothing will be the same again. I'm not sure the end will bring anyone the peace they crave.'

Maggie sat quietly beside Alex and mulled over his words. They sent a small quiver of unease through her, but it was the despair she saw in his eyes that unsettled her the most.

22nd March, 1918
Alex has asked me to the dance at the hall tomorrow evening! The Church of England is hosting it so there's sure to be a big turnout. Usually I have to go home when

Mum and Dad leave. Dulcie, being older, always gets to stay and walk home, but Alex has already asked Dad if he can see me home!!

What on earth will I wear? I'll have to raid the sewing box and pray Dulcie has left some material for me to be able to throw together a new dress!

Maggie forced herself to concentrate on her breathing as she walked into the hall that evening. She was so overcome by a mix of nerves and excitement that she could barely think straight. Beside her Alex stood tall and proud in his uniform. He was so handsome she thought she might actually swoon if she looked at him for too long.

News had travelled fast over the last few days. Alex's frequent visits to the Abbott farm hadn't gone unnoticed. Maggie tried not to feel self-conscious about the curious gazes and low whispers that followed their progress around the hall. She was becoming used to being the latest topic of gossip. It was still somewhat of a novelty that she was working in the bank. She hoped her father didn't overhear anyone talking about that tonight. She didn't want to set him off again, hearing how women just didn't do that sort of thing. To listen to him, you'd think she was breaking in wild horses or felling timber!

The hall was lit up, kerosene lamps burning brightly. It was obvious this was a big event as kerosene was under ration. Candles would not do for a dance that had attracted *dignitaries.* The dance had been organised to coincide with Alex's return home and had in fact been part of the conditions of his leave. The army was trying to sign up more men and it was hoped he could be 'the face of the war' to help secure more volunteers. The initial flood of volunteers in the first few years had dwindled to a trickle and so there was a recruiting drive under way to bring up numbers.

Streamers decorated the walls and colourful signs saying *Fight for King and Country* and *Australia! Your country needs you* were placed at the front of the stage. Maggie smiled and waved at Enid Crawford up on the stage. Enid was only a year younger than Maggie but had earned a reputation for being one of the most talented pianists in the district. She was very pretty, but painfully shy except when she was behind her piano. Mr Adams, the local music teacher, accompanied her tonight on the violin and already there were a number of people on the dance floor.

Nervously Maggie ran her hands down the skirt of her dress. She hated sewing but had done it this time out of pure necessity. She'd wished while she'd been unpicking a seam for the *third time* that she had Dulcie's ability when it came to sewing. Her sister could run up a new dress in a matter of a few hours, while Maggie had been hunched over hers most of the day and had been seriously thinking about setting fire to the darn thing for much of that time! Nevertheless, in the end she had triumphed, and as long as nobody looked too closely at the seams, everything would be fine.

She actually felt quite pretty for a change in the modest dress she wore. It was a shade of green that suited her darker complexion. She'd been lucky Dulcie hated green in any shade and hadn't used the material for herself. Given she wasn't an expert seamstress, she'd stuck to a simple straight design with a sash made of the same material that fitted nicely just below her bust and emphasised her slim waist. Dulcie had helped fix her hair into a loose bun and teased long tendrils to fall gently about her face.

'You look beautiful, Maggie,' said Alex quietly, leaning in to her.

Somehow he knew she was feeling uncomfortable and she drew strength from his quiet praise, holding her head a little higher as they moved toward the dance floor. She caught sight of her parents and saw her mother's approving smile. Her father was less animated, but his usual troubled frown was nowhere in sight tonight.

Alex took her in his arms and they began moving across the timber floor, joining the other dancers. Maggie stopped worrying about everyone else in the room and reminded herself how brief this escape was for Alex. Within a few days he'd be returning to the war and she'd only have this night as a memory when he left. Thanking the logical side of her brain for coming to the rescue, she pushed any lingering insecurities aside and allowed herself to simply enjoy the gift she'd been given.

Dance after dance they shared, and finally, at the end of a more lively number, Maggie had to stop and catch her breath. They made their way towards the chairs lined up along one side of the wall, Alex stopping to talk to familiar faces as they went. It seemed everyone wanted to have a chat with him. That was to be expected, though; having grown up in Warrial and been involved in the football club— something that was very important in the district—he was known by just about everyone and was certainly the hero of the moment. Maggie didn't mind; she was happy to see him smile and proud to be by his side.

As the MC, Mr Frederick, stepped up and made the evening's announcements, cups were handed out from large washtubs and the women from the church committee went around the room filling them with tea that had been boiled outside over the open fire. More ladies followed with milk, sugar and sandwiches from large platters.

Whilst the dancers took a breather the raffles to raise money for patriotic funds were drawn and the winner of the competition, to guess the name of the beautiful hand-made doll donated to the cause, was announced. Games of euchre were played at tables around the hall and quite a tidy sum of money was raised. Afterwards Alex excused himself for a moment and shortly afterwards Maggie glanced up at the stage as a familiar voice echoed around the hall.

'Good evening, everyone. I've been asked to come up here tonight and sing a few songs,' Alex announced almost shyly.

A cheer rose from the crowd and Maggie waited with anticipation, wondering what he'd sing. Before the war, Alex had often sung at dances and she'd listened on with pride from her parents' side, wishing secretly that he was singing those songs to her.

Alex began softly to sing 'If you were the only girl in the world', and Maggie's heart went into flutters all over again. His deep smooth voice reached out and touched her and he held her gaze from across the hall, making her feel as though they *were* the only two people in the world. His voice seemed to wrap itself around her and her heart began to pound against her chest. The thunderous applause and catcalls were an unwelcomed intrusion at the end of the beautiful song and Maggie forced a smile to her lips as she belatedly joined in the clapping.

He sang a few more songs—rowdy renditions of popular songs to boost morale—before a small parade of local councillors and other returned servicemen went up on stage.

Memories of the early recruitment drives that had enticed her brother and Alex to enlist surfaced and Maggie felt a chill run down her spine. The war had been going on three long years now, though it felt more like ten. Now, after so many boys had died or returned wounded, how could they possibly try to convince anyone else to sacrifice their loved ones to a war on the other side of the world? How many more *able bodies* were left?

'We've all read about the Germans and their Operation Michael,' said Mr Partridge, the editor of the local newspaper, speaking over the hum of voices. 'I don't have to tell you the devastating impact this German push has had on the Allies. But it's clear, ladies and gentlemen, that if we don't do something now the threat of Germany winning this war will be a reality.'

A low murmur went through the crowd. This wasn't the first time Maggie had heard those terrifying words over recent days; it was all she'd been hearing at work and on the radio, and the newspapers were full of it. Germany seemed to have the upper hand as they regained precious territory they'd lost to the Allied forces. Maggie felt ill over the number of casualties being reported; if the news was to be believed it was heading upwards of seven thousand five hundred men. It was hard to believe those kind of figures. So many lives destroyed.

As she listened to the speakers reminding the men it was their patriotic duty to enlist, Maggie fought the urge to protest. They tried to make those men who had not yet enlisted feel obligated, implying that if they didn't enlist now they'd be letting down their mates who were already over there doing their duty for their country and the crown.

It was wrong.

Alex was standing to one side of the stage as the speakers continued to use him as an example of bravery and selflessness. Maggie saw that his gaze was fixed on a point high up on the rear wall of the hall; he seemed detached from the speeches going on around him.

She could tell he hated being up there on display, but his military training held him in place, obediently doing what he'd been ordered to do. He was here to raise support and encourage the reluctant men of the district to enlist. He was a weapon in the army's propaganda arsenal, and he hated it. She could sense it. He didn't want to be part of this any more than the few eligible men squirming around her. There weren't many who fell in the bracket of age and fitness to enlist but for various reasons hadn't. Boys like Wally Simpson who stood across from her, head lowered and looking like he'd rather be anywhere else in the world. He was around Frank's age and had already lost two older brothers, one on the beaches of Gallipoli and the other on the battlefields of France. His mother, Mabel, was a hard-working woman who had lost her husband just before the war in a farming accident and still had three younger children at home. How could *anyone* expect that family to sacrifice any more? Wally was needed at home. There was no way Mabel could run the farm and take care of her younger children alone. The poor woman was still grieving for her two lost sons, for goodness sake.

From her own family's experience, she knew that keeping the family farm going was hard work when there was limited manpower available. Who was going to grow the food if all the workers were taken? There were limited returned servicemen who were able-bodied enough to cope with the heavy physical side of farming. How could they not see how illogical their mentality was?

Fresh anger swelled inside Maggie. How dare these people stand up there and demand such things! Her heart went out to Wally for the inner turmoil he must be going through, feeling obligated to fight and yet knowing he had responsibilities here at home—responsibilities far too big for a boy of eighteen to have to shoulder. Yet in these horrible days, so much more was being expected of everyone. Too much, Maggie thought.

Five

Poppy closed the computer and packed away the work she'd brought home to finish. She'd taken to leaving the office early. Between the gossip she knew was circulating and Gill just *being* there, she couldn't concentrate at work.

Thank goodness this case was almost finished. Tomorrow she would be in court most of the day and then her part in the whole process would be done. She loved the challenges her job brought, playing detective and successfully untangling the intricate webs people used to cover their financial tracks. However, money always left a paper trail and although at times it could be extremely painstaking to track down, she always felt a huge sense of achievement when she finally did.

Earlier she'd promised herself that if she managed to finish all the paperwork she'd brought home she'd reward herself with a few more pages from Maggie's diary. It was late but surely she could squeeze in just a couple of pages. She was completely hooked by the unfolding tale of a young girl's life during the First World War.

Who *was* this Maggie Abbott, and where did she fit into her father's side of the family? She decided if she got enough time tomorrow she'd give her nan's sister Myrtle a call and see what she could find out.

'Maggie Abbott?' Myrtle pondered aloud the next day. 'You know, I don't have any idea, Poppy,' came the frail reply. 'I knew a few of your grandfather's family, but not a lot about that generation, I'm afraid.'

Myrtle was the last remaining of her nan's three sisters. Poppy wasn't surprised she hadn't heard of Maggie, given she was only related to the Abbotts through her sister's marriage.

'She mentions brothers, Tom and Frank. Does that help?'

'I think your grandfather had an uncle called Tom who died during the war. But that was long before he was even born. And Frank was your granddad's father, but I can't place a Maggie anywhere.'

Poppy frowned on her end of the line. It had to be the same family and it made her sad to think that Maggie's older brother Tom, whom she'd obviously loved a great deal, had never come home from the war. She tried to imagine how hard it must have been to wave off husbands, fathers, brothers, fiancés without knowing whether you'd ever see any of them again.

Another thought occurred to her then: if Maggie had been Frank's sister, then she would have lived in the same old farmhouse her nan and pop had lived in until they'd sold it to move into town, because she knew that it had been passed down to Pop from his father and he'd always been proud that he came from such a long line of farming Abbotts.

'Leave it with me. I might remember something if I think on it for a few days. '

'Thanks, Aunty Myrtle.' The phone call left Poppy strangely dissatisfied. She'd been hoping for answers and hadn't got any. She berated herself that if she'd bothered to research her family history before now Nan would have been able to fill in all the blanks, but as usual it seemed that most of life's lessons were learned too late.

Maggie

Maggie found herself thinking back over the night of the dance all the next day. After Alex had come down from the stage, he'd seemed distant. Their connection while he'd been singing was gone and they hadn't danced to any of the songs that followed the speeches.

Confused, Maggie had sat silently, feeling Alex's withdrawal like a tangible thing. Thankfully the dance had concluded soon afterward and they had set off on the walk home.

A steady line of people had made their way along the road. Couples were scarce compared to before the war, although with more boys returning home each day there were a few romances rekindling and those couples walked apart from the rest of their friends, holding hands and sharing the last few precious moments together before having to go their separate ways. Couples like Dulcie and Gordon. Gordon had enlisted around the same time as Tom and Alex but had returned from the war injured, having almost lost a leg in an explosion. His leg had been saved, but he would always have a limp and his fighting days were over.

Maggie and Alex had been left to make their way home alone. Dulcie was already further ahead, Maggie could hear the tinkle of her laughter floating back toward them.

'It was a lovely evening,' Maggie volunteered when the only sound between them was their footsteps on the road.

'I'm glad you had a good time.'

'Alex, is there something wrong?'

Alex shook his head. 'I'm sorry, Maggie. I shouldn't have let my mood ruin the evening for you.'

'Was it the speeches?' That was when she'd first noticed he'd lost his smile.

'No. It's just . . .' Alex gave an impatient sigh. 'I'll be leaving soon . . . to go back. We're running out of time. I'm sorry about tonight. Let me make it up to you. I'll pick you up tomorrow after church and we can spend the afternoon down by the creek. Would you like that?'

Maggie swallowed nervously before answering. 'I'd like that very much.' Despite the fact he was Church of England, while the Abbotts were Roman Catholics, her parents had never held that against him. Maggie knew she was lucky that her parents were a little more flexible in their views— many families in the district would not countenance their children stepping out with someone of a different religious denomination.

That night in bed, Alex's words echoed in her mind. He'd be leaving soon. Just as quickly, she pushed it away. She couldn't bear to think of that yet, not when he was still here and she would be seeing him again tomorrow. Maggie's heart beat wildly at the thought of seeing Alex the next day. She didn't care that her father insisted Dulcie and Gordon join them—as long as she got to see him again.

True to his word, Alex arrived after church and they walked down to the Abbotts' swimming hole to enjoy a peaceful picnic by the creek. After they had eaten a lunch of cold meat and homemade bread, Dulcie and Gordon took a walk together, leaving Alex and Maggie alone.

'Tell me about the places you've seen, Alex,' Maggie said as they lay side by side on the grass. 'The nice places, not the . . .' she trailed off.

'Even the nice places aren't that nice any more.'

'Maybe not, but at least you've seen them.' She knew through Tom's letters home that Alex had been in the same places he'd been in—foreign, exotic places like Egypt, London and Paris—places she could only ever dream about seeing. 'It must have been amazing. What were the pyramids like? Did you see the Tower of London?'

Alex smiled down at her tolerantly and shifted his weight so that he lay back on both elbows.

'The pyramids are amazing, just as you imagine them. I remember staring up at them and feeling like I was a speck of dust in comparison. There was something mystical about them.'

Maggie hung on his descriptions of London and Paris and the things he'd seen whilst he'd been on leave in other places. He described things in such detail that Maggie almost felt as though she had been there with him.

'It must be nice to find some beauty, even in the middle of a war,' she said softly.

Maggie watched his features harden once more as he stared out over the water. 'The beauty is far and few between.'

'One day I'm going to go and see those places,' she told him.

When he pierced her with his dark stare, she felt her smile waver slightly.

'You think your father would allow you to travel across to the other side of the world by yourself?'

'Who knows? The world's changing. Look at Warrial. I'm a female bank teller! Who would have thought that could ever happen?'

Alex smiled. 'Then who knows what's going to be possible once this thing's over.'

They didn't talk about what would happen if the Germans won. It was too hard to comprehend, especially so far away in remote little Warrial, so Maggie pushed the uneasy thought to the back of her mind.

She closed her eyes and listened to the sound of the creek and the insects buzzing in the air. A gentle touch to her cheek made her open her eyes in surprise. Alex was leaning over her, his expression as gentle as his smile.

'I wish I could take this moment back with me.' At the confused wrinkle of her brow, he added, almost shyly. 'I wish I could capture this moment, how you look, how you smell, how you feel.'

Maggie felt her heart begin to hammer through her

chest as his fingers softly traced a path from her cheek to her throat. She didn't dare breathe in case it broke the spell. When his lips gently touched her own, everything around them seemed to still. There was no drone of busy insects, no birds tweeting merrily in the treetops above, just Alex's warm lips upon hers and a painful stab of desire inside.

Breathing heavily, Alex lifted his head and stared deeply into her eyes. 'You don't know how long I've waited for you, Maggie.'

Alex had been waiting for *her*? 'But you've never even looked at me.'

'Oh, I've looked,' he chuckled. 'And I've been waiting, not so patiently, to do something about it.'

'But . . . why? What do you possibly see in someone like me? Dulcie is—'

'Not for me,' Alex finished, brushing her hair from her forehead. 'You really have no idea how beautiful you are, do you?'

'I'm not.' Maggie swallowed past her uncertainty. No one had ever called her beautiful before. She'd been called determined, mature-for-her-age, and sometimes over-opinionated, but never beautiful.

'Ah, Maggie,' he whispered. 'You're as beautiful on the outside as you are on the inside. Do you remember the show a few years back? When Dulcie forgot to clean out the dairy?'

How could she forget? Dulcie had entered a beautiful piece of embroidery and could hardly wait to see if she'd won first place with it. She'd been so preoccupied with getting ready for the big day she'd forgotten about her chores. Furious, their father had stormed into the house to find out why they hadn't been done.

'You took the blame for that so Dulcie could go to the show,' Alex reminded her quietly.

Maggie remembered the tears that had fallen from her sister's eyes and knew it would have broken her heart after all the hard work she'd put into creating the delicate piece. She hated cleaning the dairy but she loved her sister and she couldn't stand watching her spirit break under their father's strict authority. Maggie was the child her father clashed with the most, and so being reprimanded for her forgetfulness wasn't something out of the usual. It had only occurred to her afterwards that by telling her father she was the one who'd forgotten about the chores and being banned from going to the show meant she wouldn't get to see Alex. But how could she have not done it? Poor Dulcie would have been crushed had she not been there to claim her first prize ribbon.

'She would have done the same for me.'

Alex shook his head slightly. 'Are you sure about that, Maggie? Dulcie's always been more than a little pre-occupied with herself. I don't think I'd put it to the test if I were you. No. Only *you* would have done that. You've always had a beautiful nature and I think that was the day I realised I'd fallen in love with you.'

Maggie sucked in a breath as she stared up at him in surprise. 'You fell . . . in love with me?'

'I did. And I'm more certain of it now than ever.'

Maggie stared up into his green eyes; seeing how soft they had become turned her insides to jelly. She reached up and laid her hand on the side of his face, watching as his eyes drifted shut at the touch.

'Ah, Maggie,' he whispered on a sigh, covering her hand with his own and bringing it to his lips to kiss gently.

How was she ever going to say goodbye to this man? What if she never saw him again? The thought almost crippled her with grief. She squeezed her eyes shut tightly and tried to block out the horrible thought, opening them to find him looking down at her intently. 'Please come back to me, Alex,' she whispered.

His eyes crinkled as he smiled. 'You've always been my reason to come back. Now I know what I have to fight to come back for, wild horses couldn't keep me away.'

Maggie wasn't sure her heart could contain all the emotion she felt gathering inside her, but a sudden whoop of laughter and playful squealing echoed up along the creek then and intruded upon their moment.

'Come on, that looks like fun, let's get our feet wet,' Alex said, standing up and reaching down to pull her upright.

Maggie shrugged off her melancholy feelings. She couldn't waste a single second of the time they had left together feeling sad; there would be plenty of time for that after he left. For now she would feast her eyes on the man she loved and savour every moment of him.

Six

Poppy placed the diary on the bedside table, closed her eyes and let her mind play over what she'd just read. She'd never really stopped to think how hard things would have been during the war years.

She recalled Nan talking about being a young girl during the Second World War, but it was strange that she'd never really considered how different things must have been then. *The self-centeredness of youth,* she thought with a sigh. She'd sometimes rolled her eyes when Nan had saved leftovers or reused bits of material; Nan had never liked to waste anything, and was always darning socks or patching old shirts. She'd been born into an era when resources were scarce and precious, not unlike the times Maggie had lived through. *We take so much for granted nowadays,* Poppy thought sadly.

She pictured her nan at her happiest, in her kitchen, gently humming a song under her breath as she created some baking masterpiece. There were never any packet biscuits or cake mixes in Nan's house—she made everything from scratch. Good, wholesome country cooking. Poppy's mouth actually began to water for a chunky stew and dumplings.

She wondered what Maggie had looked like. She supposed it would be the opposite to Dulcie, whose fair-haired beauty Maggie had occasionally made mention of.

Poppy had what was politely called mousey brown straight hair and her father's darker features, her eyes a deep almost navy blue framed by dark lashes that her mother had always said were her best feature. Nowadays, though, thanks to the very expensive hair stylist she regularly indulged in, she had honey and caramel highlights over a deep chocolate brown base.

Her stomach grumbled. 'Great,' she sighed, now she was craving chocolate.

She glanced at the clock and groaned at the hour. She had to get some sleep before court tomorrow. 'Goodnight, Maggie,' she said, rolling over and dreaming of a handsome soldier with mossy green eyes.

25th March, 1918
I don't know how I shall say goodbye tomorrow. Alex is leaving. I have promised to see him off, but I know there will be too many people at the station, my family included, for me to be able to say the things I long to say to him.

How can we have found each other, only to lose one another again so soon?

It feels as though the moment I saw Alex again, life as I once knew it ended. A new life has opened up before me, a life with Alex. I see children and laughter and so much love that I can almost reach out and touch it. But he's leaving me to go back to that horrible war and I am terrified that all the things I see in our future will be ripped away from me.

It isn't fair! I hate that I have to let him go. I feel like lying down on the floor and throwing a gigantic tantrum, but what use would that be? The whole country is saying goodbye to their loved ones. If only this stinking war would end!

Maggie

The train station was busy. She remembered the last time she'd been here, to farewell Tom, and Alex had been leaving as well. The platform had been packed tight with people saying their teary goodbyes to sons, brothers and husbands. She remembered Tom's grinning face; he couldn't wait to get going, off on his big adventure, Alex just as eager beside him. Looking at Alex now, she couldn't help but compare his resigned expression and feel the emptiness of loss. Those two carefree boys were long gone now.

Late last night she'd written Alex a letter with all the things she couldn't tell him today. She'd told him about the things she saw in their future and that she'd be counting down the days till he returned. She told him how much she loved him—how much she'd always loved him, even if she hadn't completely understood that's what she had felt.

'Don't open it until you've left,' Maggie said, handing Alex the envelope.

He stared at it in his hand before lifting his gaze to meet hers steadily. 'I'm coming back,' he told her firmly.

His words struck at her heart. 'I know,' she whispered, praying she wouldn't break down and cry here in front of everyone.

The stationmaster's voice rang out across the platform and Maggie stepped back to allow Alex's mother to say her goodbyes. The two women stood side by side, their gazes never wavering from the train as it disappeared down the track.

30th May, 1918
It's with a broken heart that I write in here today. I was tempted to simply lie down on my bed and cry until there was nothing left, but after two days of this, it seems there's no end to the terrible pain and torment. Our beloved Tom is dead. Mum and Dad received the telegram while I was at work and sent Mr Crawford to work to fetch me home. I've never seen Mum look so wretched, and Dad vanished out into the paddock and didn't return until well after dark. They both look like they've aged a good twenty years since they received the news. I can't imagine life without Tom in it and yet this is how it will be from this moment on. Our darling Tom is lost to us forever.

The long grass swished around the bottom of her skirt as Maggie trudged across the paddock towards her brother.

He was walking behind the plough as it dug deep trenches, turning up the dark soil in preparation for seeding.

'Lunchtime, Frank,' Maggie called.

She saw him look over his shoulder at her. Once his eyes would have lit up at the thought of food and he'd have raced across to meet her. There was no bright boyish grin now, he was just existing like the rest of them. Tom's death was a terrible blow to them all.

Maggie brought her own lunch out of the basket, happy to have an excuse to leave the house for a while. There'd been a constant stream of visitors dropping by to extend condolences and Maggie wasn't sure she could shake one more hand or summon another thank you.

'Do you remember the last thing you said to him?' Frank asked, breaking the silence as they ate.

Maggie swallowed her mouthful of sandwich; she didn't feel much like eating these days. 'To Tom?'

Frank gave a nod but didn't look at her.

'I suspect it was to be careful or something. Why?'

She watched Frank tug at some long grass with his free hand and crush it in his fist. 'You know what I said?'

Maggie remained silent.

'Nothin',' he said in an empty voice. 'I didn't say a thing. I was angry that I could shoot better than him and I was the one stayin' home milkin' flamin' cows.' He gave a shake of his head and lowered his gaze to the ground. 'I couldn't even wish him luck. What kind of brother does that make me, Maggie?'

Maggie felt her heart clench in sympathy at the torn look on his face and knew they were all reflecting on things they should have said or done. 'It makes you a younger brother who wanted to be going with him. That's all.'

'He's dead, Maggie,' he said with a bitter twist of his lips. He propelled himself to his feet and stared out over the paddock before them.

Maggie blinked back the burning sensation of tears. Slowly she stood and moved across to where Frank stood. 'It's okay to be angry—I am too. Angry at this war for taking away everything good in our lives, angry at the pain it's causing everyone . . . but don't you dare be angry at yourself, Frank,' she said. 'Tom knew you were disappointed, he would have been feeling the same way if he'd been in your shoes—he wouldn't have blamed you for not sending him off properly.'

Frank lifted his arm and swiped at his face quickly, but remained silent. She knew he was taking Tom's death hard—they were all dealing with it in their own way. Their mother had wept openly before summoning an inner strength Maggie could only marvel at as she dealt with all the visitors and continued to run the household. Their father had remained stony-faced as people came and went. Maggie knew he was grief-stricken but he would never allow anyone to see him weep—not even for his eldest son. Dulcie and Maggie tried to help their mother as much as possible, but she was like a whirlwind, cooking, cleaning—anything to keep her hands busy. It fell on Frank to continue working and for the first time ever, Maggie actually looked forward to coming out and helping him. Anything was better than the heavy cloud of misery that hung over the house.

Maggie moved forward, resting her arms on the split rail fence next to her brother. She wasn't sure how long they stood there, side by side, drawing comfort from each other, both lost in their own thoughts of the brother they were going to miss so desperately.

7th June, 1918
I have been writing to Alex every day, but have only received one letter in return. I know it must be difficult for him to write, but I miss him so desperately, I some-times do not know how I can bear it a second longer. Since Tom's death, I can't seem to ignore the lingering sense of doom I feel in my heart. I spend my spare time reading and re-reading Alex's letter—so much so that I fear I will wear out the writing and lose this most precious link with him forever.

Maggie struggled to remain seated at the kitchen table as she heard her father's utility pull up outside. Each week her father drove into town to purchase supplies and collect their mail. It was becoming increasingly difficult for her to contain her anguish as another week passed and there was no letter from Alex. She forced herself to continue topping and tailing the beans for dinner as her father handed over the mail to her mother and turned towards her with an apologetic expression. She felt tears gathering behind her eyes. Then he withdrew a tattered, grimy envelope from his back trouser pocket, handing it across the table with a small smile that vanished as quickly as it appeared.

Smiles didn't belong in their house any more, only tears.

Did the joy she felt at receiving a letter from Alex make

her a traitor to her brother and insensitive to her family's grief? She'd struggled with the thought constantly since the news of Tom's death. But life went on despite sorrow, and she thought Tom would be happy that his best friend and little sister were finding solace in each other.

Dropping the beans into the bowl, Maggie leapt from her chair and ran from the kitchen and out through the squeaky screen door. The swing tied to the branches of the massive old fig tree that she used to climb as a child was now her favourite spot to sit and dream of Alex. For the briefest of moments she stared down at the envelope; the untidy writing sprawled across its face was the most glorious sight she could imagine. To think he had held this very envelope thousands of miles away. She lifted it to her face and held it against her cheek for a moment, imagining his touch on her face.

Finally, when she could no longer wait, she carefully opened the flap of the envelope, reining in the urgent desire to tear it open and toss it aside. Nothing could be discarded; everything associated with Alex had to be kept, treasured, preserved until the day he came back to her. These things were her link to him, her only physical connection, and she treated each letter as though it were made of the most fragile and precious material.

Dear Maggie,
I heard about Tom through a bloke I know. Death is such a normal part of my day here—it has been for too long. I can't believe how long it's been since I was last a normal bloke, living in a normal house in a normal town, instead of moving from one hellhole to the next. Life over here

doesn't seem to be worth much. Until I heard about Tom I wasn't sure I was capable of crying for the dead any more. But I cried for Tom. He was a good mate and he was proud as punch of his little sister who could add up numbers faster than any bloke he knew.

I'll miss him.

What I wouldn't give to be able to see your beautiful smile now. The memories of our time together have seen me through more horrors than you could ever imagine. Mind you, I hope you could never imagine the things I've seen over here because they're beyond what any normal person could possibly picture. I don't know how I survived those times before coming home, because all I know now is when I reach the point where I think I can no longer go on I remember your face, your smile, the way your eyes light up when you're happy. I recall the sweet smell of your hair and how it reminds me of apples and sunshine, and I know I can make it through another day.

Maggie read the letter over and over in the weeks that followed. It was the first thing she reached for when she awoke and the last thing she put down before she fell asleep. He had become the missing limb she hadn't known was missing until he went away.

Then one afternoon, while Maggie was helping her brother move cattle, Frank announced he was planning to enlist. Maggie stared at him, horrified.

'But you can't.'

'I can. I'll be eighteen next week,' Frank replied calmly.

Maggie grabbed at her brother's arm and turned him to face her. 'This will *kill* Mum. She can't lose two sons, Frank, it's not fair.'

'I'm hardly going over there intending to die, am I,' he said, shaking off her hold and giving her an accusing glare.

'Neither was Tom!'

'I'm going, Maggie. I'm not a shirker.'

'This isn't about what people will *think* of you. This is about your life!'

'There are men who won't put their hands up to do their bit in this war, Maggie, but I'm not going to be one of them.'

'So it's all right to just throw away life after life in this endless bloody slaughter?'

'It's a war! I want to be part of it. I want my family to be proud of me, the way they were proud of Tom.'

'It won't make any difference if you're dead!' she cried, feeling hot tears seeping down her face.

'I wasn't asking for your blessing, Maggie. I just wanted to tell you before I tell Mum and Dad.' Maggie watched him walk ahead of her. Her brother was no longer the same carefree, larrikin kid he'd been before Tom went away to the war. None of them were the same.

She remembered how excited Tom had been when he'd signed up. If she was honest she'd have to say they all were. All those boys she'd grown up with had looked so handsome and clean-cut in their uniforms. Stopping in the street, a proud neighbour would sprout about their sons and when they were due to ship out. In the beginning there was excitement in the air. There were farewell dances held at the hall, full of hope and good cheer.

It wasn't until after Gallipoli—that strange, foreign place none of them had ever heard of before—that the brutality of war struck at the heart of their community. So many of those proud young men they'd farewelled back then were now dead. Their bodies left in a land far away from their home. Their families denied the right to say goodbye. No, there was nothing festive any more; it was gone along with their loved ones, lost on the dirt and beaches of those stinking battlefields overseas.

10th June, 1918
Four letters arrived in the mail today! Four! I've read them all, but I've found myself skimming over them quickly, too impatient to read them in detail. How am I supposed to read this many letters at once, when I am used to dissecting them, one at a time, for months on end? I cannot believe my good fortune, it's like all my Christmases have come at once!

The earlier letters were mainly full of questions. He wanted to know what was happening around town. Had she been to see his mother lately? How was her job at the bank going? There was no location on these letters, no mention of where he was. They were also not very long. Paper was obviously hard to find as two of the letters were written on small notepad paper and he'd had to write in tiny letters crammed on both sides. She made a mental note to include a few blank pages in her next letter to him.

She could tell things weren't going well. His letters were dark and sombre, and he no longer tried to cover up how bad things were by making jokes about the food or accommodation. All the letters ended with him saying how much he missed her and how he longed for the day they could be together again. She held the words close at night and echoed his sentiments.

21st June, 1918
I have tried to force myself to write but I have not been able to find the words. Maybe I'm a coward. To actually write the words down on paper will mean that they are real and I cannot ignore them any longer. I pray each night before I close my eyes that it's all a terrible nightmare. A mistake. I cannot believe that it's real, because I don't feel that it is. Surely I would no longer feel him with me if it were true? And I do. I still feel him with me. I can't believe the worst. I will not believe the worst!

Maggie hadn't eaten for three days. How had things gone so terribly wrong?

She'd received a backlog of mail from Alex and had been intoxicated by the heady excitement of being able to devour his words in such a gluttony of correspondence. Then two days later Mr Clarke, the Wilsons' neighbour, had come to the door and her father had summoned her to the lounge room wearing the gravest face she could ever imagine.

'Mr Clarke has just come by to deliver some bad news, Maggie love.'

A heavy feeling began to settle inside her stomach, and for a moment she was sure she had stopped breathing. She looked imploringly at her mother, but there was no comfort there.

'Maggie, there's been some news about Alex.'

Maggie shook her head and began to back away from her parents.

Her mother stepped forward and gently took her arm. 'Dear, he's been listed as missing in action.'

'Missing?' Missing . . . not killed. Relief flooded her body and she hoped she wasn't going to pass out with the sheer force of it.

'Yes, missing . . . But Maggie, so far there've been no survivors from his battalion. They've informed Mrs Wilson to expect the worst.'

'No!'

'Maggie. You need to accept the fact that in all likelihood Alex is dead.' Her father was not a cruel man, and somewhere deep inside she knew he was trying to help by not sugar-coating the truth, but at this precise moment nothing else registered except that they hadn't said killed in action. *Missing* was not *killed*.

She didn't bother to protest again after that. Everyone else had decided to assume the worst, but she refused. They *would* find Alex, so she remained silent. Waiting. Hoping.

She'd tried to bury herself in work, but living in a small town made it impossible to avoid the constant sympathetic glances and mumbled condolences.

Even Mr Fortescue seemed a little more understanding. He'd called her into his office and told her he'd understand if she needed to take some time off. She'd thanked him but declined. She couldn't think of anything more depressing than spending more time at home with everyone walking on eggshells around her.

Alex was not dead. She knew it. She didn't know why she couldn't accept it as everyone else had, but something inside her refused to give up hope.

Seven

The diary ended. Poppy sat up in her bed and stared at the blank page in despair. No! It couldn't just end like that. On closer inspection, Poppy noticed that pages had been ripped out. She gently rubbed her fingers along the inside spine of the book, feeling the telltale stubby remains. Why would Maggie have ripped out pages? Perhaps she'd gone on to marry someone else after Alex died and didn't want her husband or children to know about him; but if that was the case, why leave in the earlier entries about Alex? Why not rip out everything to do with him? And she had written so religiously even before Alex made an appearance; why wouldn't she have kept writing?

Damn it, she hated a sad ending to a book—even if it was a diary—and she would've liked to at least know a bit more about Maggie's life. Did she end up marrying? Having children? She frowned as she remembered no one in the family could actually recall her. Was it possible there'd been a family scandal and she'd been ostracised?

Poppy closed the diary and stared at it sadly. She'd been so wrapped up in Maggie's life that the abrupt ending felt as though something special had just been ripped from her life.

It was raining. Poppy stared out over a miserable-looking Sydney skyline and wished she could crawl back into bed. Gill continued to message her and she'd turned her phone off last night when she saw his name on the caller ID. A glance over at the clock on the lounge room wall drew a despondent groan as she realised she'd have to move now or risk being late. Poppy was never late. Punctuality was something she prided herself on.

Despite her best attempt to be on time, though, she got stuck in a traffic jam and then couldn't find a parking spot. Rushing into the building, she was about to enter the sanctuary of her office when Gill called her name and came walking over to her.

'Everything all right, Poppy?'

'Sorry I'm late, Gill. Traffic.'

Gill seemed to be waiting for her to open her office door and invite him inside. Poppy kept her back to the door— inside her office was the last place she wanted him. 'Well, it's not like you make a habit of it. Just wanted to check you were okay.'

'Why wouldn't I be?' She hadn't meant to snap, but she couldn't be bothered to mask her irritation this morning.

'I've just noticed you're not yourself lately. Let's go into your office and talk for a minute,' he said, taking a step towards her.

'Gill.' Poppy fought to keep her voice low; they were drawing attention from their workmates. 'Thank you for your concern, but I'm fine, just tired. Now you'll have to excuse me, I've got a lot to do this morning.' Opening the door just enough to slide through, she quickly closed it before Gill could follow her. When she heard his footsteps walking away, she breathed a small sigh of relief.

She couldn't continue like this, though. She knew she would have to face up to him before the end of the day. That's what she should have done to begin with, before things got so uncomfortable and . . . messy. She'd been hoping he'd get the message that she wasn't interested. Clearly that was not going to happen any time soon.

With her head buried in spreadsheets, Poppy jumped when a tap at her door sounded late in the afternoon. 'Come in,' she said, looking up to see Gill standing in the doorway.

'I wondered if you wanted to get some dinner?'

Dinner? A quick glance at the clock on her wall gave her a start. *Six thirty? Holy cow.* She hadn't realised it had gotten so late. 'Ah, no, thanks. I'm just going to finish up here and get home.'

'Poppy. We need to talk.'

Poppy bit back her irritation and knew the time had come to end this thing.

Gill crossed to her side before she could get to her feet, and leaned across, trapping her in her seat. 'I know you've been avoiding me, and I know why.'

'I'm avoiding you, Gill, because you've been making me uncomfortable.'

'It's because of the other night,' he said, cutting her off before she could continue. 'Look. If you're worried about me being married, don't be—my marriage is a sham. My wife and I have been drifting apart for years. We've been waiting for the kids to get old enough before we do anything about it.'

'Gill! For goodness sake, stop it,' Poppy demanded. 'I'm not interested in a relationship with you! It was a mistake. It should *never* have happened and it's *never* going to happen again.'

For a moment she thought she'd finally gotten through to him, that he'd back off, embarrassed by his assumption, but she was wrong. He did seem to get it, but he didn't react in the way she'd anticipated. His face contorted into a fierce scowl.

'You goddamn tease!'

Poppy's mouth dropped open in astonishment.

'You've led me on all these months! You know you have. How can you deny it after the other night?'

'It wasn't supposed to mean anything, Gill.' She tried to push Gill back so she could stand up—his close proximity was alarming her—but he refused to budge.

'Wasn't supposed to *mean anything*?'

'We'd both had too much to drink. It was a *big* mistake.'

If ever there was a night she wished she could go back and change it would be that night. One of the cases she'd spent months on had finally come to a successful end and she'd been in high spirits, celebrating with most of the office after work at a nearby pub. It had been one of the biggest cases she'd ever worked on and she'd had every right to be celebrating; even a few of the big bosses had turned up to congratulate her. She'd been too restless to go home when the others had called it a night and Gill had been the only one who'd wanted to join her for another round.

Looking back, going out alone with her married boss hadn't been the smartest move. She hadn't been thinking of him in any other way than a willing drinking and dancing partner, but somehow the drinks had just kept coming and her better judgement had left her to it. She'd woken up in the early hours of the morning and found herself in a motel room, next to her naked boss.

She'd left without waking him and caught a taxi home. She hadn't been able to recall the last time she'd had a hangover quite so bad and she'd slumped under the shower, feeling very sick and more than a little sorry for herself. How had it come to this? How had she made such a stupid mistake?

She was usually so careful about avoiding awkward situations at work. She usually stuck to one-night stands and casual relationships, which she justified to herself as her way of keeping men at a distance and maintaining her independence. And then she'd made the mother of all mistakes. She'd slept with her boss.

'A mistake?' He glared at her.

'What else can you call it? I certainly never intended to sleep with you, Gill.'

'That's not the message I was getting,' he snapped.

'Oh for goodness sake! It was only ever flirting, it didn't mean anything. I flirt with all the guys, Gill. It's just a bit of fun.'

'I see. So you sleep with me and then we just move on like nothing happened?'

'That bit wasn't supposed to happen. That's what I've been trying to tell you, but you're not listening to me.'

'Because I can't just *forget it*, Poppy. That night was—'

'Don't.' Poppy held up a hand in warning. 'Look, I'm sorry you got the wrong impression, but you need to hear me now when I tell you there's nothing between us, Gill. It was a bad decision on both our parts.'

'Do my feelings count here at all? I think I'm falling in love with you, Poppy.'

'No.' His words sent a flurry of panic through her. He was starting to scare her. She had done nothing to give Gill any reason to believe she had those kind of feelings for him. 'There's nothing else to talk about.'

'Poppy, wait.'

She saw his shoulders slump as he realised there was no hope of recovering the situation.

Poppy grabbed her purse from the cupboard next to her then crossed the room quickly to open the door. She felt ill.

'Poppy,' Gill called again from her doorway as she reached the deserted reception area. 'Just wait.'

'I can't work like this any more, Gill. If you don't let this go, I'm going to make a complaint to the company.'

For a moment he looked shocked before he gave a bitter snort. 'You think they'll believe anything you say?'

'*What?*' Poppy gasped, surprised.

'Come on, don't act so shocked. Everyone knows you sleep around. I can find a dozen witnesses to testify that you like to party and sleep with men you've picked up on a night out. We've all seen you in action.'

Oh, for the love of God! Once! She'd only ever done that in front of workmates once. She'd accepted a dare from some of the guys after work one Friday night to see how long it took to pick up a guy at the bar. It was a stupid thing to have agreed to, but it had all been in the name of fun, and it had happened over *two years ago.*

'I'm pretty sure they'd take this seriously, Gill. And more to the point, I think your *wife* would take it very seriously. I want you to leave me alone.'

She didn't wait for his reply. She stepped into the elevator and began jabbing at the door-closed button urgently. It wasn't until she was locked safely inside her car that she began to shake.

Curled up on her lounge later that evening, Poppy reached a decision. She didn't want to deal with Gill any more. She felt a deep humiliation at the picture he'd painted of her reputation. She was under no illusions that her work-mates talked about her behind her back, but it was another thing altogether to have it thrown in her face. It shouldn't have worried her, she knew she worked as hard or harder than anyone else in the office and deserved every promotion and accolade she had received. It shouldn't matter what a bunch of people she worked with thought about her, except it did.

Damn it. When had it started mattering? Maybe she should have accepted more of the girls' social invitations, but she'd never been a girly girl, into day spa treatments and shopping trips. She liked night life and, yes, a few drinks, but somehow it always seemed to be the guys from work she ended up hanging with. She knew some of the women on staff didn't like her. She wasn't stupid, she'd seen them whispering and laughing together, and been aware of conversations stopping when she walked into a room. It hadn't really bothered her that much because she was happy with her job and her life. She did what she wanted, when she wanted, without having to answer to anyone.

But tonight, hearing Gill talk about her like that made her take a long hard look at herself. Maybe if she'd tried to get along with the others and had made a few more friends she'd have someone on her side to stand up for her against his hurtful allegations. Shoulda, woulda, coulda.

Well, she wasn't going back to that office tomorrow. She needed some time away from Gill so he could hopefully work out whatever the hell was going on in his head. Only a few weeks ago human resources had been onto her to use up some holiday time and she'd been avoiding giving them an answer. She could take some time off and head out to Warrial. Immediately the instinct to shy away from dealing with her nan's things sent a predictable sick, empty feeling to the pit of her stomach, but the urgent need to be somewhere familiar and comforting and safe, to run back to Nan's, overrode the need to protect her emotions. She'd been putting off sorting through Nan's things and this was the perfect opportunity to make herself do it. She needed to get away from the city for a while.

Eight

Poppy squinted against the blinding glare of the late-afternoon sun as she drove along the narrow country road. Patchwork pieces of bitumen disappeared beneath her tyres, quick-fix measures against a few bad years of flood damage. Hitting a pothole, Poppy cringed at the loud crunch of tyre meeting wheel well and eased her foot off the accelerator.

She tried not to think about the last time she'd been along this road. Flashes of that visit went through her mind: the hospital; her nan's frail hands, the skin almost paper thin, still so warm and comforting; then a few days later, the church, flowers and wellwishers. The thoughts still managed to swell her throat with emotion.

She supposed she should be grateful that she'd made it out here in time to see her nan after her stroke. In all honesty, despite the fact the doctor had told her on the phone that she should prepare for the worst, she hadn't believed she'd lose her nan so fast.

The first stroke had been rather mild—she'd only experienced tingling down one side—but it had been the fall she'd taken that had done the damage. However, while she'd been in hospital she'd gone on to have smaller strokes and eventually a much larger one that had left her unconscious until she passed away peacefully a few days later.

A bend in the road brought a moment of relief from the fiery sunset, and Poppy eased her grip on the steering wheel, able to relax back in her seat. She'd been driving since eight am. She'd stopped a few times for coffee and a stretch, but once she was in the car she liked to keep going. Nine and a half hours was a long stretch and she was looking forward to getting to her nan's house.

Large gum trees lined the roadside and threw long shadows across the road ahead. It was all so familiar and yet somehow different. Had the place changed, or was it her?

Her phone gave a small bleep from the depths of her handbag on the seat beside her, but Poppy didn't bother to reach for it. She knew who it was—Gill had been leaving messages all day. She was still too angry and humiliated by his words to even think about talking to him, even if he was her boss. She'd spent the previous day organising her work files and arranging her leave. She took with her a few things she could work on away from the office, the rest she'd left with detailed notes on Gill's desk. There wasn't much: she was pretty much up to date with all her cases. She'd contact him once she was set up at Warrial and only if it had something to do with work. Human resources hadn't been happy about her abrupt departure but, once the idea to leave had taken root, she wasn't about to let something like paperwork hold her up. She explained somewhat bluntly that she was taking her leave and had left it at that.

The shadows ended and farmhouses began to appear closer to the roadside, until a few kilometres further and they were side by side and lining wide, quiet streets.

Warrial. Population 1165. The welcome sign had been recently erected and a freshly planted circle of bright flowers grew beneath it. In fact, everywhere Poppy looked there were signs that things had been revamped around the small country town. Warrial had gone through a few rough patches over the years. Time and a slow decline of the population had left the place looking neglected and rundown for a while. But the town was in much better shape nowadays. The community had bound together and formed a town-pride group who had taken on the job of beautifying the main street, planting gardens at the entrance to the town and maintaining the nature strips. Neatly mowed lawns had replaced the old overgrown garden beds, and although there were still some empty shopfronts, a few new businesses had opened and there was no sign of the neglect that had befallen the small town in the past.

Poppy pulled into the driveway of the white weatherboard house and turned off the engine. For a long while she remained in the driver's seat and stared at the house. She knew it was irrational to sit here and wait, but she just couldn't make herself move. She wanted so desperately for that front door to open and for her to see that gentle face beaming out a welcome. With a heavy heart, Poppy climbed out of the car. There wasn't going to be any welcoming hug that smelled of baby powder and perfume. No smooth hands cupping her face and looking at her, *really looking at her*, as though she were someone's entire world.

Taking the keys from her handbag, Poppy tried a few before finally managing to locate the correct one and opening the front door. A musty yet familiar smell enfolded her as soon as she stepped inside the house. No one had been here since the day after the funeral and the old house was in desperate need of a good airing. She moved through the house, opening windows and pulling back curtains, and memories of her grandmother flooded back to her.

Nan had lived here for over thirty years after selling the property she and Pop had worked since the day they'd married. Their son, Poppy's father, had not been interested in farming, so they'd had no other option but to sell and move into town once the place got too much for them.

Nan had loved having the company of neighbours close by and the convenience of walking to shops and social meetings at the CWA, but Pop had pined away at the loss of his beloved farm and he'd never adjusted to town life. Two years after moving from the farm, he'd died.

Poppy paused as she walked into Nan's bedroom. It was almost eerie the way everything was exactly as it had been the day Nan had been taken to hospital. The bed was neatly made and a cardigan lay draped over the back of a chair, just where Nan had left it. It was almost as though even the house were awaiting her return. Poppy hadn't had the heart to touch anything after her last visit. Her mum had come out for the funeral and had even offered to stay and help pack up the house, but Poppy hadn't wanted to do it then. She just hadn't been ready. There was no way she could have packed her nan's things into boxes and wiped away her memory, all within days of burying her.

Poppy's gaze fell onto the dressing table where a fine layer of dust lay undisturbed. She knew that must be driving her grandmother insane. 'Tomorrow, Nan,' she promised, heading out of the room and down the short hallway towards the kitchen. She'd give the place a clean tomorrow. All she wanted now was a nice hot cuppa and a chance to catch her breath.

Searching through the pantry, she managed to find a tin of condensed milk and a small jar of instant coffee. Letting the cold water run for a few seconds, she waited until it ran clear before cleaning out the jug and refilling it. She smiled at the familiar chipped cups her nan had always used and felt a comforting warmth spread through her like a hug. It felt good to be back here.

The phone inside her handbag vibrated on the benchtop once again and Poppy looked at it, annoyed. What part of *I'm not answering your bloody phone calls* didn't the man get?

The strange feeling that things in her life were beginning to unravel nagged her once more. Maybe it had to do with the diary, or maybe she'd been pushing her emotions aside for too long, and this was the universe's way of telling her it was time to start dealing with them.

She knew she hadn't properly grieved over Nan's death. Her mother had warned her not to go off and shut everyone out like she always did, but that was the only way she knew to deal with grief. She'd never been one to openly show her emotions. Besides, she hadn't had time to break down, not then. She'd had that huge case to deal with, the one she'd finally won months later; maybe that was why she'd gone overboard that night; maybe it had something to do with releasing her locked feelings. She shook her head angrily; there was no point trying to find excuses for her stupid behaviour. She'd got drunk, slept with her boss and now she had to deal with the consequences.

The click of the jug boiling sounded loud in the quiet house. As Poppy carefully sipped the hot contents, the sweet milky taste brought back happier memories of cold winter mornings sitting with Nan on the back verandah watching the sunrise. The steady tick-tock of the old timber clock on the mantelpiece soothed Poppy as she sat and drank her coffee. When she'd finished, she realised with a start that it had gotten dark. Winter wasn't far away and the days were getting shorter. A slight chill touched her shoulders and she walked back through the house and closed all the windows. That was enough airing for now.

Poppy was grateful she'd gone through the hassle of changing over the electricity before she'd left town after the funeral. She hadn't known when she'd be back to sort out the house, so it had been safer to leave it connected. Thank goodness she had. Sitting here in the dark with no electricity or hot water for a shower would not have been a wonderful way to end a long day of driving.

She supposed she would eventually have to work out what she wanted to do with the place. The financial side of her brain weighed up the value of the property and what it was worth on the market. It would give her some cash to invest elsewhere if she sold it, and she had to wonder about property values in Warrial. While the town was in okay shape now, there wasn't exactly a population boom going on. She didn't regret her decision to buy Nan's house, but it was never going to make her any money. If she sold it for what she'd paid for it, she'd be happy and she could then reinvest the money in something that would guarantee her a healthy return. However, the emotional side of her brain was reluctant to give up her last link with her grandmother. Regardless of what decision she made, the fact still remained that she had to go through Nan's things and decide what to do with them all.

Too tired and emotionally wrung out to deal with it tonight, she decided against making anything for her dinner and opted instead for an early night. Things would look better in the morning, she told herself firmly, and then smiled as she recalled the countless times Nan had uttered those very words to her.

Finding some sheets that smelled like lavender soap folded neatly inside the linen press in the hallway, Poppy made up the bed she'd always used in the room at the back of the house.

God bless hot water, she thought as she stood beneath a steaming shower a few minutes later. Poppy let out a sigh of contentment as she slid in between the clean sheets. Maybe all in her world wasn't perfect at the moment, but it was nice to be able to take comfort in the small things. Lying here tucked up in the same sheets she'd had as a child, and smelling the familiar scent of lavender soap, she could almost imagine she was a carefree eight-year-old again.

'Night, Nan,' she whispered into the darkness, closing her eyes and letting the soft hum of a lullaby somewhere in distance sing her to sleep.

Nine

Poppy awoke to the sound of thumping.

It took a few moments to orientate herself to her surroundings, but as the thumps grew louder she threw back the blankets on her bed and hurried to the front door.

Kicking her toe on the corner of the hallway skirting board, Poppy gave a painful cry and limped toward the door, opening it to stare in disbelief at the audience of faces before her.

'Good morning, dear. Did we wake you?'

Balancing on one leg, clutching her throbbing toe tightly in her hand, Poppy blinked up at the grey-haired woman mutely.

'Jim, take a look at the poor girl's foot, she might have broken something,' another woman cut in from behind the first woman. Leaning closer she added, 'Jim's very good with livestock.'

Livestock? Poppy's startled gaze flew to meet that of a somewhat amused, nicely built man whose presence she hadn't registered until this moment. He wore jeans and a long-sleeved shirt. The cuffs had been turned back and rolled up a little way, revealing tanned forearms, dusted with light hair.

'Bernadette, how about we give Miss Abbott some room,' he suggested.

Miss Abbott? She tried to recall the last time she'd been referred to as Miss Abbott, and how did this man know who she was?

'Good idea. How about a nice cup of tea and a scone?'

She must have slipped and hit her head. Who were these people and what were they doing offering her tea and scones? The trio paraded through the doorway, completely oblivious to her stunned reaction, and Poppy found herself standing alone in the open doorway, watching their backs as they disappeared into her kitchen.

Hobbling as fast as she could after them, she was amazed as she watched the two women deftly unpack a small feast from within the depths of a large basket, which the man they'd referred to as Jim had been carrying. True to their word, a plate of scones was revealed, along with small containers of cream, jam and golden syrup.

'We didn't think you'd have much of anything here, so we brought along a few meals to put in the freezer and some staples to get you through until you find time to go down to the store.'

This could not continue. 'I'm sorry, but, I have no idea who you all are or what you're doing here.'

The woman who'd spoken first waved off her concern

with a small chuckle. 'Oh, you poor dear, here we are barging our way inside and we haven't even introduced ourselves. I'm Bernadette, and this is Alice. We're members of your grandmother's CWA branch. We were at her funeral, but I suppose you were too overwhelmed on the day to remember us.'

'And this is Jim Nash,' Alice put in.

Poppy let her gaze drift back to the man standing off to one side. She tilted her head slightly. 'And are you in the CWA as well, Jim?'

She watched as a slow smile curved his lips and for the briefest of moments Poppy felt her sardonic exterior waver slightly.

'Nope, I'm just the local stock and station agent.'

Of course he was. It made complete sense that the local stock and station agent was tagging along with the dynamic duo here. She really wasn't ready to cope with this first thing in the morning. *Seriously, she wasn't.* Just then Poppy glanced down at herself and realised she was standing barefoot in her bright yellow duck-print pyjamas. Gritting her teeth, she refused to acknowledge how ridiculous she must look, especially in front of this man who seemed to find her so amusing.

'Would you like me to take a look?' he offered, glancing down at her swollen red toe.

'No, thanks. It'll be fine.'

'It could be broken, dear. Maybe you should sit down and let Jim take a look.'

'No, no need. I just stubbed it, that's all.'

'Well, sit down and have a nice cup of tea,' said Bernadette, placing a cup on the kitchen table and waiting expectantly for her to take a seat.

Poppy gave a small sigh and sat down. Maybe it was the grandmotherly appeal of the two women as they fussed about her, putting away the meals they'd brought and setting down the scones in front of her, that threw her off guard. Or maybe she was still in shock at having three strangers making themselves so at home in her grandmother's kitchen. Whatever it was, she found herself sitting meekly at the table as the two women fussed about her.

The aroma of sweet black tea wafted up from the cup Alice placed in front of her, and suddenly Poppy realised she was ravenous. She took a bite of the biggest scone she'd ever seen. The cream was fresh and the jam made her tastebuds tingle in delight. She scoffed down both halves more quickly than could possibly be considered polite but she couldn't help herself.

'Well, ladies, if you don't need me to carry anything heavy back to the car, I'd better be getting to work,' said Jim.

Poppy licked her fingers and wiped at her face self-consciously. So that's what he was doing here. He was the Good Samaritan kind of guy—the kind of man she avoided like the plague.

'Nice to meet you, Miss Abbott.'

'It's Poppy. Miss Abbott makes me sound ancient.'

'Nice to meet you, Poppy. If you need anything while you're in town, just give me a yell.'

'I'm pretty sure I won't need anything, thanks,' she said, dropping her gaze from his smoky grey eyes.

She heard the front door close and summoned a polite smile for the two CWA women now seated across from her. Well, this was certainly cosy.

'How did you know I was here? I only arrived yesterday afternoon.'

'Joyce Howard lives across the road, in number thirty-two. She saw you arrive last night and noticed the lights on in the house. She called me but it was a bit late to come around then.'

Thank God they drew the limit somewhere, Poppy thought with a silent snort.

'How long will you be in town for, dear?' Bernadette asked, before daintily biting into a scone.

Distracted by a smudge of cream on the woman's top lip, Poppy had to concentrate to answer the question. 'I'm not sure. It was a bit of a rushed decision to come up here, but I'd imagine it's probably going to take a week or so to get things sorted.'

'You won't be staying then?' Alice asked.

'Stay? What, for good? Oh no.' *Good God no!* She couldn't even contemplate living in a town like Warrial. What did people even *do* here? There were barely any shops, and the nearest regional town was at least a ninety-minute drive away.

'That's a shame. We could use some new blood in town. We're losing so many of our young people.'

'Yes, well, I guess people have to find work and earn a living.' She could understand why most of the kids would run away as far and fast as they could once they finished school here. She'd spent her fair share of time in towns like Warrial over the years. With her stepfather working in the bank, they'd averaged maybe three years per town. By the time Poppy was twelve, she'd decided she'd cried enough tears over lost best friends to even bother making them any more.

She'd learned her lesson early in life, and it was probably one of the most important ones to learn: don't let anyone close enough to get attached. It might sound harsh, but look at all the pain she'd saved herself. She'd have become an emotional wreck if she'd cried her heart out over each and every transfer her family had made until she'd been old enough to leave school. 'Well, we'd better be going, we just wanted to make sure you were settled in. If you need a hand going through the place, you just call us. It's not an easy job to pack things away.'

Poppy swallowed past a tightening of her throat at the woman's sympathetic tone. 'Thank you. And thank you for the food; you really shouldn't have gone to all this trouble.'

'Rubbish. You're Elizabeth's granddaughter. She'd have done the same thing for any of us. We take care of each other, you know that. Or have you forgotten how we do things out here?'

The question caught her off balance. 'Well, I've been away for a long time, and it's not like I was ever really a local to start with.'

'You belong here, missy,' said Alice seriously. 'Your father, God bless his soul, was born and bred here, as were your grandparents and their parents. Don't you ever forget it. Blood is thicker than water.'

Poppy watched the two women walk down the pathway towards their car. Alice's parting words shook her more than she cared to admit. *Belong? Her?* Poppy Abbott didn't belong anywhere.

Ten

Poppy wandered around the house with no idea where to begin after her unexpected visitors had left. She did, however, decide to get dressed, on the off-chance anyone else decided to pop around and welcome her to town. Other than that, though, very little else seemed to get accomplished.

Flicking on the jug, she had a renewed surge of gratitude when she saw the milk, butter, eggs and loaf of bread Bernadette and Alice had left behind for her, not to mention the remainder of the scones, jam and cream. *That really was very nice of them,* she thought. At least she wouldn't have to go down the street today. She had enough supplies to last a few days at least.

She took her coffee outside to see what state the backyard was in while she made a phone call.

It was a pleasant surprise to find that she didn't have to

fight through a jungle in order to get to her grandmother's small outdoor table and chair set. In fact, as she pressed the numbers on her keypad she realised the lawn had been *recently* mowed, but before she could do more than frown in confusion at the discovery, her mother answered the phone.

'Poppy! Hello, love, what's wrong?'

'Why would there be something wrong?' Poppy answered, a little put out that her mother thought she'd only call if she had a problem. 'I'm just checking in. I'm at Nan's. I've decided to make a start on the clean-out.'

'Really? What's brought this on?' Her mother sounded suspicious.

'Nothing. I just had some time owing to me and decided to come out and do it.'

'You would tell me if anything was wrong?' Her mother was sounding anxious now. Somehow she always knew when Poppy wasn't being absolutely truthful.

'Mum, there's nothing wrong, stop worrying, I'm a grown-up now, remember.'

'Tell me that again when you have kids of your own—if you ever get around to having kids of your own.'

'It's way too early in the morning to be having that old conversation, Mum. I just wanted to call and let you know that I was in Warrial. I'll call again soon.'

She'd just disconnected the call when the phone lit up and Gill's name flashed across the screen.

With a low sound that was halfway between a growl and a groan, Poppy pressed the answer button and waited.

'Poppy? Is that you?'

'Gill,' she acknowledged.

'I've been trying to call you.'

'I've taken some time off to sort out some personal business. I told you that in the note I left on your desk. I've also cleared it with human resources, so if you have any problems I suggest you go see them about it.'

'Tell me where you are, please. We need to sort this thing out.'

'Gill, I'd appreciate it if you'd keep this professional. I'll be in touch via email. I've brought along the last of my open cases to work on and I'll send them through to you as soon as I've finished writing up the reports.'

'Poppy, if you'd just give me a chance—'

'I'll be in touch, Gill.' Poppy pressed end and placed the phone on the table, relieved she'd managed to remain calm and professional. Barely five minutes passed and the phone buzzed, flashing a notice that she had one new message. She didn't bother reading it; instead, she headed for her grandmother's vegetable garden.

The veggie patch that had once been so lovingly tended had gone to seed. It was strange not to see the neat rows of lettuce and spinach and onions and the bright red tomatoes on the staked vines, tied with old stockings. Not for the first time, Poppy wished she'd been blessed with her grandmother's green thumbs, but she had a sad little collection of wilted brown corpses lined up against the wall of her apartment block to attest to her lack of horticultural ability.

The swing remained, though, the same one that had hung here her entire childhood. Poppy placed a hand on the worn timber seat and gave it a small push. The sun felt warm on her back and for a moment she closed her eyes and listened to the gentle breeze high up in the old gum trees.

This was the only place she'd ever felt she could truly be herself. Between transfers, Warrial had been her home base. This was where Christmas and school holidays had been spent, regardless of where in the country her step-family was living at the time. At least she had been able to rely on that much in her life—that and her nan's love. She knew her mother loved her, and she was lucky she had made sure Poppy never lost touch with her father's family, but at times her concern could be a little stifling. It didn't help that Poppy always felt somehow inferior to her step-siblings, who seemed always to be doing something amazing. She couldn't help but feel dejected that her own career, hardly something to be sneezed at, didn't seem to rate in comparison to her siblings, both of whom were doctors. She tried not to take offence, but it was hard to ignore the less than subtle comparisons she'd lived with since the day her mother remarried. Her mother had always wanted *more* from life. She could remember fights between her parents from a young age and it hadn't been until she was older that they'd made more sense. Her mother had constantly picked at her father to take more pride in his life. Go for a bigger promotion, update their car . . . buy a bigger house. She often wondered if they would have remained married had her father not died in that accident.

She'd never really warmed to her stepfather; he was a somewhat aloof man and she didn't like that her mother seemed to be always trying to please him. She'd finally found a man in the right social circles that she'd always wanted to be in, and yet now it seemed that he was the one always snipping at her to be *more*. Poppy supposed if her mother were truly unhappy that she'd have done something about it.

The last time she'd brought up her observations though, her mother hadn't spoken to her for a week afterwards, so now she just kept her mouth shut and led her own life.

It wasn't like she was an impulsive teenager, and yet her mother seemed to always be waiting for her to make some terrible mistake. She was a qualified forensic accountant. She was paid a lot of money because she was good at what she did; yet while other people viewed her as an intelligent, hardworking professional, to her mother she would always be her slightly troublesome child.

Back inside, Poppy faced a tough choice. Where to start? At first she headed towards Nan's bedroom, but she didn't make it past the threshold before she turned abruptly on her heel. It was too hard to think about removing all those clothes that she could still picture her grandmother wearing; the whole room still smelled like her and she wasn't ready to face that yet. The spare room, which Nan had also used as a sewing room, had wall-to-floor cupboards packed with the things her grandparents had brought with them from the farm. Generations of memories, things that couldn't be left out in a shed for rodents to chew their way through.

Poppy had always dreaded looking for things in the spare room cupboard. It was like a tightly packed jigsaw—once one little piece was removed it had to go back in exactly where it had come from or it simply wouldn't fit. It had always smelled funny to her as a child and gingerly opening the first door now, she realised it *still* smelled funny.

It smelled old. She'd never really understood why her grandparents had bothered to hold on to all these old boxes filled with papers and old school books of her father's. She'd always wondered why people feel a need to hold onto these things for so many years. It's not as though they were ever going to be worth anything. To her analytical mind, it just didn't make sense. That was before she'd started reading Maggie's diary though. Now she was hoping against hope that somewhere in these old boxes she'd find those missing pages. It was a long shot and in truth she really wasn't expecting them to be there, but try as she might she couldn't stop thinking about Maggie and what had become of her. She hated an unsolved mystery! Maybe the diary pages wouldn't be there, but she might find something else that would help fill in the blanks.

She had no real idea what she was going to do with all this stuff once she'd gone through it, but staring at it wasn't going to make it organise itself. Reaching up she began to pull down boxes.

Inside the first few were more photo albums, old ones, way before her time. As she flicked through the browning pages, Poppy realised that hardly any of them had names or places written on them. These people were her family but she had no idea who they were. They'd all been long gone before she was even born. Without Nan or Pop to point out who was who, they became little more than strangers. Poppy felt sad. No one ever thought ahead to a time when they would no longer be around to fill in the blanks.

Arming herself with some cleaning cloths and hot water, she wiped out cupboards as she continued to sort through the boxes. Maybe she should call her Aunty Myrtle to see if she wanted any of this stuff. There were albums with old photos of Nan as a young girl. There was also some jewellery Myrtle might like to have. Poppy had already taken the rings and some of the beautiful opals her Nan had favoured, more for sentimental value than anything else. She'd like Myrtle to have the rest of it, rather than get rid of it.

The sound of the next-door neighbour's lawnmower starting up outside the window made her jump. Crossing the room, Poppy was in the process of reaching up to shut out some of the noise when a figure passed in front of the window, making her let out a scream at the unexpected appearance.

With her hand still over her heart, she stared at the startled face looking back at her as the lawnmower's engine died with a splutter.

What the hell was Jim Nash doing here?

Leaning out the window, Poppy reacted instinctively, her body launching into fight mode as adrenalin surged through her. 'What do you think you're doing?'

'Sorry. I tried knocking on the front door, but I guess you didn't hear me. I always give your grandmother's lawn a mow when I do mine.' He hitched his head in the direction of the fence.

'You scared me half to death.' He might very well be doing something nice, but the fact still remained that he'd almost given her a heart attack.

'Took a few years off my life too, I reckon. Last time I heard a scream like that was when some guy in a hockey mask was chasing a woman on the big screen.'

Poppy realised she was staring. Earlier he'd been dressed in jeans and a work shirt, but this time he wore an old faded T-shirt that seemed to fit him like a second skin. He'd looked rather good in his work clothes, but they hadn't highlighted those arms or how wide his chest was. 'You live next door?'

'Sure do.' He looked down at the ground for a moment before lifting his grey eyes to meet hers almost uncertainly. 'Your grandmother was a very special lady.'

His words caught her off guard, instantly dissolving her irritation. 'Yes, she was.'

'I saw you at her funeral. I wanted to let you know how sorry I was for your loss, but I thought you might have had enough condolences for one day.'

The thought that this stranger had been able to read her so well was a little disconcerting, but at the same time she appreciated his insight. She wasn't sure she could have handled hearing one more, 'What a beautiful service.' Beautiful? What was beautiful about a funeral? She could still feel her stomach turn at the sickly sweet smell of all those flowers mingling together in the small church. So many people had wanted to speak to her, to say how sorry they were, and all she had wanted to do was find a quiet place to hide away and cry.

'Sorry, I don't think I really remember anyone from that day. There were so many people there.'

'Your grandmother touched a lot of people's lives in this town. Everyone loved her.'

Poppy wasn't sure what to say, his quiet words filled her with both great pride and a terrible emptiness. Her eyes began to sting.

'Do you need help with anything?'

'Not really, thanks,' she said. 'I'm just doing a bit of cleaning and sorting things at the moment.'

'Well, let me know if you need a hand.'

'Thanks,' she said with a smile. Brushing her dusty hands against her jeans, she felt suddenly awkward.

'Okay, well, I'd better keep going before it gets too dark.'

'Do I need to fix you up for the mowing?'

The look he sent her somehow made her feel as though she'd insulted him. 'No. I've always mowed your grand-mother's lawn. I don't do it to get paid.'

'Oh. Okay then,' Poppy stammered. 'Well, thanks. I'll see you later.' She stepped away from the window and pulled it shut, muttering to herself as she made her way to the bathroom. Why did she feel so self-conscious whenever she was around this guy? He wasn't even her type, for goodness sake. He was so clean-cut and wholesome. She'd have never paid him the slightest bit of interest if she'd met him on her own turf. Okay, maybe she would have at least *looked* at him; the guy was kinda hot, in a clean, country-boy way.

Poppy sent her reflection in the bathroom mirror a stern frown. 'Get a grip, girl.' With a pointed look, she turned off the taps, wiped her hands and headed into the kitchen to see what the good ladies of the CWA had left in her freezer for dinner.

Eleven

Poppy had finished airing out the house. She'd vacuumed and dusted, bleached and scrubbed the old place to within an inch of its life and finally it was starting to feel lived-in again. She was taking a break in a warm spot in the back yard, her laptop in front of her, when the peaceful tweet of birdlife was rudely interrupted.

'You're ruining my life!'

Poppy glanced over her shoulder at the theatrical yell and cringed at the slam of a door somewhere inside the house next door.

It was the first time she'd heard anything from Jim's house. She wondered what was going on. A lovers' spat perhaps? She didn't know if the guy was married or not. He didn't wear a wedding ring, but that didn't mean much. A trickle of discomfort ran through her and she forced her thoughts back to the computer screen and the various jobs listed on the employment site she'd been perusing. She'd been thinking about her options as she'd cleaned. She loved her current job, but when she thought about going back to the office, where no doubt her sudden absence was causing even more whispers, she felt sick. Of course it could be that Gill had just been trying to hurt her when he'd told her everyone thought she was a tramp, but now that he'd said it, she couldn't seem to shake it off. She didn't like feeling powerless like this; she was used to being able to do her job without worrying what her colleagues thought of her. It wouldn't hurt to see what her options were.

Hers was a specialised field of accounting, but thankfully in high demand. She knew a few of the companies advertising for a forensic accountant position and could immediately discard a couple, having heard stories about high staff turnover and unhappy working conditions. That still left quite a few interesting possibilities. It was ironic that for a person who had loathed moving around so often as a child, she still seemed to do it quite a bit as an adult. There were a few major differences, though; nowadays she moved on her terms and not when someone else decided. There was also the simplicity of being able to pack up and go without the need to disrupt anyone else. When she was bored with one place or job, she just moved on to another.

Her career had given her opportunities most people would dream of. She'd worked in New York for a few years before travelling around the UK between jobs, one of the advantages of having a well-paid career. Maybe that was why she became restless—it wasn't that difficult for her to leave when she became bored or if things got too complicated ... *like making a stupid, drunken decision to sleep with your boss.* Maybe it was time for another change. Maybe this is the way she needed to approach packing up Nan's house, thinking of it as a fresh start.

Poppy's thoughts were interrupted by a thump against the old timber fence somewhere down the side of the house. She blinked in surprise when a young girl, barely in her teens, rounded the corner of the house. She was dressed in jeans and a T-shirt that was too tight, and she came to an abrupt halt when she saw Poppy.

'Who the hell are you?' she demanded.

Poppy let out an incredulous snort at the girl's accusatory tone. 'I think I should be the one asking who the hell *you* are, given this is my house.'

'It is not. I know who owns this place and it's *not* you,' she said, putting her hands on her hips and eyeing Poppy suspiciously.

For a young kid, she was certainly not intimidated by much, Poppy thought with a grudging mix of admiration and annoyance. 'This was my grandmother's house, and now it's mine.' For a moment Poppy thought she saw a slight waver of the girl's tough exterior, but in a flash it was gone.

'You could be anyone. How do I know you're not just some squatter?'

Was this kid serious? Whatever happened to respecting your elders, for goodness sake! She would never have dared speak to an adult like that when she was a teenager. *Oh my God,* Poppy groaned inwardly. She was sounding just like her mother. 'I think you'd better run off back home now.'

'I think we should call the police and make sure you're not some criminal.'

Right. That's it, Poppy thought, closing the lid of her laptop and pushing back the chair with a loud scrape. 'I think we should go and have a chat to your parents instead. Where do you live?'

'As if I'm telling you.'

'Fine. We'll just go ahead and call the police and I'll have them take you back home.' Rude little . . .

'Do what you want, I couldn't care less.'

'Lacey!' They turned their furious gazes back to the fence, where Jim Nash was standing, his expression thunderous.

'Get your butt back home right now, young lady!'

'You can't make me.'

Poppy's gaze switched between the two faces like a spectator at a tennis match.

'Don't push me, Lacey.'

'I'm sick of you telling me what to do all the time. I'm not a baby!'

'Then stop acting like one. I'm not going to ask you twice.' All the petulance in the world couldn't ignore the fact that this was an order Lacey would be wise not to ignore.

Poppy didn't realise she'd been holding her breath until she felt it leave her body in a small rush of relief as the young girl sent a snarl of indignation their way, before stomping down the side of the house. A few moments later they heard the front door of Jim's house slam shut.

Jim rubbed the back of his neck with one hand. 'Sorry about that.'

Poppy shrugged and looked around for a tactful excuse to escape the backyard.

'That was my daughter, Lacey. She never used to be like this. I'm not sure what's gotten into her lately.'

The poor guy really did look miserable and more than a little perplexed by it all. 'How old is she?'

'Thirteen, though she thinks she's twenty-one,' he said dryly.

Poppy offered him a commiserating look. 'That'd explain it then. Hormones,' she said.

'Great.' He seemed to have paled slightly.

'It's a girl thing.'

'I'm not that great with girl things.'

'Well, I guess it's easier for mothers to deal with than fathers.'

'Unfortunately I don't have that luxury.'

Instantly Poppy wished she could take back the words. 'I'm sorry, I didn't think—'

'Oh no. Lacey's mother's still around, just not around *here*. We're divorced and Lacey lives with me.'

'Oh.'

'It was just easier before this teenage stuff came along. I'm still trying to get my head around it all.'

'By the time you do, she'll probably have outgrown it, so I wouldn't worry too much.'

'God, I hope so,' he said with feeling.

Poppy backed away from the fence. 'Well, good luck,' she said. She could safely say this was one occasion when she was more than a little relieved she didn't have children.

Poppy stood at her grandmother's bedroom door again. The spare room had been sorted and the cupboards cleaned.

She'd gotten boxes from the shed and packed all the old stuff Pop had brought into town from the farm and begun putting stickers on the things she thought should be either sold or given away to Vinnies. There wasn't a great deal to take to the tip—her grandmother wasn't a hoarder of rubbish—just a lot of family hand-me-downs accumulated from a farmhouse that was well over a hundred years old. *The house where Maggie would have grown up,* Poppy thought wistfully. It was good she had the cleaning to take her mind off things, but Maggie never seemed to be too far away from her thoughts.

She hadn't counted on all the emotions being back in this little house had brought, or all the quiet contemplation that allowed her far too much time to think.

While she wished for the comforting presence of her grandmother, she was almost relieved that she wasn't here. There wasn't much Poppy had ever been able to hide from her astute grandmother. There was no way she'd be able to face the look of disappointment on her grandmother's face if she'd been here and learned the reason behind Poppy's sudden appearance in the tiny backwaters of Warrial.

Everyone knows you sleep around. The words kept running through her mind, each time bringing with it a renewed sense of shame and embarrassment. So she wasn't into the whole find a nice husband and settle down and have kids thing. Big deal! That was her choice. So what if she went out with a few different men occasionally? The thought of settling down usually gave her hives; but surely that didn't make her a tramp? Slowly she moved through her grandmother's room, lightly running her fingertips across the embroidered bedspread as she crossed to the

99

large wardrobe doors. Pulling one open she was immediately launched back to her childhood as smells swirled around her, so powerful in their familiarity that it felt like an embrace and her heart squeezed painfully in response.

Reaching out she touched the soft pink material of a dress her grandmother had loved; she lifted the fabric to her face as memories took her back to a much happier time in her life. Poppy didn't realise she was crying until she stepped away from the cupboard and saw a damp patch on the sleeve of the dress.

Closing the door softly, she left the bedroom untouched.

Twelve

Poppy hit send as she emailed the last of the reports she'd been working on for her client and gave a huge sigh of relief. She'd remained professional in her dealings with Gill. She'd tried to limit their contact to email correspondence as much as possible, but there had been a few occasions when he'd called with questions about some of the work she'd left him with. Most of the things she knew full well he could have worked out himself, and that he'd only used them as an excuse to call her. When he'd tried to bring up anything not related to work, she'd managed to shut down the conversation; however, the fact he was still trying to talk about 'their relationship' was beginning to bother her. It was becoming clearer to her that she would have to find another job.

When her stomach began to rumble, she wandered into

the kitchen to see what she could scrounge up for lunch. She'd gone through the CWA ladies' food faster than she cared to think about—if she kept eating at this rate she'd be the size of a house before too long. Standing in the quiet kitchen, it suddenly felt all wrong. This had been such a hive of activity in her childhood. There had always been music playing softly in the background or voices on the radio. The sound of dishes being washed in the sink. She remembered how Nan had told her that when her father had been a boy, this was the time they'd spend chatting about his day at school, as they washed and dried the dishes. She and Nan had done their fair share of talking over the dishes as well. There was something calming and methodical about the chore. There had always been something delicious-smelling in the oven, Tupperware containers filled with good old-fashioned staples like jam drops and fruitcake waiting on the bench.

Tears sprang into her eyes, but she blinked them away. She didn't want to cry, didn't want to accept that all she had left of Nan were memories. She thought that if she let herself start crying now she might never stop.

Opening one of the kitchen cupboards, Poppy automatically caught the large stainless-steel bowl that fell out at her, then cringed at the loud crashing of tins and saucepans as the ones she hadn't managed to catch clattered to the floor.

It was funny how many memories tumbled out as she surveyed the mess of bake ware at her feet. She remembered standing on a chair at the bench alongside Nan while she mixed and measured and baked. There were no recipe books for her grandmother. No measuring cups or scales, just her hands and eyes to judge amounts. Baking with Nan had been something that Poppy had loved and she wondered now when she'd allowed herself to get too busy to cook? She couldn't remember the last time she'd made anything other than an omelette or a stir-fry. She never baked for the simple pleasure of it; she wasn't even sure she remembered how.

During her childhood, especially after she'd been to stay with Nan on holidays, she'd return home and bake up copious amounts of biscuits and slices, cakes and desserts. Her mother had always thought she might go into some kind of cooking-related career once she left school, but it had never eventuated. Her love of maths had taken precedence over her love of cooking. In fact it had always baffled her that despite being so meticulous about numbers she could completely disregard them when it came to cooking. Nan had taught her to cook by feel, not measurement. A cup was irrelevant, instead it was a handful of this or a dash of that.

Poppy hesitated as she was about to put a battered cake tin back in the cupboard.

She wanted to cook something.

A bubble of excitement began in her stomach at the thought, but a quick glance in the fridge reminded her that she'd need to restock first. Poppy gave a decisive nod at the tin she still held in her hand, then put it down on the bench and grabbed her car keys.

Downtown Warrial. You could throw a rock and not hit a single person. A few cars were parked here and there along the wide, quiet main street. It looked pretty much as she remembered it growing up. Warrial was old and much of the architecture dated back to the late nineteenth century, which made it seem as though you were stepping back in time. The wide street was divided in half by a nature strip. A large town clock dominated one end and a war memorial sat in the centre. Trees and gardens filled in the spaces between. At the bottom end of town was the police station and the school and Poppy could hear the muted sounds of children playing. There was a café and a post office, a grocery store and chemist, a butcher and a baker and, more than likely, there'd once been a candlestick maker too. A few offices were scattered along either side of the street, along with empty old buildings that would have once housed banks and council offices.

Parking her car, she waited for a rusty white ute to drive past, lifting a hand automatically in response to the driver as he idled past, before crossing the main street.

She headed into the small, independently owned grocery store and smiled as she recalled trying to pull a fast one on Nan a few times—picking out foods she'd never been allowed to have at home but telling Nan her mum bought them all the time. Nan hadn't believed her for a second, she was sure, but she usually bought for them for her anyway.

Poppy picked up a carry basket and made her way down the aisle, gathering ingredients as she went. Flour, caster sugar, eggs. Poppy ticked them off in her head, going over the recipes she planned to tackle when she got back to the house. The basket became heavier, piling up high with items she suddenly realised she needed.

She walked past the long freezer in the centre of the store and surveyed the very limited selection of frozen meals. There were a few chicken teriyakis that had ice encrusted on the lids. Other than that it seemed the good people of Warrial weren't big on buying frozen meals. She couldn't block out her grandmother's disapproving *tsk* at her laziness. *You can cook something better than this, young lady.*

A stirring for a nice big steak prompted her to make a mental note to stop by the butcher when she was finished in the grocery store. Quickly buying the rest of her staples, she took the basket to the slightly overweight middle-aged lady at the checkout and unloaded them onto the counter.

'You must be Elizabeth's granddaughter then?' the woman said.

It shouldn't shock her that everyone seemed to know who she was around here, but it still managed to give her a small jolt. 'Yep. That's me.' The woman had a vaguely familiar face; she'd probably been working here for years.

'I remember you coming in here when you were just a little thing,' the woman told her with a smile. Poppy glanced down at the ample bosom to see a faded name tag which read *Doreen*. 'Your grandmother used to talk about you all the time. You should have seen her when she knew you were coming home for holidays, she'd be in here buying up all your favourite things. I could always tell when she was expecting you.'

Poppy remembered. They'd count down the sleeps over the phone before she'd get here, and the pantry was always stocked with food when she arrived.

'So you moving into your grandmother's house then?'

What was it with these people? 'No. Just cleaning it out until I decide what to do with it.'

105

'It's a big job. My hubby and I had to go through his mother's old place a few years back. My God, the woman had some stuff! Lost count how many trips to the tip we did.'

'This isn't quite that bad. It's mainly just cleaning the house and packing away Nan's bits and pieces.' *Throw it all out?* Poppy didn't have a particular fondness for her grandmother's furniture, but she could never throw it out. It was part of her childhood memories of her grandmother.

Poppy thanked Doreen and walked out of the store. She slid on her sunglasses and looked up the quiet main street, locating the butcher shop. 'Now for that steak,' she murmured.

The butcher shop was exactly as she remembered it. The smell of raw meat greeted her like a slap to the face as she walked inside.

'Hello, love. What can I get you today?' The butcher looked like an ex-boxer, with his nose slightly off-centre and no sign of a neck.

'I'd like a steak. The biggest one you've got,' said Poppy.

'Music to an old butcher's ears,' the man smiled as he selected the cut of meat and wrapped it in paper. 'Now, you know how cook this?'

Poppy raised an eyebrow, unsure if the man was serious or about to pull her leg. 'I was planning to use the frypan.'

A look of horror crossed the butcher's face. 'I can't believe I just heard that. You can't cook a prime piece of meat like this in a *frypan*.' He said the word as though it tasted bad. 'This needs to be cooked on a barbie over hot coals.'

Okaaay. 'I guess I could find a barbecue somewhere,' she said, handing over the money and reaching to take hold of the brown paper bag with the meat in. For a minute the butcher didn't let go of the parcel and Poppy shook her head slightly in exasperation. 'I promise I won't cook it in a frypan.'

He seemed satisfied with that, and released his hold on the bag. 'You won't regret it.'

Outside, Poppy glanced up and saw Jim Nash crossing the road and coming towards her. 'Hey there,' he called.

'Hey.' Poppy found herself staring at his broad shoulders beneath his work shirt. Gone were the T-shirt and jeans. Today he looked as though he'd stepped from the pages of a RM Williams catalogue—the quintessential country professional, complete with worn akubra and boots.

'Finally run out of food?'

'Yeah. Thought it was about time I ventured out of the house. I've had the strangest craving for a steak today.'

'Steak, huh? Do you know how to cook it?'

Him too? Seriously? Did they think people from the city couldn't cook? 'I'm sure I'll figure it out.'

'How about you bring your steak over tonight and I'll cook it for you.'

'Oh no. I can manage, thanks.'

'You sure? That looks like a pretty big steak.'

Oh for goodness sake! 'If I run into trouble I'll let you know.'

'If you're sure.'

'I'm positive. Thanks. See you around.'

She turned to walk away, only to find he'd fallen into step with her. Stopping to glare at him, Poppy once more encountered that amused glint in his eye as he cocked an eyebrow at her questioningly.

'Do you mind? I *can* find my way home, you know.'

'Well, that's good to know. I'm just heading back to my office,' he said, nodding his head towards the open doorway with *Nash's Stock and Station Agents* written across the top.

Poppy grimaced at her stupid mistake and, once again, felt like an idiot.

'See you around, Poppy. And let me know if you need a hand with that steak.'

Clenching her jaw, she refused to glance back, but his soft chuckle followed her as she made her way to the car. She'd show him! There was an old barbecue in the backyard. She'd go straight home now and clean it up. They'd soon see who was laughing when the smell of steak sizzling drifted over his fence tonight!

Poppy reached up to the top shelf of the pantry and pulled down a stained old cookbook. Its hardback spine was cracked and some of the pages had come loose, but the faded chequered notebook had been her grandmother's pride and joy.

Inside were recipes that had been handed down from her grandmother and great-grandmother. Poppy had always loved it. She remembered Nan bringing it down to show her how to read a recipe, even though she never used it while she cooked. She didn't need to. She'd made the recipes so often they were a part of her.

Poppy had loved carefully flipping through the old book and reading the little tips and notes Nan had faithfully written down. Things like how to get rid of stains on clothing with a cleaning fluid made up of ammonia, glycerine and alcohol. A cure for diarrhoea and, bless her cotton socks, even a cure for drunkenness! This one made Poppy smile as she read through it. *Sulphate of iron: 5 grains; magnesia: 10 grains; peppermint water: 11 drachms; spirits of nutmeg: 1 drachm. Dose: 1 teaspoon to be taken in a wineglass of water twice a day. Highly recommended,* had been underlined in dark pencil beneath the recipe. Poppy chuckled and turned to the back of the book where the recipe for Nan's famous sponge cake was located.

'All right, Nan, let's see how much of this I remember,' said Poppy, positioning the cookbook on the bench for easy reference while she gathered the ingredients together.

'Eggs at room temperature,' said Poppy softly, having remembered to leave the carton of eggs she'd bought out of the fridge. Once, Nan would have only used her own chook eggs, having put the hens on a special diet before cooking for a show event or special competition. The chooks were long gone now, so store-bought eggs would have to do. Carefully separating the egg yolks and whites, she picked up the heavy old whisk and began to whip the whites. Nan had never used an electric beater when she was making a sponge. She'd done it the old-fashioned way, the way *she'd* been taught as a girl. It was damned hard work, but Poppy had always enjoyed it. Once you found a rhythm it became easier. It was actually rather therapeutic.

Once the high peaks formed, she added the sugar then the yolks. Sifting the dry ingredients into the mixture, she then carefully folded it until it was only *just* combined. Sliding it gently into the oven, mindful of keeping the air bubbles intact, Poppy finally released her breath in a long sigh.

'Fingers crossed, Nan,' she said with a nervous glance at the closed oven door.

Thirteen

Poppy swore under her breath as smoke stung her eyes and clogged her throat.

This shouldn't be that difficult, she thought, frustrated that the fire she'd built in the pit beneath the old brick barbecue refused to do anything but billow out smoke. She'd been trying to light it for close to an hour. In the end she'd resorted to using some metho she'd found under Nan's sink and the last of the box of matches. 'Don't try this at home, kids,' she added under her breath. 'Poppy, my girl, you'd never make an arsonist.' At this rate, she'd still be out here cooking breakfast! Her hair and clothes stank of smoke and her eyes felt gritty.

'Should I call the fire brigade now?'

She didn't bother to turn around; she'd been almost expecting that deep voice all afternoon. So much for tantalising his tastebuds.

'Are you going to cook it or incinerate the poor thing?'

'How was I supposed to know it wasn't a gas barbecue?'

'The lack of a gas cylinder wasn't a giveaway?'

'I didn't realise until I came out to cook that it was this primitive.' Why was she explaining this to him? It was none of his damn business.

'Are you really going to waste your steak on that? Come on, bring it over here and I'll fire up mine.' He didn't bother to wait for her reply, dropping to the ground on the other side of the fence and vanishing—presumably to pull out his man oven.

Fine. He was right on one point. She really didn't want to waste all that money. Dragging the hose over, Poppy made sure the last of the fire—or rather, the *smoke*—was out before heading back inside to collect her steak from the fridge and, on a whim, the plate with the sponge. Catching a whiff of her smoky shirt, she made a quick detour and changed her clothes. She wasn't trying to make an impression, she told herself firmly as she walked past the mirror in the hallway, she was just showing common courtesy.

The front door of the Nash home was open, but before Poppy could knock, Jim called for her to come down the side of the house. She followed a neat pathway leading to a paved entertainment area and tidy, manicured lawn. On a small deck that stepped up from the paved dining area, Jim was standing, tongs in hand, beside a stainless-steel monstrosity of a barbecue that looked very large and very expensive.

'Yeah, I know,' he said with a slightly abashed grin when he noticed her expression. 'It's my one real indulgence. We do a lot of barbecuing.'

'So it's not one of those overcompensating things then?' she asked dryly.

'Maybe,' he shrugged with a grin. He held a hand out for the plate with the steak.

'I brought dessert,' she said looking down at the cake and feeling a little self-conscious. This was the first time she'd shared her cooking with anyone in a very long time.

'That looks great. I really miss your nan's cooking,' he said and she caught a wistful smile briefly cross his face as he stared at the cream-filled sponge. 'There's wine or beer. What can I get you?' he asked over his shoulder as he turned and carried the cake inside.

'Wine would be great, thanks.'

She followed him across to the paved area where a table was already laid with three place settings. As Jim poured her a glass of wine she said, 'You didn't have enough time to set this table and light up that barbecue in the few minutes it took me to come over here,' she said suspiciously.

'Nope. Set it when I got home from work.'

'You were that confident I'd agree to come over?'

'Nope, I was counting on you hanging out for that steak too bad to say no.'

Poppy wasn't sure if she should be flattered or insulted. She could have got that barbecue working if she'd really wanted to.

'So how's it going over there?' Jim said. 'Making any headway?'

Poppy followed him back up to the barbecue. 'Not really. I'm cleaning as I go, but I don't want to throw out anything until my mum has a chance to go through it. This is more of a work break for me, I guess.'

'Your grandmother used to talk about you all the time. She was very proud of you, you know.'

Poppy took a hasty sip. *Would she still be proud of me if she knew I'd slept with a married man—my boss, no less?* The thought didn't sit well at all. Why was this bothering her so much? She'd never stopped to consider if her nan would approve of the choices she'd made before, so why did it matter now? It felt like Nan was her conscience. Even as this occurred to her, she bristled. Yes, she regretted that night, but for some reason she could not shake the niggling feeling that the whole thing with Gill was some kind of wake-up call.

'So you knew Nan pretty well?'

'I don't know what I would have done without her,' he said, looking away. 'I can't count how many times she came to my rescue with Lacey. I'll never be able to repay the kindness she gave to that kid . . . and to me. There'd be days when I'd come over to pick up Lacey, a million things on my mind, what with work and raising a kid by myself, and she'd make me sit and have a cup of tea with her,' he smiled at the memory. 'Then somehow she'd get me talking and before I knew it she'd have put things into perspective for me and I'd go home feeling like a huge weight had been lifted from my shoulders.' He looked across at her and smiled again. 'She was one of a kind.'

Poppy felt her throat close up as she struggled to keep her emotions in check.

'So you're some bigshot accountant?'

'I don't know about bigshot, but I'm in an area that's specialised.'

'What do you do?'

'I'm a forensic accountant.'

'And what does that involve?'

'We track and analyse data to find missing funds. We can trace illegal business activity and fraud.'

'In the private sector or the government?'

'Both. I've worked with governments to track down missing money from unsavoury characters. It's not really as glamorous as it sounds. I'm stuck behind a computer most of the time.'

'So you track down shonky businessmen and stuff like that?'

'Yeah,' she said nonchalantly.

'Terrorists? Do you do that too? That would be a major concern nowadays, wouldn't it?'

'I wouldn't be allowed to comment on that even if I had,' she said, biting back a grin.

'Really? So you're like some detective spook type accountant?'

'Spook?'

'You know, undercover agents and all that. Tracking down terrorists and finding out where all their drug and arms money is coming from?'

Poppy lifted an eyebrow mysteriously but only smiled. 'Sure, if you want to make my somewhat less-than-exciting job sound exciting we can go with that.'

'So what else do you do?'

'We present the evidence we find in court.'

'So does that mean you work for the police?'

'We work *with* them, not *for* them. Usually we have to appear in court as expert witnesses and present the data as evidence, so we tend to work closely with both the police and lawyers during trial investigations.'

'Wow, that sounds exciting.'

Poppy smiled. 'I enjoy it, though it's tedious—lots of analysing numbers and poring over thousands of files and cross-matching records, emails, phone accounts, bank statements. It's pretty intensive.'

'Sounds it. What made you decide to go into that line of work?'

'I love numbers. I was one of those geeky kids who loved maths at school. I became an accountant at first, but after a while I wanted more of a challenge, so I went back to university and got a job with a major accountancy firm who specialised in forensic accounting,' said Poppy. 'What about you? What made you become a stock agent?'

'Nothing very exciting. Born and bred in Warrial. My family had properties all over the place where we raised cattle.'

'So you have a lot of family here still?'

'Just a few old aunts and uncles. My parents were killed in a car accident when I was in high school.'

'That must have been hard,' Poppy said quietly.

He shrugged in that offhand kind of way she knew men sometimes did to hide their feelings. 'It was tough, but I finished school, went away to uni, got married and then came back and eventually took over my granddad's business. He was the stock agent around here for years.'

'So you hang around saleyards?'

'I buy and sell livestock for clients. Clients use me to find them the best returns on their livestock. And I source livestock when people are looking to buy. I'm kinda like a sharebroker, but dealing in cattle instead of shares.'

Poppy liked the quiet pride in his voice. He might think his job wasn't very exciting, but it was clear that he loved it.

'Lacey! Dinner,' Jim called.

Poppy heard a muffled reply and then footsteps eventually coming from the hallway inside the house. Lacey appeared in the doorway; she looked so young and innocent until she opened her mouth. It was hard to believe such an angelic-looking child, with long straight hair and big round eyes, could have such a bratty attitude. She stared at Poppy with a frown. 'What's she doing here?'

'Lacey. Watch your manners or you can turn around right now and go back to your bedroom.'

The teen seemed to be weighing up whether it was worth giving up dinner before thinking better of it and pulling out a chair at the table.

'Can I do anything?' Poppy asked, feeling awkward as she stood by the table and watched Jim placing the meat he'd cooked on a big platter.

'Nope. Just take a seat. I'll be right back with the spuds and salad.'

Poppy sat and fiddled with the stem of her wineglass. She felt the hostile gaze of the young girl across the table and steeled herself to make conversation. 'How was school?'

'A waste of time.'

'What year are you in?'

'Eight.'

Poppy remembered Year 8. It was even worse than Year 7. She'd spent most of her school life in the library reading—it was just the town name that changed, the schools were all the same. Thank God they all had a library. 'Do you know what you want to do when you leave school?'

116

'Get as far away from this hole of town as I can.'

Poppy took in the young girl's pretty face—which was hidden behind far too much makeup—and commiserated. Maybe Lacey wasn't the loner Poppy had been growing up, but she recognised in her that same tough outer shell that protected something very fragile.

'There are plenty of worse places to grow up,' Jim snapped, coming back outside with a bowl of green salad in one hand and a potato bake in the other.

'Worse than this? I doubt it.'

'This looks really nice,' Poppy put in quickly to avoid a fresh outbreak of father-daughter hostility. 'Thanks for saving my steak.'

'No worries. We eat out here most nights—except when it gets too cold in winter.'

'Did you do all this yourself?' Poppy asked, indicating the landscaped backyard.

'Yeah. Bought the place cheap and renovated it. I want to sell it eventually and move out to a property I'm running a few head of cattle on. But for now it's easier to stay in town.'

'Yeah, it's bad enough now. Moving all the way out to the middle of nowhere would be like going to prison,' Lacey muttered.

'Which is why I'm seriously thinking about making the move sooner rather than later,' Jim put in.

Poppy wondered how Jim coped with this constant hostility. Surely it wasn't this bad all the time? She kept her head down and concentrated on eating.

'How's the steak?' Jim asked, watching her from across the table.

'Delicious. You certainly know how to use a barbecue.'

'Don't ask me to cook anything else. I'm pretty limited in the kitchen—unlike you, if that cake on the bench inside is anything to go by.'

'Oh no. I don't really cook either. That's actually the first thing I've made in years.'

'Yeah? How come you don't cook?'

Poppy shrugged. 'It kind of seems a waste to cook when it's just me.'

'Why do you smell like smoke?' Lacey asked abruptly.

Jim shut his eyes and seemed to be summoning the strength to cope with his daughter's rudeness.

'I was trying to light the barbecue before your dad invited me over here tonight.'

'Who can't light a barbecue?' Lacey scoffed.

'Well, it wasn't a gas barbecue,' said Poppy, trying hard to keep any defensiveness out of her voice. She'd like to see this kid try to light a fire. On second thoughts, the obnoxious little brat probably could.

She headed home, pushing open the front door and locking it behind her.

The sponge had been a huge success. Poppy had felt a warm glow of pride as Jim had bitten into the cream layered cake and groaned his appreciation. She couldn't deny there was something fundamentally satisfying about a man's enthusiastic approval of one's cooking skills. Shaking off her goofy smile, she reminded herself that she hadn't cooked the sponge for Jim. She'd just taken it over as a thank you for cooking dinner.

She ran a deep bath and poured in some shampoo when

she realised she didn't have any bath bubbles. Sinking into the hot water, she breathed a sigh of relief. Maybe it was all the physical activity she'd been doing, cleaning out her grandmother's house, but she hadn't felt this tired in a long time. It was the good kind of tired—the physical, aching-muscle kind of tired, not the mental kind of tired she was used to. Eventually she dragged herself out of the bath and got into her pyjamas.

Looking at her watch, she rolled her eyes as she realised it was barely nine pm and she was in her PJs already. So much for a glamorous social life!

Fourteen

The slam of a door somewhere nearby jolted Poppy out of a deep sleep. Lying still, she listened for any further sounds but only heard the rattle of a four-wheel-drive starting up and reversing out of the driveway next door. Clearly it was just another day in paradise for Jim and Lacey.

Poppy sighed and rolled over, trying to get back to sleep, but after a few minutes she realised that was not going to happen. Her gaze fell once more on the diary on the bedside table and she reached out to pick it up.

Poppy loved reading Alex's letters to Maggie. It was remarkable to think they had been written in a trench somewhere in France during the First World War.

Dear Maggie,
Thank you for the socks. I got them today. They're very welcome, let me tell you—nothing quite like

a nice pair of dry socks to put on your feet. They don't stay dry for long, though. And I don't even care about the dropped stitches you said you were worried about—knowing you made them with your own two hands makes them the best pair of socks I've ever owned.

Things have been quiet here for a change. Just the odd artillery round going off to keep things interesting. It won't last, but it's nice for now. I'm getting lots of letters written. Thanks for keeping an eye on Mum. She said you came over for a cuppa the other day and brought her some milk and veggies. I like thinking of my two favourite girls sitting at the kitchen table and looking out for each other. Soon I'll be home to take care of you both.

I love you, Maggie. You're the first thing I think of when I wake up in the morning and the last thing I think of at night. Your letters mean the world to me and I know you worry about me, but know that everything I do is to ensure I get home to you safely.
All my love,
Alex.

Closing her eyes, she could almost hear the sound of cannons and gunfire around him as he wrote his letters. Poppy ran her fingers over the paper carefully, trying to imagine all the places this letter had been. 'If only you could talk,' she murmured wistfully.

She tried to picture Alex, balancing the paper on his knees as he scribbled down his innermost thoughts. *Had he spoken to Maggie like this,* she wondered. Had he been the kind of man who had been able to tell Maggie how much he loved her? Or would he, like so many men, have felt like an idiot if he'd dared speak those words out loud?

She could picture Maggie lovingly reading and re-reading these letters while she waited for him to return. Poppy felt her smile melt from her face as she remembered the last page of the diary.

> *21st June, 1918*
> *I have tried to force myself to write but I have not been able to find the words. Maybe I have been a coward. To actually write the words down on paper will mean that they are real and I cannot ignore them any longer. I pray each night before I close my eyes that it's all a terrible nightmare. A mistake. I will not believe that it is real, because I do not feel that it is. Surely I would no longer feel him with me if it were true? And I do. I still feel him with me. I cannot believe the worst. I will not believe the worst!*

Surely this meant Maggie had been told Alex had been killed? But something about the desperate tone of that last entry made Poppy doubt this. Was it just a young woman's attempt to deny the truth? Why had all the following pages been ripped out? What had Maggie written in there that was so bad it had to be destroyed?

Poppy stopped reading as the phone rang.

'Hello, dear, you weren't still in bed, were you?' said a familiar voice when she picked up the receiver.

Poppy opened her mouth to protest but didn't get a chance.

'I heard you were out and about yesterday in town, and I was just calling to ask if you'd like to come along to our next meeting.' It was one of the women who had turned up on her doorstep that first morning, but her name escaped Poppy for the moment.

'Oh. No. Thanks. I'm pretty busy at the moment,' she lied, looking around the house for something that needed urgent attention.

'I was hoping you'd come along to the meeting as a guest speaker. Your grandmother spoke so highly of your career. She always meant to get you to come along and give a little talk about it,' the woman said with a wistful sigh. 'I guess that goes to show we should never put things off.'

Guilt rippled through Poppy. Nan had actually asked her a few times, but she'd brushed it aside as something trivial and silly. She didn't have time to come all the way out here to give a talk to a bunch of bored CWA ladies. She'd worked alongside ASIO, for goodness sake!

Now she felt terrible. She'd put off far too many visits she should have made and now it was too late. What kind of self-centred idiot did that? It was hard to swallow the truth that *she* had done that.

Nan had never harped on it, had never sounded disappointed when Poppy had declined, citing a thousand and one reasons why she couldn't, but looking back now, Poppy knew it must have hurt Nan's feelings.

'Umm, well, I guess I could take a break and come along to your meeting if you'd like,' Poppy offered, clearing her throat.

'Oh lovely! Well, it's tomorrow. Pop down around ten o'clock, by then we'll have dealt with all the business items and be ready to sit back and enjoy a talk and a cuppa.'

'Great. I'll be there,' Poppy said weakly. Bernadette! That was the name she was trying to think of, but it was too late, the woman had said her goodbyes and hung up. Poppy replaced the phone with a sigh and looked outside. The sun had given up trying to fight its way through the dull looking grey-white clouds that covered the sky outside the window and a light pattering of rain began to fall. 'Great,' Poppy murmured dismally. The day was matching her mood perfectly. Retracing her steps back to the bedroom, she pulled on a warm cardigan and slid back into bed. She'd leave this world far behind for a little while and step back into Maggie's, where things were a whole lot less complicated.

The following day Poppy pulled out the closest thing she had to professional attire—a pair of black pants and a white T-shirt—then pulled her hair back and fastened it at her nape with a large silver clip. It wasn't ideal—she probably needed a suit jacket—but it did the job.

The CWA hall was a small white weatherboard building that also served as the local baby clinic and home to various other groups, judging by the large sign out the front with the various organisations and their meeting times. Opening the childproof gate to the yard, she walked inside, placing a hand to still the butterflies that suddenly fluttered inside her stomach. It didn't make any sense. Why would she be nervous of a few older women sitting in a hall? She'd appeared in front of courts and military tribunals, given evidence to a room full of high-profile officials. By comparison this was nothing, so why were her hands suddenly feeling clammy and her knees wobbling?

'And here she is now!' Bernadette spoke up as she caught sight of Poppy.

There were quite a few people in the crowd, definitely more than she'd been anticipating. She recognised one or two of the smiling faces but most of them were unfamiliar. Focusing on Bernadette, Poppy put out a hand, which was swiftly ignored as the woman pulled her into a tight hug, filling Poppy's nostrils with strong-smelling perfume.

Straightening awkwardly, Poppy did her best to smooth her hair back and regain some composure. She'd make a note to keep an eye on body language in here today and sidestep any further public displays of affection. She wasn't one of these touchy-feely people, especially with complete strangers. She preferred to keep people at a distance. Her mother would say this was on a personal level as well as a physical one.

Taking the small stage at the front of the hall, Poppy introduced herself and gave a spiel about her job, what it involved and some of the situations she had found herself in. As she let her gaze drift around the room she spotted the other woman who had arrived that morning with Jim and Bernadette. *Alice, that was it,* she thought. The woman smiled encouragingly, giving a nod every now and again to let Poppy know she was paying attention. There were a few women who looked to be in their forties, but the majority of the women were older. The building had a musty smell, that wet timber kind of scent that seemed to linger in these old places. The sun streamed in through cloudy glass windows, and part of the stream fell across the stage where she stood, hitting her like a spotlight. Within a few minutes she was quite warm and could feel a small bead of sweat roll down the back of her neck.

At the completion of her short talk, she was surprised when a sea of hands immediately rose and she found herself plied with questions that continued for close to an hour.

'So you mentioned matrimonial disputes, what does that mean?' a blonde-haired woman in the middle of the front row asked.

'In some divorces, usually involving quite a bit of money or multiple businesses, one of the parties may hire a forensic accountant to trace investments the other party may be trying to hide in order to keep them from being included in the divorce settlement.'

'You thinking of hiring Poppy here to see if Albert's holding out on you, Patricia?' another woman asked from a few rows back and most of the younger members chuckled. She noticed that Bernadette turned sideways in her seat to flash a disapproving glare their way.

'You mentioned fraud earlier?' another woman asked.

Poppy nodded. 'I sometimes get called in by a business who suspects an employee is stealing from them. I have to investigate the nature and extent of fraud and sometimes, if they aren't sure who it is, I have to identify the perpetrator.'

'How do you do that?'

'It takes a lot of digging and tracing records back to a source. I have to locate bank account transactions and things like that. It's called following a paper trail.' She smiled and relaxed as she realised the women were

genuinely interested and she enjoyed the challenge of trans-
lating the terminology into laymen's terms. 'I can also be
involved with personal injury claims, for instance, in the
case of a motor vehicle accident. We have to assess
the economic losses that may result when a person loses the
ability to work due to injuries sustained in the accident.
There's lots of different areas we work in and we have to
be up-to-date with all kinds of legislation, legal issues and
procedures. Basically we have to know quite a bit about
the law in order to do our job. It's not just tax and finding
loopholes,' she added dryly.

During question time Poppy noticed a few of the women
disappearing into a small room, bringing out plates of food
and depositing them on a long table at the rear of the hall.
Once the questions were wrapped up, a swarm of people
zeroed in on the goodies.

Poppy tried to think of the last time she'd seen so much
food. There were cakes and scones and slices of every
description, as well as dainty little sandwiches and quiches
with melt-in-the-mouth pastry. Everything that Poppy
tasted was delicious.

Poppy gratefully accepted a cup of coffee from Alice,
balancing her plate and the cup awkwardly.

'Thank you for coming here today, dear. I haven't seen
this much curiosity since we invited the local doctor to
come and give a talk. Poor man, he spent half the morning
giving out medical advice and the rest of the time trying to
avoid the infected big toe Harriet Brown was determined
to show him.'

'Well, I'm glad I'm not a doctor then.' The two women
shared a smile.

'Your grandmother would have been very proud of you coming here today,' Alice said softly.

The soft, fluffy lamington Poppy was eating turned to cardboard in her mouth. 'I should have made the effort sooner,' she said.

Alice tilted her head slightly to consider the young woman. 'Everything can be put off until tomorrow when you're young,' she shrugged.

Poppy smiled sadly. That was certainly true. She'd never spent time pondering what it would be like when Nan was no longer around. It just hadn't seem possible that one day she would lose her grandmother.

'Actually, Alice, I'm trying to find some information about a woman I'm pretty sure must be related to me. Her name was Maggie Abbott. Her diary was in with some photo albums of Nan's. I started reading it and just as it got interesting I found out someone had ripped out the ending!'

'A diary?' she asked, her gaze locking onto Poppy's.

'Yeah. It's from 1914. I couldn't believe it when I found it. I've been half-hoping I'd find the rest of it somewhere at Nan's . . . but so far nothing,' she shrugged. It was actually quite a disappointment; she really would have loved to have found the missing pages.

'Well, sometimes old things like that fall apart over the years.'

Poppy thought that was an odd thing to say—there was quite a difference between pages that had fallen apart and pages that had been ripped out. 'Does the name mean anything to you?' she persisted.

'That was all before my time, dear.'

Poppy frowned. 'What was all before your time?'

'That era. It was all before my time,' said Alice, delicately brushing the remaining crumbs off her lap.

'I wish I'd found it earlier. I'd have loved to ask Nan about it.'

'Perhaps you could start researching your family tree,' Alice suggested.

'I've never really been interested in that kind of thing before. I'd never even thought about it before I found the diary.'

'It's very rewarding. I've gone all the way back to 1642 with my husband's family.'

'Wow.' The more she thought about it, the more Poppy was attracted to the idea. She'd look into it—at least she might be able to find out who Maggie Abbott was, if only to put her into context on her family tree.

'So what do you think about Jim?' Alice cut in on her thoughts.

The sudden change of topic caught Poppy off guard. 'He seems nice. He was certainly very good to Nan. It's hard to find neighbours like that any more.'

'I mean, what do you *think* of him?'

That he fills out a pair of jeans in all the right places, she thought. 'He seems nice enough,' she said.

'He's a real gentleman. You won't find many men like him around nowadays.'

And that was the reminder she needed to kick herself back into reality. Nice guys were not her thing. She liked men who didn't complicate her life. Ones who didn't need anything more than she had to give. Nice men were dangerous.

Fifteen

Poppy lay out in the sun on an ancient-looking banana lounge she'd dug out of the garage and hoped the plastic straps would hold her.

The plastic creaked as she shifted her weight and Poppy braced herself in case it fell apart, but when nothing happened she let out a sigh of relief and went back to reading Maggie's diary.

In Maggie, Poppy had found a kindred spirit. She sympathised with her frustration in society and the restraints it had put on women back in 1918. Change had come to Australia, and watching it unfold before her eyes on the pages of this young woman's diary was truly an amazing experience.

As Poppy reached for the margarita made with limes she'd picked and squeezed that very afternoon, the plastic beneath her bottom gave a loud snap. She squealed in surprise as a sharp stab shot through her thigh and she fell through the frame of the old banana lounge with a painful thump.

Poppy found to her dismay that she was wedged inside the frame of the lounge up to her armpits. She had the glass in one hand and the diary in the other, and she didn't think she could put the glass down without it smashing on brick pavers. The old steel frame of the lounge was pushing against her thigh, and the more she tried to wriggle out, the more it dug into her.

Next door, she could hear movement inside the house. She wasn't sure who she hoped it was more—Lacey, the teen witch, or Jim. With a shake of her head, she realised she was going to have to call for help. There was no way she would ever be able to live this down, but her leg was hurting.

'Hello?' she called, but there was no response. 'Hello!' she yelled louder, her patience wearing thin. 'Goddamnit, Jim!'

'Poppy?' Jim's deep voice called only moments before she saw his head appear above the fence. 'Whoah. What are you doing?' His bemused chuckle did nothing to restore her good temper.

'Oh, I don't know, making scones. What does it bloody well look like I'm doing?'

'Well, at first glance,' he said, heaving himself over the fence effortlessly and dropping to her side, 'I'd say you were flat on your arse holding a cocktail, but I could be wrong.'

Poppy gritted her teeth and shut her eyes. It was a funny situation. She should just smile and make light of it. It could happen to anyone. It just never usually happened to *her*. 'The chair broke, and I'm stuck. Could you give me a hand?'

Jim stood in front of her, hands on his hips, staring down at her with a grin on his face. 'I always wanted to rescue a damsel in distress.' He took the glass from her hand and put it on the ground behind him.

'Could you please hurry up,' she said between gritted teeth. 'The frame's digging into my hip.'

Leaning over her Jim ran his hands down her waist to where her hip was wedged into the frame and his smile slipped as he realised she wasn't kidding. 'Why didn't you tell me you were hurt?'

'I'm stuck! I figured that was indication enough.'

'Can you feel your hip?' he asked, looking at her face strangely.

'Yes,' she told him. The truth was, with each passing second the pain was getting worse.

'Okay, just hold still, I'm going to try to bend it a little and see if I can straighten it enough for you to get out.'

As Jim struggled to get a hold on the frame, each slight movement intensified the pain in her hip. She bit down and tried not to cry out.

'This isn't going to work. I need you to stay still while I go and get something to cut through this frame. Don't move, okay? I'll be right back.'

'I'm not going anywhere!' she muttered, trying to reach her thigh to rub it, but there wasn't enough room and each movement hurt.

Jim came back, carrying a pair of long-handled cutters, which she eyed uncertainly. 'What is that?'

'Boltcutters. I have to cut through the frame.'

Poppy noticed he'd brought along a box with a big red cross on the lid. A sudden rush of clamminess washed over her and Poppy felt the colour draining from her face. Oh no, she remembered feeling like this once before when she'd had to have a blood test, right before she fainted.

Jim glanced up at her and she saw him take stock of her condition. 'It's okay, I'll have you out in a jiffy. Don't you pass out on me, Poppy.'

She didn't bother saying anything—she felt sick, and what were these horrible little black dots floating before her eyes?

She heard Jim grunt as he wrestled with the boltcutters, and then a moment of excruciating pain as the frame fell away, releasing her from its cruel grip. Immediately Jim was by her side, lifting the broken and mangled frame away from her. 'Easy. Don't try and get up. You need to lie down for a minute. The frame punctured your skin a bit and I'm just going to—'

Poppy didn't hear anything after that, slipping instead into a dark, quiet void.

'How are you feeling?'

Jim's voice sounded close by, but all she could manage was a groan.

'You didn't strike me as the fainting type.'

She opened her eyes. 'I've never had a piece of garden furniture try to eat me before,' she murmured. *Well, this is humiliating.*

'Take it easy,' Jim warned when she tried to sit up. He ducked his head to get a better look at her face. 'At least you've got a bit of colour about you now.'

Her hip hurt and she leaned sideways a little to see what the damage was. Her cargo pants had a big gaping hole at the hip and a padded dressing had been applied beneath.

'Sorry about your trousers. I had to rip the hole bigger to get to the wound. Speaking of which, when was your last tetanus shot?

Oh my God, a needle? Was she imagining it or was the blood once more rushing from her face. 'I have no idea. I don't think I've ever had one, or not that I can remember.'

'Really?' he asked doubtfully.

'I don't get hurt often,' she protested.

'We better get you to the hospital. That old chair had some nasty-looking rust on it, and that puncture wound went pretty deep.'

Poppy held up a hand and stopped him. 'I don't want to know.'

'Okay, tough guy, let's get you to the cruiser. Can you walk, or do you want me to carry you?'

Poppy shot him a look that told him she'd rather crawl than be carried. 'I'll manage.'

He slid an arm around her waist before she could utter a protest. Poppy found it difficult to concentrate with his big body pressed tightly against her good side, and his warm hand burnt a hole through her shirt at her waist. The upside was that this distracted her from her throbbing hip.

As she eased into the front passenger seat she let out a small gasp, 'Oh no!'

'What?'

'The diary. I've left it outside.'

'Diary?'

'I was reading an old diary out the back this afternoon.

It must be still out there. I can't just leave it. It's really old.'

'I'll go back and check. Wait here,' said Jim, closing the door and moving off at a long-legged lope around the back of her house. He returned a few moments later and slid into the driver's seat, handing her the leather-covered book before starting the vehicle.

Poppy gave a sigh of relief. She wasn't sure when this little book had become so important to her but the thought of losing it filled her with dismay.

Sitting in the emergency department of the hospital was an eye-opening experience. For a small rural hospital, it was certainly busy. People came and went while Poppy and Jim sat on hard plastic seats in the waiting room. An ambulance brought in a young boy who'd had a quad bike accident, a small child sat looking hot and miserable on his mother's lap, and a man in his twenties held a towel around his arm having come off second best to a barbed-wire fence. Poppy averted her gaze from the dark patch of colour seeping through the towel and prayed they'd attend to him soon.

She'd told Jim repeatedly that he didn't need to stay with her, but he refused to listen and was casually flicking through an old issue of *Women's Weekly*.

Poppy opened up the diary.

'So what's the story with the diary then?' Jim asked.

'It was in with a box of things I took home with me after the funeral.'

'Is it your grandmother's?'

Poppy shook her head. 'It belonged to Maggie Abbott and it was started back in 1914.'

'She was a relative of your Pop's then?'

'Apparently, but I'd never heard about her before.'

'Well, that's pretty cool.'

Poppy glanced at him and saw that he seemed genuinely impressed. 'Yeah, it is. I've never been all that interested in family history, but there's something about Maggie. I feel a . . . I don't know . . . a connection with her. I know that sounds stupid—'

'No, it doesn't,' he cut in.

Poppy shrugged uncomfortably. She wasn't sure why she was talking about these weird feelings with someone who was, really, little more than a stranger. Maybe it was some kind of bonding experience between trauma patients and their rescuers.

'There's nothing stupid about feeling a connection with your past. The Abbotts have a long history in this town. You should be proud of that.'

'I've spent so long in different places I've never really felt as though I belonged anywhere, even here. I've got all this family history but it doesn't feel like it's mine. I didn't grow up here the way my father and grandparents did. I used to envy that about locals like my nan, the way they'd refer to places like "the old Goodwin store" that hadn't been the old Goodwin store for over fifty years and yet everyone still knew it by that name. I don't have that connection with the town.'

'Yeah, I get that. Then again, you've seen a lot more in your life than most locals, so I guess they'd envy *you* that.'

'Maybe.'

'So what's in the diary? Any juicy gossip?'

'Better than that,' Poppy said with a smug smile. 'It's like a novel. It's got everything—romance, drama, and there's also an element of mystery.'

'Mystery?'

Poppy nodded. 'Some of the pages are missing at the end. They've been ripped out. I've been hoping they'll turn up in an old box somewhere at Nan's.'

Just then her name was called by a friendly faced nurse and she handed over the diary to Jim for safekeeping.

'You sure you don't want me to come in and hold your hand?' he asked.

'I'll be fine. Thanks.' She hoped she sounded more confident than she felt. She really hated needles . . .

Sixteen

'Today would have to have been the single most embarrassing day of my life,' Poppy moaned, resting her head against the window of Jim's Landcruiser. His soft chuckle did nothing to reassure her she was overreacting.

'Could have been worse.'

'Really? Because falling through a chair, having to get rescued by my neighbour, passing out, and then throwing up in the ER when I caught sight of my own blood was just about as much as I can handle in one day.'

Way to impress the guy, Poppy.

Impress? She wasn't trying to impress anyone. Or was she? Well, a fat lot of good it'd have done if she was.

'You were, however, very brave while they stitched you up,' he pointed out.

'Did I hurt you?' she asked rolling her head across to

look at the deep gouge marks on his hand. Oh yeah, not only had she proven just how much of a sook she was in front of the doctor and nurse, she'd gone and begged them to call Jim in to hold her hand. She still didn't know what on earth had possessed her to do that; she pushed it to the back of her mind to think about later. She felt humiliated enough without going into that.

'What, this?' He lifted his hand off the steering wheel and waved it under her nose? 'Nah, it might scar a little, but they say women dig scars, right?' he grinned.

Poppy managed a weak snort. 'Whatever. My scar's going to be way cooler than yours.' Although the two stitches the doctor had put in were hardly impressive.

The painkillers she'd been given were making her drowsy and the sound of the road beneath the tyres was almost hypnotic as she shut her eyes for a few minutes.

Poppy thought for a moment she might be about to faint again when she opened her eyes later. Everything around her seemed to be moving in and out of focus and she felt as though she were floating, until she realised she was not floating, she was being carried. She moved to untangle herself but Jim's deep voice reverberated against her ear that lay against his chest. 'Don't wriggle or we'll both go arse up . . . and I think we've had *enough* time in the ER tonight.'

'I can walk, you know,' she protested.

'And ruin my one and only chance to play the hero? No way.'

'You shouldn't be so nice to me,' she murmured and for a moment wondered if she'd actually said it out loud or just thought it.

'Why?' he said softly.

'Because you're *too nice*. Don't you know nice guys finish last?' she sighed. This wasn't entirely an unpleasant sensation; not drunk, but very sleepy.

'So I've heard,' he said, before asking which room she was sleeping in. As he lowered her to the bed, Poppy gave a sigh of contentment. 'But you know, the *reason* nice guys finish last is because we always make sure ladies finish *first*,' he said, planting a kiss on top of her head and leaving the room quietly.

Poppy was too tired to open her eyes, but she felt a smile settle on her face at Jim's parting words. *Well, well, well,* she thought. *Jim Nash was just full of surprises tonight.*

The next day, Jim dropped by to check on her.

She reassured him she'd changed the dressing just as the nurse had instructed, but for a minute there she thought he might insist she show him. 'Would you like a coffee?' she said to distract him.

'Sure. Thanks.'

She felt his eyes on her.

'Are you okay? You look like you've been upset.'

'I'm fine.'

'You sure? Because it doesn't look that way to me.'

She'd been reading through the letters before he arrived and feeling sad that Maggie and Alex had been separated by the war, perhaps forever. She was sure it was her hip making her feel like such a sook; the painkillers had worn off in the night and it was painful to move.

'It's stupid, and you'll think I'm crazy if I tell you.'

'What? You don't think I've already came to that conclusion? Nah, come on, tell me.'

Poppy took her time spooning the coffee into the two cups before she answered. 'It's the diary.'

'What about it?'

'I've read through it three times and each time I get more upset and frustrated.'

'What do you mean?'

'I *need to know* what happened to them. Did Alex die in the war? If he didn't, what happened to him? What happened to Maggie?'

'You do realise it's something of a moot point anyway, don't you? I mean, everyone from that era is long gone now. It's not as though you're going to find them alive and well.'

'I know that. It's the *principle* of the matter. I told you it was stupid. Forget I even mentioned it.'

'Okay, I'm sorry.' He put his hands up in mock defence.

Maybe he didn't understand after all. Or maybe she was a little crazy to be obsessing over an old diary, but for some reason it was important to her. She felt as though she *knew* Maggie and Alex. She wanted to know what had happened to them.

'You could go out to the cemetery to see if you can find her grave,' Jim suggested.

'I really don't like cemeteries,' she said, suppressing a growing unease at the thought. She hadn't been out to the cemetery to visit Nan's grave since she'd been back. She hated to think of her grandmother buried under the ground. She was glad her father had requested his ashes to be scattered out to sea. It helped a little to think of him like that rather than in some box in the earth.

'You could order her death certificate.'

She'd considered applying to Births, Deaths and Marriages but it just seemed so . . . clinical. It was Maggie's *life* she wanted to know about, not her death. Had she been happy? Had she had children? Had she married someone else after Alex's death? And if so, had she loved *him* as much as she loved Alex? She wanted to hear the answers from Maggie herself and nothing else would do.

'Oh hello, dear,' said Bernadette, catching Poppy as she stepped from her car two days later.

Damn. She'd just ducked down the street to pick up a few things and now she'd been sprung by Bernadette. 'Hello.'

'I was planning on dropping in on you this afternoon.' The starched uniform the woman wore was so white it was almost blinding in the glare of the morning sunshine. Poppy slipped her sunglasses from the top of her head back onto her face and read the insignia embroidered across the woman's left breast. *Warrial Bowling Club.* A matching white hat, with a wide, surprisingly trendy-looking turned-up brim, was perched on top of her head.

Poppy got the impression she'd somehow managed to disrupt Bernadette's carefully laid plans. 'Oh. I guess I've saved you a trip.'

'Yes. Never mind.' She opened her oversized white handbag and withdrew a folded piece of paper, which she handed over to Poppy. 'It's an invitation,' she said briskly. 'To our annual fundraising morning tea next week,' she added.

Poppy skimmed the paper and wondered irritably why the woman had bothered to give her a printed invitation if she was only going to tell her everything on it anyway.

'We all bring a plate, which is judged and then auctioned off for charity.'

'A plate,' Poppy repeated weakly. 'I don't really cook. I mean, I don't have a lot of experience cooking for other people. Not like *this*.'

'Hmm . . . well, I suppose, as an exception, I could cook something on your behalf,' she said, seeming to ponder the possibility.

Poppy's eyes narrowed suspiciously when the woman lifted her sly gaze.

'If you gave me Elizabeth's special sponge cake recipe, maybe I could whip it up for you.'

Poppy knew her grandmother was very protective of her recipes and had spent many a day listening to her kindly Nan get quite snippy when talking about the other competitors in various bake-offs over the years. She suspected Bernadette had been one of those competing cooks. An image of her grandmother spluttering in outrage at the thought of revealing her special recipe to one of her fiercest competitors made Poppy bite back a grin.

Easy, Nan. I wasn't going to give it to her! 'I'd forgotten about Nan's sponge recipe,' Poppy said slowly. 'I think I might see if I can throw something together.'

'Well, if you're sure, dear.' The woman didn't even bother to hide her doubtful expression. 'I'll be off to bowls, then. I'll see you at the morning tea.'

Poppy swore under her breath as she realised she'd been baited into accepting the stupid invitation. What was with these people? Why were they always roping her into things? She was only here temporarily! Well, she'd just not show up. What were they going to do? Send out a search party for her?

Shrugging off her frustration, Poppy decided to take a walk down along the river, just behind the town centre. It was a popular place for locals and tourists—well, those who ventured out this way—to sit and have a bite to eat. There was a small park up one end and picnic tables scattered along the length of a rock breakwall that reinforced the riverbank against flooding and erosion. Finding a quiet corner, Poppy withdrew an apple she'd brought along, crunching happily as she took in the wide river and bright blue sky above.

Her peace and quiet was interrupted by a chorus of giggles and noisy chatter from a group of teenagers who emerged from beneath the bridge. Poppy watched the two males in the group—their jeans hung low, exposing boxer shorts—kick an empty drink can like a soccer ball between them, showing off for the two girls with them. The smell of cigarette smoke wafted across and she gave a *tsk* of annoyance that even after all this time some kids still didn't get the 'don't smoke' message. As she got a closer look at the group, she recognised a familiar face. Lacey Nash.

She thought about making a run for it to avoid being seen but realised there wasn't time. Great. The last thing she wanted to do was become tangled up in an ongoing battle of wills between father and daughter.

She resigned herself to the inevitable as Lacey spotted her. Fear, guilt, suspicion and then anger all flashed across the young girl's face in rapid succession.

Poppy decided to play it cool and remain silent. After all, this wasn't her child. If Lacey wanted to give herself lung cancer that was Jim's business, not hers.

'What are you doing here?' Lacey demanded.

'I could ask you the same thing. Shouldn't you all be in school?'

'It's sport.'

'Really? Since when was wagging considered a sport?'

'Wagging?' The other girl sniggered, and the two boys gave nervous giggles.

'We don't call it that any more,' Lacey snapped.

'Well, excuse me for having better things to do with my life than keep up with what kids are saying in high school,' said Poppy, tossing her apple core into the rubbish bin beside her. 'Well? Run along, you're blocking my view.'

'So I suppose you're going to go straight to my dad to tell him, aren't you?'

'It's none of my business,' said Poppy, holding the girl's defiant gaze.

'Yeah, right.'

Poppy stood up. 'I really do have better things to do with my time than care what a bunch of kids are up to.'

Lacey made a scoffing sound, then turn and walked away.

Poppy watched as the four of them headed back towards the main street. *Ah, to be young and rebellious,* she thought wryly.

Eventually she wandered back along the shady main street. Many of the shopfronts were originals and were now heritage listed. Maggie and Alex had probably walked along this very footpath all those years ago. If only these buildings could talk what an amazing story they'd have to tell. This little town had seen so much of Australia's history unfold—wars, droughts, floods—and still it remained as proud and sturdy as ever.

In amongst all Nan's photo albums Poppy had come across old photos of Warrial. If it hadn't been for the old-fashioned cars parked along the street and the clothing people wore, the photos could have easily been taken today, so little had changed about the town.

Poppy stopped outside an old stone building on the corner of the main street which looked like an old bank. The date in swirly figures high up on the front of the roof read *1905*. This date proved that the building had been around during the war. The only other banks in town now stood empty, but the dates etched into their brickwork told Poppy they hadn't been built until the mid 1920s, which would have been too late to have been where Maggie worked in 1918. With a rush of excitement she realised this *must* have been Maggie's bank. The building now housed a government aged-care service, but the outside still looked very much like an old bank. There were no banks in Warrial now. They'd all closed after exchanging staff for ATM machines in the early nineties, realising how much money they could save if they got rid of banks in rural communities across the country. Poppy remembered the uproar when the last bank left town. It had been hard on the older members of the community like Nan; many of them didn't drive any more and there was no public transport to the bigger regional areas, making getting into a place like Glenwarren difficult if they needed access to a branch. Progress, it seemed, didn't take small rural towns into consideration.

Poppy stopped and placed a hand against the warm bricks of the old building and closed her eyes for a moment. A flutter of excitement ran through her as she pictured the young woman excitedly climbing these very same marble steps to head into work on her first day. *The first female teller in Warrial.* A surge of pride swelled inside Poppy at the thought.

'Good for you, Maggie,' she whispered, then with a sad sigh pushed away from the post and headed back to her car.

Seventeen

Poppy carried her groceries to the back door and frowned as she noticed a brown paper package on her doorstep.

Putting down the plastic bags she'd been carrying, she picked up the parcel and turned it over in her hands. There were no postmarks or stamps, so it hadn't been delivered by the postman.

Unlocking the back door, she dropped the parcel into one of the grocery bags and carried them all inside. Having unpacked her shopping, Poppy reached into the last bag and withdrew the parcel.

She grinned as she dug through the useful-box drawer, recalling how her grandmother had named the drawer after the ABC program *Play School* and the craft box they used on the show. If you were looking for sticky tape, pipe cleaners, matches, glue, marker pens or envelopes, they could be found in the useful-box drawer.

She cut through the string that secured the brown paper wrapping and carefully removed the small white box inside. She lifted the lid and gasped.

There in the bottom of the box was a small pile of papers secured by a ribbon threaded through two holes someone had punched in them. They were the same pages as Maggie's diary.

Poppy sat down at the kitchen table and stared at the box in disbelief. Where had it come from? Who had delivered it, and why now? Biting her lip, she suddenly realised she didn't care! She'd figure that out later.

With hands that had begun to shake with excitement, Poppy carefully lifted the pages out of the box and placed them on the table. Inside the pages, just like inside the diary, there was a folded letter. Poppy opened it and started to read, but quickly refolded it and put it back in between the last few pages where she'd found it. She was going to make herself read this in order.

Making a coffee, she settled onto the lounge and began reading.

12th August, 1918

It has been a most extraordinary week. Mr Fortescue has employed a new teller. His name is Mr Walter Hicks and he is truly the most infuriating man I have ever had the displeasure to meet! I suppose in his own way he could be called quite handsome, although I'm certain if one was to ask him he would most definitely assure you he was! He seems to think he is some kind of charmer, and more than one of our older female customers appears to be quite taken by him. I am left speechless at some of the women this scoundrel has managed to fool.

He has even had the hide to ask me to accompany him to the dance this weekend. As if I would be tempted to lower my standards to do such a thing!

Maggie

It didn't seem to matter how rude Maggie was to this man, he simply didn't take offence. If anything it only seemed to incite him further!

It didn't matter how many times she turned Walter Hicks down, he just continued to flirt with her and, what was even more unsettling, she was beginning to expect it.

There had been no further word on Alex, and as the weeks turned into months, something inside her began to grow numb. It was hard to maintain her faith that he was still alive when there was no news of him, and slowly her hope crumbled. Her parents' vigilant concern for her made her feel as though she were walking on eggshells. She understood they were worried about her, but their constant need to watch over her was making her feel claustrophobic. She hated that she felt so angry and hateful inside most of the time, and she was desperate to have just a moment of peace. Just *one* day where she wasn't completely consumed with worry that Alex would not be found. She had no appetite; she was eating only to stop her mother nagging; she had no interest in anything other than going to work and then shutting herself in her room at night.

Everything annoyed her. She lashed out at her sister and parents when they tried to draw her out of her misery. She knew they had enough to worry with Frank now fighting in a place called Péronne, in France, but she was beyond consoling. The only thing she wanted was Alex.

She didn't like the person she was becoming but she had no idea how to stop it. Then one day Walter asked her to accompany him to a dance and she surprised herself by accepting.

Sitting on the end of her bed the evening of the dance, she listened to her parents' hushed whispers outside. She knew what they were saying. They were relieved she seemed finally to be putting Alex behind her and moving on, but on the other hand this Walter Hicks fellow was beginning to ruffle a few feathers about the place. He was seen with a different girl each time he went out and he was a regular at the Star Hotel, and not always in the company of the most respectable of women. This was not the kind of man they wanted to be associated with their daughter.

Maggie just needed to escape for a little while; to dance and sing and let the music stop her thinking for a few hours. Walter seemed to know all too well how to take a person's mind off their worries. He was surprisingly good company and had an uncanny knack of knowing just the right thing to say to distract her from her thoughts. He was a fine dancer and showed impeccable manners. Maggie was forced to admit that maybe her first impression of the man had been a tad harsh.

26th August, 1918
Walter is like a bad habit I can't seem to give up. When I'm with him I feel like a different person. He appreciates my intelligence and treats me like a sophisticated woman, not

151

a simple country girl. And I like being this different person. It's so much easier being her. She hasn't lost a brother or a man she still loves so much her heart aches and cracks a little more each day. The girl I become when I'm with Walter doesn't have anyone but herself to think of . . .

Poppy

Poppy stopped reading and knew instantly what Maggie meant. Hadn't she, too, invented a new persona to deal with her own sadness? In school she'd accepted the taunts and bullying that came with being the new girl, and a geek at that, which was why she preferred to spend her time in the library. But at university things changed. Suddenly she wasn't in the minority; the place was full of geeks. And guys seemed to find the aloofness she'd perfected over the years attractive. With the first few stirrings of interest she'd slowly allowed herself to play up this aspect of herself. No longer locking herself away in the library, she embraced this new-found freedom and no one would ever have suspected that hiding inside was that lonely little girl who never quite felt like she belonged anywhere.

By her early twenties she'd worked out she needed to avoid the nice guys. She wasn't interested in settling down and giving up her independence, so the bad boys were who she went for. They weren't interested in long-term either, and she didn't care about flowers and romantic dinners. When she wanted some excitement, she found a guy. No one got hurt. It was a heady feeling once you embraced it. If you had no one but yourself to care about, then you could do anything you liked.

Maggie

Maggie was setting the table for Sunday lunch. Dulcie was standing with her back towards the window, watching her thoughtfully.

'Whatever is the matter with you, Dulcie? Here, make yourself useful and finish laying out the cutlery. Walter will be here soon and I want to fix my hair before he arrives.'

'You really think he's the one then?'

'What?' Maggie almost dropped her mother's antique serving dish that she had been taking from the china cabinet.

'Walter. You two are serious then? Going steady?'

'Of course not. Why would you say such a daft thing, Dulcie?'

'You spend every weekend with the man and he clearly adores you.'

'We're just having a bit of fun, that's all.' She looked at her sister warily. 'Why do you ask?'

Dulcie shrugged. 'I heard a rumour the other day, that's all.'

'About what?'

'Walter. He's apparently quite wealthy. He'd be a good catch.'

Maggie clicked her tongue, annoyed. 'Maybe if Gordon did more than sit around listening to gossip down at the Star, he'd get more work done.'

'Gordon is a decent man. He works hard. I'm just saying that if a well-off gentleman was paying me attention I'd take the opportunity to get out of Warrial.'

'Well, this is none of your concern, so I would advise you to worry about your own love life, not mine.'

'So you do have feelings for him!'

153

'No,' said Maggie, gritting her teeth. 'I do not. Not those kinds of feelings anyway.'

'Well, if you're not serious about Walter, then you'd better let him down gently before he makes a fool of himself over you. And you're not getting any younger, you know. You need to find a decent man before it's too late. Come along to the dance next week with me and Gordon and let's see who we can find for you. There are more and more boys coming home every day.'

Dulcie froze as she caught sight of Maggie's shocked expression.

'I didn't mean . . . Oh look, Maggie, there's no point beating around the bush, is there? Alex is not coming back and you have the rest of your life ahead of you. You need to find someone to settle down with before you turn into an old maid.'

Maggie gripped the back of the chair tightly, fearing that if she didn't she would pounce on her sister like a feral cat. How dare she assume to know what was best for her? None of them knew the pain she carried around inside her; none of them knew the emptiness that was with her day and night. Only Walter managed to make her forget her troubles. He was the only thing that didn't remind her of Alex.

'Mind your own business,' she snapped at Dulcie and stormed out of the room. She felt a moment of regret at the heartless person she'd become, then ruthlessly pushed it aside. The old Maggie was long gone, along with any joy or hope left in her world.

At the dance that weekend Maggie held on tight and let the music take her far away. Walter's arms held her steady and she allowed her sorrow to be disguised in laughter and singing. She tried to ignore the look in Walter's eyes. She pushed away the uneasy feeling that she was giving him some kind of false hope. She didn't want to acknowledge that; if she did, then she knew she'd have to put an end to these dances, and if she did that, she'd be forced to sit back in her room and think about Alex day and night, and it would surely send her crazy.

Pausing to catch their breath between dances, Maggie and Walter lined up for a drink.

'So, mate, when are you planning on joining up?' Maggie glanced over at the speaker, her good mood evaporating instantly. Doug Crawford stood with two other young men, Pat Sanders and Tommy Edwards, all having returned from the war with missing limbs. She had grown up with all three.

Walter smiled but didn't comment.

Maggie felt a wave of animosity encircle them and she tugged on Walter's sleeve urgently. 'Walter, I'm really not thirsty, let's go outside.'

'We'll stay here and wait. It won't be much longer.'

The other men exchanged glances and Maggie saw Doug's jaw clench. 'You think you're too good to serve your country then? Is that it? Scared to swap your fancy clothes for khaki like a real man?'

'I have no quarrel with you, Doug. I don't want to cause a scene when everyone's here to have some fun. Don't you think it's high time we all had a little bit of enjoyment in our lives?'

'Oh pardon me, so sorry you've had to live without *enjoyment* lately. It must have been terrible back here, safe and sound and sleeping in your own comfy bed these last few years. Do you want to know how we've been sleeping?'

'We all appreciate the sacrifice you've made. But the country doesn't just stop when you all head overseas. Believe it or not, people are needed here to keep things running to pay for you lot to go over there.'

It wasn't the right thing to say. Doug, like many of the other returned soldiers, was having a terrible time trying to settle back into normal life. Maggie remembered the pride she'd seen on the faces of Doug's parents at the dance they'd thrown for him before he left, and she'd watched only the other day when Doug's father had turned his face away as his son stumbled up the main street on his prosthetic leg, on his way to the pub again.

It was hard for all of them to adjust to these men returning home, so achingly familiar and yet so very different to the boys they had been when they'd left. It was going to take time and a great deal of understanding from the community, but in Maggie's mind it did not excuse this outright bullying of a man just because he hadn't joined the armed forces to fight. Many did their bit for the war effort back home, and Walter did have a point, men were also needed on the home front. She had wondered why he hadn't jumped at the chance to see the world, as most of the boys she knew had, but it was none of her business. People had their reasons.

'Cowards aren't welcome here. I expected better of you, Maggie. Tom and Frank would be ashamed to see you out here flaunting yourself in front of everyone with this spineless excuse of a man.'

'What gives you the right to speak about someone like that?' Maggie demanded, outraged that the man could attack a person's character so publicly and without provocation.

'Losin' my leg for my country gives me the right,' Doug said, leaning close to Maggie and slapping the artificial leg beneath his trouser pants.

'We've paid for a ticket just like everyone else,' Walter told them, moving to stand in front of Maggie, his previously jovial mood replaced by a flush of deep anger.

'You're not welcome here. Leave or you'll regret it.'

'It'd almost be worth seeing you try to remove me.'

It all happened so fast: one minute Walter was smiling, the next moment his smile had been wiped from his face by a strong right cross, quickly followed by a roar of outrage from nearby patrons. Maggie stumbled backwards out into the cool night air, her hand around her throat as she caught flashes of arms, legs and bodies as men rolled and tumbled about the floor.

Dulcie came running outside, hurrying Maggie toward Gordon's old truck, pushing her sister into the cabin as Gordon half-dragged, half-carried a beaten and bloody Walter towards them. Tossing him up onto the tray in the back, he slammed the driver's side door shut behind him and took off. A hail of abuse was thrown after them as they drove away.

Once the vehicle pulled up at the Abbotts' farm, Maggie hurried around to the back to help Gordon lift Walter from the tray and get him inside. In the light, she was relieved to discover the damage wasn't as bad as she'd at first feared.

'Oh my goodness. What's happened?' The girls' mother bustled into the kitchen, immediately taking charge of the situation, issuing orders to everyone and carefully cleaning up Walter's bloodied face.

As his wife administered first aid, Maggie's father asked questions, listening closely to Gordon and Dulcie's rehashing of the event. When Walter had been cleaned up, Maggie's father escorted him to the vehicle outside, Gordon following silently.

Maggie knew nothing good was going to come of this evening's fiasco and she braced herself for her father's return.

'You won't be seeing that boy again and that's the end of it.'

'But, Dad—'

'I said,' her father raised his voice, silencing her protest, 'that's the end of it. And on Monday you'll be handing in your resignation at the bank.'

'You want me to give up my job at the bank? No, Dad, that's not fair!'

'With Frank overseas, you're needed here on the farm more than ever.'

Maggie felt her heart sink. She saw how her poor mother had grown old with hard work over the years. Tending children and working alongside her husband on the farm had aged her faster than her contemporaries in town. How many times had Maggie stared at the women in town who lived in their tidy little houses with their neat little gardens and well-tended lawns and thought of her poor mother? She knew her mother would have dearly loved to be pottering around in a pretty little flowerbed instead of bending over in the field, picking beans and watermelons, hard physical labour with hours spent out in the hot sun. Her beautiful porcelain skin had turned leathery and brown after being exposed to the elements all these years. Maggie didn't want a life like her mother's. She wanted freedom and excitement, recognition for being as smart as any man, and as capable in business.

'Please, Dad, let me ask around town for another job. I'll do *anything*, just don't make me work on the farm.'

'I can see that allowing you to work at that bank was a mistake. You seem to have forgotten where you come from, girl. This farm brings an honest living and puts food on the table. You think sitting inside that fancy bank and adding up figures is somehow better than the work your family does here?'

'That's not what I think at all. But I love numbers. Mr Fortescue himself said I'm the best clerk he's ever had. Please, Dad, this is what I'm good at, it's what I love.'

'In case it's slipped your mind, there happens to be a war going on. Do you think those boys over there are happy about lying in stinking trenches all day? Do you think that the ones who've been killed are sacrificing their lives so that you can sit back and be choosy about what kind of job you do?'

'I'm no good at farm work, Dad.'

'Well then, you'll have plenty of time to practise. You can take over the milking first thing in the morning.'

And that was the end of the conversation.

Eighteen

The front yard was today's task. Although the lawn was kept neat and tidy thanks to Jim's regular mowing, the flowerbeds that ran across the front boundary line were beginning to look rather scraggly. She didn't know much about gardening, but she knew enough to know the difference between a weed and a plant, so she hoped she wouldn't do too much damage.

'Nan would be horrified if she saw the state you were in,' Poppy murmured as she surveyed the garden bed, wondering where to start.

'Do you always talk to yourself?'

Poppy glanced up to find Lacey standing on the other side of the little brick fence, arms crossed, a smug smile on her face.

'I wasn't talking to myself. I was talking to the plants,' she said.

'Weird.'

'Did you want something?' Poppy asked after a few moments.

'No. I'm just bored, that's all.'

'There are plenty of weeds to go around,' Poppy offered without looking up.

'I'm not that bored.'

Poppy ripped at the weeds harder, absolutely certain now she never wanted children.

'How come you haven't said anything to Dad about the other day?' the girl finally asked, kicking at the dirt on the other side of the fence with the toe of her shoe.

It had been two days since she'd sprung Lacey and her friends skipping school and had actually forgotten all about it. 'Like I said, it's none of my business.'

'I thought adults were supposed to care about stuff like that. Doesn't sound too responsible to me.'

'So you want me to go and tell your father you were wagging school and smoking?' Poppy asked.

'Well, der! Of course not. But most other grown-ups would have dobbed me in.'

'You know, your attitude is really annoying.'

'*Now* you sound like a grown-up,' Lacey muttered. 'So how come you never came out here to see your nan much?'

Poppy's hand hesitated over the next patch of weeds. 'I was away a lot. I lived overseas for a while.'

'I know. Nan used to show me your letters sometimes.'

'You called her "Nan"?' A lump began to form in Poppy's throat as she continued weeding.

'Well, she wasn't my real nan.'

Poppy could imagine Nan filling in as a surrogate grandmother to this young girl. Being a nan was what she did best. Poppy thought back to all those warm hugs and quiet moments that had meant so much to her growing up and she was glad Lacey had had Nan there to help fill in some of the emptiness left by losing her mother. *Not to mention the void Nan had to fill when you grew up and decided you were too busy to come back and visit,* a little voice snapped.

'She was like my real nan, though,' Lacey added, almost as though she felt a need to defend her relationship to Poppy.

Poppy smiled softly. 'It's okay, I don't mind sharing her. I'm glad she had you to take care of. It was her most favourite job ever, spoiling kids. Did she ever make you fairybread butterflies?'

Lacey looked up with a surprised light in her eyes. 'Fairyflies,' she said and a rare smile touched the young girl's lips, before she dropped her gaze once more and continued kicking at the ground.

'So you never answered my question . . . how come you didn't tell Dad?'

'Because it's up to you if you want to ditch school and ruin your health. Personally I'd be more impressed if you'd show a bit more respect for yourself.'

'What's that supposed to mean?'

'You seem like a smart kid. I'd be concentrating more on using my brains to get out of town and get a good job than throwing away my education to smoke all day.'

'School's boring.'

Poppy shrugged. 'Being stuck in a dead-end job in town is more boring.'

'It's all right for you, you've *got* a life. Nan always talked about how well you were doing and how rich you were. I'm stuck here for years before I can leave.'

What on earth had Nan been telling everyone?

'Nan said *that*?' Poppy eyed the girl dubiously.

'Well, *something* like that,' she muttered, and Poppy realised it had probably been nothing like that at all.

'You think I got *my* life by skipping school and hanging out with boys who wear their jeans down around their ankles? You have to work for things you want in life. They don't just fall in your lap.'

'Now you sound like my father.'

'Then he's obviously a very smart man.'

'You like him, don't you?'

Poppy's hand stilled on the clump of grass she'd been about to pull from the ground. Man, this kid could throw her off-centre. 'Sure I like your father. Not many people look out for their elderly neighbours the way he did,' she hedged.

'No, I mean *really* like him.'

Poppy's eyes widened in surprise. What? 'No, not like that,' she said a little too hastily.

'You do so.'

'I do not.'

'Do so.'

Honestly, how old was she again? 'I'm not interested in your father *romantically*,' she corrected.

'I think he likes you,' Lacey taunted.

Poppy began to feel flustered by the direction this conversation was headed; she had no idea what to do to rein it in. 'Look, if you're not going to help me weed, then you'd better go and find something else to do.'

'For a minute there I thought you were cool, but I guess I was wrong. I've got better things to do anyway.'

Poppy watched as Lacey turned on her heel and marched back home. She had the sudden suspicion that the girl had been trying to reach out to her, but Poppy had no idea how to help. How was she supposed to help a teenager? It had been a long time since she'd been one, and anyway, did she look like an advice columnist or agony aunt? With a frustrated sigh, she went back to her weeding.

What she really wanted to be doing was reading the rest of the diary, but she'd put herself on a strict diary diet. She'd been tempted to just keep reading yesterday, but she knew she had to ration herself. After this there were no more diaries—she knew because she'd been through all of Nan's boxes and hadn't found any. She couldn't bear to reach the end and still not know if Maggie had her happily-ever-after. Not yet. She was rationing out her allotted diary reading time to make it last for as long as possible.

Poppy glanced up as the big four-wheel drive idled to a stop in the driveway next door, and she tried to ignore the flutter of awareness that quickly followed. She'd been out here longer than she'd anticipated. Weeding was not something she did often. In fact, she couldn't recall the last time she'd actually done any weeding. But once she'd started, it had been rather therapeutic. Unfortunately it was pretty warm, and she could only imagine what a sight she looked with her sweaty T-shirt and messy hair.

'Who's winning?'

'It was touch and go there for a while, but I think I might have the upper hand now,' she said.

'Hadn't picked you for a gardener.'

Poppy looked over at him leaning out his window. He was wearing a grin that made her lose her train of thought. 'I have many talents you don't know about,' she said.

'Yeah, apparently.'

Gathering up the weeds, Poppy couldn't stop thinking about a hot shower and glass of wine, but she was surprised when, instead of heading inside after his day at work, Jim came over and helped her heap the weeds into the green waste bin she'd dragged from the backyard. 'Thanks.'

'You look like you could use a drink.'

'I think I could use a shower more.'

'Well, I was thinking of getting you a drink, but if you need a hand with the shower instead—' he started, then chuckled at Poppy's narrow-eyed glare, holding his hands up and backing away slowly. 'Take your time. I'll get the drinks and be waiting out the back when you're finished.'

Poppy did take her time under the shower, enjoying the hot water and soaping up a lather of lemon-scented soap to wash away the dirt and sweat.

Towelling her hair dry, she quickly ran a comb through it and ruffled it with her fingers before pulling on underwear, jeans and a T-shirt she'd found after digging through the folding she hadn't gotten around to putting away earlier.

She shouldn't be enjoying these little neighbourly get-togethers so much. It would be far wiser to put a stop to all this before Jim got the wrong idea. She didn't want things to get complicated.

'Here she is, and just in time,' said Jim, handing her a nicely chilled glass of wine. Poppy took a sip, forcing herself not to scull the lot in one go. Who knew gardening was such thirsty work!

'Thanks, I've been thinking about this all afternoon.'

'Looks like you've been pretty busy. Does all this yard work mean you're planning on putting the house on the market soon?'

'I'm still not sure what I'm going to do with it yet. I just couldn't stand looking out at all the weeds a moment longer.'

'Your grandmother loved her flowers.'

Poppy smiled at the memory. 'Yeah, she did.'

'Hey! Get back here, young lady,' Jim called as he caught sight of his daughter about to head towards the front door.

'What?' Lacey came to the back of the house, her hands on her hips.

'You are not leaving the house in that get-up. Go back and get changed.'

She was dressed in a short skirt and a top that had been tied to expose her midriff, but it wasn't the outfit as much as the thick makeup that worried Poppy. Lacey definitely didn't look like a thirteen-year-old.

'What's wrong with what I'm wearing?' she demanded. 'I'm going to Tia's.'

'Not like that you're not, and get rid of that stuff off your face while you're at it.'

'It's just makeup.'

'Go change. Now.'

'I don't have anything else to wear,' she groaned.

'I just bought you new clothes a few months ago.'

'Exactly, I have nothing decent to wear.'

'Lacey, you either get changed now or you can forget about going over to Tia's altogether.'

'God! You make my life so miserable! You ruin every-thing!'

Lacey stormed back into the house and Poppy winced as a door slammed a few moments later.

She tried to put herself in Jim's position. It must be hard for a father of a teenage daughter in this day and age. It was never an easy age, but trying to keep up with them when they had mobile phones and the internet at their disposal would be a nightmare.

'Sorry about that,' Jim sighed, sitting down on the chair opposite her and running a hand through his hair. 'I just don't know what I'm going to do with her. You saw how she was dressed just then. Would you let her go out looking like that if she were your kid?'

Poppy smiled sympathetically. 'I know it's not what we'd probably choose for her to wear, but fashion is a relative thing, you know. It changes. I can understand her wanting to fit in with the other kids.'

Jim shook his head. 'There is no way I'm letting my daughter walk around town looking like a hooker. I don't care if I have to lock her in her room.'

'Do you pick out her clothes all the time?'

'Well, she comes with me, but the stuff she wants isn't even practical. I've always bought her clothes and she never used to complain before.'

'That was before she became a teenager.'

Jim sighed, tipping his head to rest against the back of the chair. 'It really doesn't seem that long ago.'

'Look, I'm no expert on kids, so take or leave this advice, but maybe you could compromise with her next time you go clothes shopping—you know, give in on one or two things she likes if she agrees to something reasonable you choose.'

'Maybe you're right.'

Poppy shrugged.

'You know what I reckon might work?'

'What?' asked Poppy cautiously, suddenly not liking the way he was eyeing her thoughtfully.

'I reckon she needs a female influence. Someone like you to go shopping with her.'

'Oh no. No, no, no,' said Poppy, shaking her head forcefully. 'I'm the last person you should be asking to do that. I don't know anything about kids and I probably shouldn't really be trusted to go shopping with one. In fact, I'd be a very bad influence.'

Jim chuckled at her alarmed expression. 'Relax, Poppy, they don't bite.'

'I wouldn't want to bet on that.'

'Come on, be a sport. I really need help here,' he said quietly.

'What makes you think she'll listen to me, or even want me to go shopping with her for that matter?'

'I'm willing to bet she'll listen to you more than me when it comes to fashion.'

Footsteps stomped down the hallway and the two adults looked up to see a pouting Lacey, standing hands on hips, waiting expectantly for her father's approval of her outfit. 'Happy now? I look like a freak!' she said to her father, lifting her arms and twirling around in her outfit.

Poppy tried to keep a neutral expression as she took in the frilled skirt and T-shirt with a large bow on the front.

'Do you see what I have to put up with?' Lacey demanded, looking at Poppy in exasperation.

'What? There's nothing wrong with that outfit. Pink's your favourite colour!' Jim cut in.

'That was when I was six!' snapped Lacey. 'You make me so angry sometimes, Dad!' she added, then turned on her heel and walked away, calling back over her shoulder, 'I'm in high school, for goodness sake, not kindergarten!'

The front door slammed, leaving Jim scratching his head. 'Was it really that bad?' he asked Poppy with a bemused look.

Poppy squirmed as she thought about her answer. 'It's not horrible, but it's not exactly what the other kids are wearing either, so I can see how she might be feeling a bit . . . different.'

'That's because the other kids are wearing next to nothing!'

'I'm sure there's a compromise.'

'Great, what are you doing tomorrow?'

What have I gotten myself into now? wondered Poppy. But before she could come up with an excuse, Jim had organised a time to pick her up and left to get a refill on their wine. Fantastic.

Nineteen

The nearest decent shopping centre was Glenwarren, a good ninety-minute drive away. Surprisingly, the trip wasn't as awkward as Poppy had been expecting. She'd been wondering what on earth they'd talk about for that long trapped in a vehicle with a thirteen-year-old, but that problem was solved soon after reversing out of the driveway when Lacey put her earphones in and stared out the window in silence.

Jim, on the other hand, was a great companion. They chatted about music and movies and even, surprise, surprise, books. They had an animated discussion about Matthew Reilly's Scarecrow series—Reilly was one of Poppy's favourite writers—and discovered a few more authors they had in common. Looking at Jim while they talked, she thought he was very much the epitome of still waters running deep. *What else is hidden beneath this man's surface,* she found herself wondering, before quickly pulling back on the reins. *Whoah. What am I thinking?* She did not have time for deep waters at this point in her life.

At the entrance to the large department store Jim announced, 'Okay, ladies, I'll meet you at the checkout.' Before either of them could protest, Jim waved goodbye and headed off to find a new pair of boots.

Lacey and Poppy stood staring after him with matching looks of dismay. *Well,* Poppy thought, *they'd just have to take the plunge and get it over with.* 'Where do you want to start?'

'Dunno.'

'Well, what do you need?' she tried again.

Lacey shrugged. 'Dunno.'

Poppy bit back an irritated sigh and reminded herself she was the adult and probably should not resort to a tantrum in public. 'Okay,' she said with exaggerated patience. 'Let's just see what we find.'

'Fine.'

Poppy led the way towards the women's section and began scouring the racks. 'How about this?' She held up a print dress in shades of pale blue. 'And you can put something like this over the top.' She grabbed a denim vest and held it up in front of the dress.

She saw Lacey considering the outfit. 'What about this?' the girl countered, reaching for a floral printed dress and holding it up next to the vest.

'Sure, that works too. Want to try it on?'

Lacey gave a drawn-out sigh before reaching for the garments. 'I guess.'

Well, don't get too enthusiastic, Poppy thought.

'I like these.'

Poppy turned around and stared at the skimpy denim shorts Lacey held up. Jim would have a fit if he saw his daughter prancing around town in something like that. 'I don't think hotpants would impress your father, but maybe you could find some other shorts.'

'Oh wow, look at these.' Lacey held up a pair of ripped denim cut-offs that looked second-hand, but they were longer than the previous pair and Poppy decided to call in the compromise.

'Okay, as long as you swap that T-shirt—which is way too low-cut—for three of these T-shirts.'

'They're so boring, though. They're like, plain.'

'You want your dad to come and pick something instead?' Poppy asked.

'No,' Lacey groaned. 'Fine, I'll wear the stupid T-shirts, but only if I can have a miniskirt and this top.'

'Where are you going to wear a slinky silver evening top like that? Are you planning on going to the Logies this year?'

'But I like it,' insisted Lacey.

Poppy took in the stubborn tilt of the young girl's head and knew she was going to have a hard time talking her way out of this one. 'It won't go with anything you've already got. Look at these tops. You could mix and match all this stuff and get twice the outfits, whereas if you get that it won't match anything and you'll have fewer things to wear.'

Poppy bit back a sigh as she saw Lacey wasn't about to budge. 'Go try all these on and we'll see.' Maybe she could distract her long enough to get away with it. She hurried

Lacey toward the change rooms and waited outside the door.

'How's it going in there?' she asked after a few minutes.

'I can dress myself, you know. You don't have to stand there like a prison guard or something.'

'I want to see what it all looks like on you.'

There was a long-suffering sigh from the other side of the door and Poppy had to bite back a smile. Apart from the infuriating lack of logic in Lacey's choice of clothing, Poppy was actually enjoying helping her put together a wardrobe.

Finally the door opened and Lacey stood, hands on her hips, waiting for Poppy to pass judgement. 'Well?'

'That looks great. Do you like it?'

'S'all right, I s'pose.'

'Okay, next outfit.'

'Do I have to try them *all* on?'

'Yes, now hurry up,' she said and, ignoring the mumbling from inside the change room, went out to see what else she could find while Lacey was changing. Handing over another two outfits, Poppy took the ones Lacey had already tried on and dropped them into the basket.

'Do you date a lot?'

Poppy frowned at the change room door. 'Not really. Why?'

'Just wondered. It must be pretty exciting living in a big city. Do you go out to nightclubs and parties and all that kinda stuff?'

God, when had she last been to a nightclub? 'Not any more.'

'I guess once you get old you don't want to do that as much.'

Excuse me? Old? 'I wouldn't say I was too old for night-clubs,' Poppy protested weakly. Was she?

'Well, you're the same age as my dad, aren't you?'

'How old is he?'

'Thirty-seven.'

He was only four years older than her. 'That's not old.'

'Are you serious?' said Lacey, sticking her head out of the change room and looking at Poppy oddly. 'He's almost forty.'

Poppy took the clothes Lacey had finished trying on and added them to the overflowing basket. 'We better get going. Your dad will be waiting.' *And I must be due for a nanna nap soon,* she added silently.

True to his word, Jim was waiting near the front of the store, and Poppy smiled as she walked past him. 'While you're going through the checkout, I'm going to grab a few things.'

'I'll meet you at the café out the front and shout you a cuppa,' he said, taking the basket of clothing from her.

'You haven't seen how much that lot's going to cost you yet, cowboy. I may be shouting you!'

Poppy tipped out the cake onto the wire cooling rack and gave a small cry of frustration as it crumbled apart. Why was this happening? This was her third attempt at making a sponge. The first one had had an enormous crack across the top, the next one hadn't risen.

'Damn it! What am I doing wrong, Nan?'

There was a hesitant rap at the back door and she looked up to find Jim standing on the doorstep with a strange look on his face. 'Everything okay?'

'Does it look like everything's okay to you?' She gestured around wildly at the kitchen bench littered with cakes in various stages of completion.

'What are you doing?' He pushed the screen door open warily and moved inside.

'I'm cooking!'

'Okay,' he said slowly as he took in the state of the kitchen.

'It's not working.'

Jim nodded slowly. 'I can see that.'

'Well?'

He gave her a bemused look. 'Well what?'

'What am I going to do? Help me fix it.'

Clamping his hands on his hips, Jim seemed to be weighing up his options. 'At the risk of losing a limb here, why are you doing this?'

'Bloody Bernadette duped me into making Nan's special sponge cake for the fundraising auction tomorrow. *Tomorrow,* Jim!'

'Okay, calm down,' he said gently, as though approaching some kind of wild animal.

As a matter of fact, the state she was in, she did feel like a wild animal, and she was ready to snap. Why was she doing this? She had nothing to prove to these women. What the hell was happening to her? If only her colleagues could see her now. Cool, calm and collected Poppy Abbott freaking out over a cake! Well, ex-colleagues, she corrected with a small flutter of panic that she pushed aside quickly. She'd finally sent off her resignation that morning. The more she thought about it, the more she realised a change was in order. She usually had a job to go to before she left, but this time she didn't have that luxury. There was no way she could go back to working with Gill—not now, it would be too uncomfortable. Once the idea to move had taken seed though, she found she was kind of excited about the possibilities. She felt a small measure of relief that at least she could finally put Gill behind her, but for the first time in her adult life she wasn't completely confident about where she was headed.

'This sponge cake. Is it the same one you cooked the other day?'

'Yes.'

'Well, what's the problem? That one was perfect.'

Poppy stared across the bench at him, trying to control her irritation. 'I don't know what the problem is,' she said with exaggerated calm, 'that's why I'm finding this a little difficult to deal with.'

'What did you do last time?'

'The same thing I've been doing here for the last three bloody attempts! But it's not working!'

'Obviously not the same thing if it's not working,' Jim pointed out reasonably.

Poppy looked down at the cake tin in front of her and seriously considered throwing it at him.

'You just need to find out what's different about this time. Run through what you were doing last time.'

'I sure as hell wasn't this stressed last time.' She had actually enjoyed making the first sponge. 'This is ridiculous!' she muttered, throwing her arms in the air. 'I followed the damn recipe—' Poppy stopped abruptly. She followed the recipe. If this cake was going to knock those CWA ladies' socks off she had to stop following the recipe and cook like Nan. 'That's it!' she looked up at Jim as the revelation hit her.

'You know what you need?' said Jim, moving around the bench towards her.

'I need to start again after I've cleaned up this mess.' Poppy was oblivious to Jim's further suggestions, already focusing on where she'd gone wrong.

'But first you need a drink so you can unwind, which brings me to the reason I came over here in the first place.'

'I don't have time for a drink. I need to get this stupid cake cooked.'

Jim watched as she began running water in the sink and stacking in the dirty cake tins and mixing bowls. 'What are you doing?' she asked when she realised Jim was resting his hip against the other end of the sink patiently.

Holding up a tea towel, he flapped it at her with a grin. 'Helping.'

'You don't have to do that. Really. I'm fine now. I think I know where I went wrong.'

'Yeah, well, I was raised better than to walk away from a neighbour having a breakdown. Besides, the quicker we get this cleaned up, the quicker we can have a drink. You need to chill out for a while before you tackle this again. Trust me. I know a thing or two about cooking competitions.'

'You?' Poppy scoffed as she began washing a large mixing bowl.

'I'll have you know I've been called on to judge the odd cake bake-off in my time.'

'I can imagine you'd have hated every minute of that,' she said, having already discovered his weakness for home baking.

'Speaking of which, what are you going to do with all this leftover cake?'

'How do you feel about trifle?' she asked. It was a good thing he seemed to like it because after this disaster he was going to be eating it for a month!

It was midnight by the time Poppy carefully tipped her cake out of its tin onto the tea towel-covered rack. She'd gone online to research tips and tricks of show cooking and discovered you didn't want cooling-rack marks on your cake. Biting her lip, she opened her eyes to face the outcome. A smile spread across her face as she stared at the perfectly round, perfectly even-coloured sponge before her. No cracks, no crumbling, no sugar spots. It was perfect!

1st September, 1918
I no longer have the job I love and people are quite happy to let me know that it wasn't proper for Mr Fortescue to have given me the job in the first place! It's like they take great delight in my fall. They want me back in my place. It unsettles people around here if things change too suddenly. I have nothing as the old Maggie, no Alex, no job, no life—I am nothing. Sometimes I think maybe Frank had the right idea after all. At least he got a chance to escape.

The mood of the diary had become noticeably different. Over the last few months Maggie had lost her bubbly personality. She had a lot to deal with between her younger brother leaving to go overseas so soon after losing Tom, and all on top of Alex missing. Poppy's heart went out to her.

How much more could a person lose? She was beginning to wonder if Maggie would ever be able to pull herself out of this depression that seemed to be setting in. There were pages of poems that Maggie had taken to writing which hadn't been in any previous entries. They were full of grief and frustration, sometimes rambling on for pages in messy, hurried writing as though she couldn't get the words down fast enough.

She barely mentioned the farm work any more, although there would have been plenty of it with Frank away. There were no more little snippets about how much she loathed various aspects of it. Poppy had come to realise that although Maggie hadn't particularly enjoyed working outdoors, her comments had always carried a slightly amused undertone. Now, even that was gone.

Poppy imagined the concern the rest of the family must have been feeling. She felt sorry for poor Dulcie—clearly she was trying her best to help Maggie take her mind off things, but it seemed she received little thanks for it judging by the 'Why can't everyone just leave me alone?' double underlined after one particularly frustrated entry. How on earth were Maggie's parents coping with all this? They'd already lost one son, another was on the front-lines in France and their once vibrant, outspoken daughter was now shutting them out of her life.

Twenty

Poppy wiped her palms down the side of her skirt nervously as she sat in the front row of the CWA the next morning. She'd driven here as though she had a newborn baby in the car, with the cake, securely packed in a cake carrier, strapped in a seat belt on the front seat. She wasn't taking any chances, not when she'd spent the entire night cooking the son of a—

Her thoughts were interrupted as Bernadette bustled past her carrying a large cake box.

'Poppy,' she smiled, stretching her thin lips in a tight red smile. 'So nice to see you turned up.'

'Bernadette.' Poppy watched as she handed her cake over to the woman at the front of the room who was in charge of taking the entries out to the kitchen for judging.

There was quite a crowd filling the hall. It seemed these events were very popular in Warrial.

'Isn't it exciting?'

Looking up, Poppy found Alice taking a seat beside her. She placed a cool hand on Poppy's wrist and gave it a friendly squeeze. Poppy smiled. She really did like Alice; there was something so grandmotherly and comforting about the woman. 'What did you enter?'

'Scones. I'm a scone maker,' she smiled.

'Were those your scones you brought around the morning I arrived?' Poppy asked.

'Sure were.'

'Then I'm glad I didn't enter scones. I'd hate to be up against you.'

'Oh rubbish. And what did you end up entering?'

'Nan's sponge cake.'

Alice gave a surprised chuckle. 'This should be interesting then, dear.'

'What do you mean?'

'Bernadette thought she'd be home and hosed this year in the sponge category.'

'Oh. Well, chances are she still could be. I'm really not much of a cook. I haven't done any for years. I just thought I'd see if I could remember anything Nan taught me.'

Alice gave Poppy's hand a gentle pat and smiled. 'You've done her proud just by entering.'

Poppy blinked back a sudden stinging sensation in her eyes, and turned her attention back to the front of the room where a small procession of people was filing out from the kitchen and heading up onto the stage.

Poppy's eyes were instantly on the tallest and most

masculine of them and she returned Jim's smile as he took up his position at the microphone.

'Ladies and gentlemen, we have an impressive selection of baked goods up for auction today, but first we need to award the places for each category. First place in the jam and pickles category goes to Eleanor Kirby.'

Poppy joined in the applause and watched as a tall, thin woman made her way to the podium to collect her ribbon.

'No surprises there. Eleanor always wins,' Alice commented quietly. 'You should try her tomato chilli jam.'

Tomato chilli jam? Here she was thinking you could only get strawberry and marmalade.

'Next category is scones and this year's first place ribbon goes to Alice Partridge.'

Poppy gave a loud cheer and clapped excitedly as Alice gracefully stood and accepted her ribbon.

'Which leads us to the final category, and my personal favourite, sponge cakes. This year the judges noted there was an increase in the number of entries and there's also been a nomination to call this prize the Elizabeth Abbott Award of Excellence, in memory of one of the most celebrated sponge cake cooks this district has even known.'

Poppy was touched by the CWA ladies paying respect to her grandmother in such a thoughtful way. She shared a smile with Alice and felt a surge of warmth and love spread through her. She knew Nan would have approved.

'Well, well, ladies and gentlemen, it seems the Abbott women must have something in their blood when it comes to sponge cakes! This year's first place ribbon goes to Poppy Abbott!'

No. Way.

'It's you, dear. Go on, go collect your ribbon!' Alice said pushing at her arm excitedly.

Walking up to the podium, Poppy accepted the ribbon with trembling fingers. 'Seriously?' she asked Jim as he grinned down at her proudly.

'Seriously.'

Waving the little blue ribbon above her head at the crowd, Poppy couldn't help the grin that almost split her face in two.

The auctioning of the baked goods and jams went on for the next half an hour or so and Poppy found herself appreciating Jim's good-natured humour and the ease with which he fitted into this close-knit community. *He really was a good man,* she thought as she chuckled along with the crowd as he sorted out bids and entertained the crowd with his auctioneering. The man could charm an Eskimo into buying ice, and soon he'd secured a rather impressive total for the fundraising event.

Later, as the crowds dispersed and the remaining people flocked around for coffee and morning tea, Poppy found Jim at her side.

'Here she is, Warrial's sponge cake queen,' he quipped.

'Jim, was it completely ethical that you were one of the judges?' She'd been trying to avoid Bernadette's glare ever since collecting her ribbon.

Jim gave a chuckle at her worried frown. 'I was *one* of the judges and I had no idea which one was yours, Poppy. I promise. Remember, I only saw your disasters, not the end result.'

Well, that much was true. Going by the cakes he'd seen lying about her benchtop like crime-scene victims, there was no way he'd have guessed the final product came from her kitchen. She felt relieved that she'd indeed won it fair and square, and could now look Bernadette in the eye and smile.

Shaking her head, Poppy was beginning to wonder if she'd somehow slipped and hit her head. A few weeks ago she would have laughed if anyone had suggested she'd be winning ribbons at CWA cook-offs. What on earth was happening to her?

Twenty-one

Opening the diary as she curled up on the lounge with a glass of wine that night, Poppy was just getting comfy when she read the next entry and let out a small yelp, almost spilling the contents of the glass over herself. Staring at the diary she re-read the first line and felt herself grinning like a fool.

22nd September, 1918
The most amazing news came today . . . I still cannot believe it, I'm almost afraid to get my hopes up . . . but Mrs Wilson came running to our house this after-noon with a telegram to say that Alex is alive! I was speechless as she wept and laughed and hugged me

tight . . . I think I may be in shock. He's alive! Alex is alive!

25th October, 1918
Today is the day Alex returns home. His mother went to bring him home from Sydney. I haven't been able to write, I haven't been able to do much of anything other than weep with joy for the last few days. I can't believe in a few short hours he'll be home.

Maggie

Maggie ran as fast as she could. She didn't hear the pounding of the gravel beneath her shoes, her own heart beating like a bass drum. All she heard were the words, *Alex is home.* It was a miracle. Her heart sang with pure joy and relief. All along she'd known, deep down, that he hadn't been dead, but it had been hard to keep that belief in the face of so many months of silence.

Even since the telegram had arrived they'd been waiting anxiously. Alex had been located in Switzerland, having been traded to the Red Cross by the Germans and lost to the system for many months.

Arriving at the front verandah of the Wilson house, Maggie paused to catch her breath before knocking on the door.

From behind the front door she heard the shuffle of footsteps and held her breath as the door opened a little way and Mrs Wilson peered through the gap.

'Good morning, Mrs Wilson. I just heard that Alex is home. I'm sorry it's so early, but I just had to come straightaway. Would it be all right if I had a short visit with him?'

She saw the woman's usually cheery face crinkle with worry.

'I promise I won't stay long, I know he'll be wanting to rest.' She heard the unmistakable plea in her voice but was too excited to care how pathetic she sounded. All she knew was that inside that house Alex was alive and she needed to see him, touch him, to make sure it wasn't all some cruel trick.

'I'm sorry, dear, but he's sleeping at the moment.'

'I just want to see him for a moment, Mrs Wilson. I promise I won't wake him.'

But the woman shook her head slowly, and Maggie felt her heart sink to her knees. 'He's in a bad way, dear.'

'I just . . .' Tears pricked her eyes as the adrenalin left her body in a deflated rush.

'He needs some time to adjust to being home again, Maggie.'

'I understand. Please tell him I was here.'

'I'll do that, dear.'

The door closed in her face and she stood blankly for a moment.

Turning away with a heavy heart, Maggie retraced her footsteps home, disappointment dragging her shoulders down and bowing her head as reality pushed aside her moment of elation. What was she doing? She'd given up on Alex, moved on with her life. Without a doubt he'd soon hear about her recent shenanigans with Walter and know she'd given up on him just like everyone else had. She felt shame wash over her at the thought.

Suddenly she stepped into a hole in the dirt road and a sharp pain ran up her leg as her foot twisted.

With a small whimper, she limped her way across to a nearby tree, its huge branches spread out in what almost seemed a welcoming embrace. Maggie didn't bother to stem the flow of tears as they fell from her eyes in large, fat drops. For a minute, hearing Alex was alive, nothing else had seemed to matter. Now, as her ankle throbbed, and large sobs racked her body, she realised just how foolish she'd been. While Alex had been God only knew where, probably in pain and mortal danger, she'd been out dancing. The angry rebellion that had been pushing her forwards all these months suddenly vanished. She hated the person she'd allowed herself to become.

After a few minutes, Maggie wiped angrily at the tears on her face. None of that mattered now. Alex was home. She'd do everything in her power to help him through this and then it would all be right again.

Twenty-two

30th October, 1918

Today I finally got to see Alex. I tried to prepare myself but I couldn't stop the small gasp of dismay when I saw his wounds. His face was scarred from surgery and his head was still bandaged. My poor Alex has lost an eye. He suffered terribly from malnutrition in the months he was taken prisoner by the Germans; and then he was sent by train to a Red Cross camp in Switzerland once it became obvious his wounds would not enable him to be returned to active duty. I'm under no illusions they were doing it for humane reasons. They were obviously trading for their own wounded, perhaps because they know the end of the war is near. How he managed to survive with such terrible wounds, I'll never know. The doctors have assured his mother that with proper care he will return to good physical health and already he's gained back some of the weight he lost, but he is still painfully thin and gaunt, nothing like the proud man I farewelled all those months ago.

Maggie

Maggie sat gingerly on the seat by the bed, trying to keep her expression neutral, although she knew he'd seen her shock when she'd first walked in. He'd turned his face away from her after that and refused to look at her again.

'Alex, I—' *I what?* What did she say to him? It all sounded so trite now. He clearly did not want to be lying here so helpless and weak in front of her and her heart went out to him.

'Can I bring you anything?' she offered quietly.

Alex didn't move, his gaze remaining stubbornly fixed on the wall across the room.

After a few minutes, when the silence stretched to breaking point, Mrs Wilson came into the room and placed a gentle hand on her shoulder. 'Alex needs his rest, dear. Give him time.'

Maggie was torn. She longed for Alex to just look at her, to say something, anything, but he refused to even acknowledge her. Maggie stopped at the doorway and turned back to face him. 'I won't go away, Alex. I'll be back when you're feeling stronger.'

'Don't,' he whispered harshly.

She willed him to look at her, but still he refused, and her heart twisted painfully inside her chest. 'How can I not? My God, we thought you were dead!'

'I should be!'

'Don't say that! How dare you say that, Alex Wilson!' she told him gruffly, moving back to the foot of his bed. 'How dare you say that when we've been here praying and worrying every single day you've been gone? Do you think Tom would wish himself dead? You came back, Alex. Tom didn't. You owe it to him to be grateful that you're alive.'

'Grateful?' He raised his voice, but even that had lost most of its strength. 'I should be grateful I've lost an eye and wilted away with about as much strength left in me as a day-old babe. Don't tell me how grateful I should be when you have no idea what I've been living through.' He winced as a ripple of pain ran through him, and Maggie moved to comfort him. 'Don't! I don't want your sympathy and I don't want you to come by any more.'

'All right,' she said, straightening and lifting her head. 'I won't come by until you're stronger, but I won't give up on you, Alex. I'm not going away, so don't think you've seen the last of me.' She crossed the room without looking back, but hesitated at the door once more and whispered, 'I've missed you, Alex. I'm glad you're home.'

Poppy

Poppy hadn't been able to put the diary down since she'd discovered Alex had returned. She'd had to go back and re-read the paragraph just to make sure she hadn't imagined it. How amazing would that have been for Maggie and his family? After having given him up for dead, they eventually get word out of the blue that he's alive!

191

Her heart went out to both Alex and Maggie. The pain in Maggie's entries following Alex's return was undeniable. She was still so deeply in love with the man and he was turning her away. Poppy could understand Alex's frustration, though. What must he have seen in the war? What had he gone through in all those months with such horrific injuries? How had he even survived?

The next few entries were filled with Maggie's growing distress at Alex's progress. True to her word, she continued to wait for Alex to heal. Over time, it seemed he did improve and she began to visit again. He moved from being confined to bed to sitting out in the garden and eventually he was up and doing light duties around his mother's yard. He joined the local RSSILA, Returned Soldiers' and Sailors' Imperial League of Australia, which Poppy had decided she'd look up and find more about it. She'd discovered this was the original organisation now known as the RSL, with their clubs a fixture in just about every country town in Australia.

Alex, like many of the men retuning from the war, found himself lost and unsettled once he returned home. It must have been hard to adjust to peaceful life in a small rural town having spent so long under the threat of constant harm or death in some foreign country.

The old tensions between those who'd volunteered to fight and those who'd remained at home became a divide within the community. Some returned soldiers found that they could no longer do the jobs they'd done before. Injuries made it impossible for them to return to the physical labour of farming or trade work, and many of their jobs were already taken by men who had stayed behind, or sometimes even women. These men who had once had a clear role in life had returned home to find there was no longer a place for them.

Maggie had gone through changes of her own after Alex's return. Since she'd stopped seeing Walter she seemed to have gone back to the old Maggie. Her entries were full of Alex and his progress, but Poppy found herself wondering at Alex's attitude as it was expressed in Maggie's entries. He seemed so unlike the man who had written those love letters. Maggie often wrote that he was cold towards her to the point of being cruel. This was not the same Alex who had written so lovingly to her whilst he was away. Maggie sounded as though her heart was breaking, yet she was obviously determined not to give up on the man she loved.

1st November, 1918

I see Alex improving every day. He was chopping wood this morning when I called by to visit him. I didn't announce my presence immediately; I wanted the chance to watch Alex unobserved for a change. I haven't had the opportunity to really look at him as it still seemed to make him uncomfortable.

He wore only a singlet which was soaked through with sweat as he swung the axe in slow, methodical strokes. Angry red welts on the back of his arms disappeared beneath the fabric and I knew they were the scars from shrapnel wounds he received when he lost his eye. He wore a patch to protect the wound from bright sunlight, and it gave him a very rugged, pirate look that wasn't altogether unattractive. His hair, sleek with sweat, was shorter than it had been— his mother must have given him a trim.

When I approached him and said hello, he flew into the most dreadful rage and I was quite shocked by it. I hadn't meant to startle him, but somehow I did and I remembered too late how I'd overheard Mum and Mrs Brown talking over tea about Charlie Mack, who has just come home and is jumpier than a rabbit in a cage of hunting dogs, taking cover behind a car when a truck backfired on the street and getting quite hysterical. Shellshock is the term I've seen in the newspaper. Alex stormed off inside and his mother came out to say that it was best I left him alone for a while.

This seems to be happening more and more often. The slightest thing seems to send him off in a temper. And yet there are times like the other day when he actually smiles, and then I see the old Alex trying to emerge, but he's gone again just as quickly and I have to turn my back and leave him to cool down.

Poppy was seated at her nan's kitchen table going through the job-search websites when a shadow appeared at the back door.

Looking up, she found Lacey standing on the back step peering through the screen at her. 'Hi.'

'Hi. Can I come in?'

Surprised by the unexpected visit, Poppy shut down her computer and waved the young girl inside. 'Anything wrong?'

'No. Why?'

Poppy raised an eyebrow at the defensive tone, but didn't comment. Obviously Lacey had something on her mind and she'd tell her when she was good and ready. 'Do you want a drink of something?'

'Coffee?'

'Are you allowed to have coffee?'

'Yeah. Why wouldn't I?'

Did kids drink coffee at thirteen now? She tried to cast her mind back to how old she was when she'd begun drinking coffee but she couldn't remember. She hesitated for a second, but reasoned it wasn't as though she was plying the child with alcohol or anything. If worst came to worst she'd be a tad hyperactive for the rest of the morning.

'Where's your dad?'

'At work.'

'Oh.' The man certainly worked long hours, even on Saturdays it seemed. Poppy put the jug on and pulled down two coffee mugs. 'So what's up?'

Lacey shrugged, toying with the table runner in the centre of the kitchen table. 'They're just weird!'

Poppy raised an eyebrow. 'Who are?'

'Boys.'

'Ah. I see. So what's his name?'

Lacey glanced over at Poppy quickly before dropping her gaze back down to the table. 'Jacob.'

Spooning the granules and the sugar into the cups, Poppy took her time making the coffee, then crossed back to the table with their mugs. 'So what has Jacob done?'

'Nothing. That's just it, he's done nothing.'

'What was he supposed to have done then?'

For the first time since meeting her, Lacey seemed awkward and self-conscious and that vulnerability softened something inside Poppy.

'I heard he liked me, and I kinda told him that I liked him, but he hasn't done anything.'

Uh-oh. 'You mean as in, he hasn't made any moves?'

'Yes.' Lacey's eyes lit up slightly. 'I don't get it. Does it mean he doesn't like me back? Or do I have to do something? I just don't get it.'

'Maybe he's just shy.'

'He's had heaps of girlfriends before.'

'Oh. Well, maybe he thinks you're different. Maybe he really likes you and doesn't want to do anything to scare you off.'

'You think?'

'Maybe. But if you're worried, why don't you just ask him?'

Lacey plucked at the material in the runner once more. 'I don't really know what to say.'

Poppy sighed inwardly; oh to have teenage dramas as the worst that could go wrong in your life. 'Well, start off asking if he feels the same way you do.'

'What if he says no?'

'At least you'll know one way or the other and you can move on.'

'How do you know if you're ready to go, you know . . . further with a guy?'

'Further? What? As in . . . sex?'

'Yeah,' Lacey shrugged, tracing an invisible pattern on the table.

Poppy looked toward Jim's house frantically. Surely this was beyond neighbourly duties? The kid was thirteen years old, for goodness sake. Were thirteen-year-olds really having sex? She was so out of touch! And she certainly wasn't equipped to have The Talk with someone else's daughter!

'I can't ask anyone else. Dad would freak out if I asked him, and my friends' mothers would all go running to Dad to tell him I was about to do something stupid.'

Poppy winced. The poor kid was reaching out for help, how could she turn her back on that? 'I'm not sure how you know when you're ready. I guess you just . . . know,' she finished lamely. A disappointed expression crossed Lacey's face and Poppy sighed. 'Is this boy Jacob pressuring you to have sex?'

'No. He hardly even *talks* to me yet.'

'So you're just curious about the whole sex thing?'

'Yeah, I guess.'

Curiosity was normal, *right*? What she wouldn't give for a book on dealing with tricky questions from teenagers right now. 'Look, what I *do* know is you should always listen to your gut instinct. If at any point you're unsure about something, it's always for a good reason. Sometimes you can be in a hurry because all your friends are saying they've done stuff. But you know what? The majority of the time the girls who are boasting about all the stuff they've done haven't done anything.'

'How do you know that?'

'Because when you do, you know, take things further with a guy,' Poppy stumbled on the words and battled to keep from becoming flustered, 'if it's right, you don't want the whole world to know about it. It's special. And that's the way it should be. The boys who talk about it, they aren't the ones you want to be hanging around. If they can't respect what they're doing then how are they going to respect you?'

'What if you really want to see what it's like?'

'My advice to you would be to wait. I won't lie to you, sex is an amazing thing, it can blow your mind with the right person. But you really don't want your first time to be with some thirteen-year-old kid who has no idea what he's doing. And trust me, there is no way a thirteen-year-old knows what he's doing.' *Okay, maybe that was a little too much information,* Poppy thought as a grimace crossed the girl's face. 'I think you'll regret it if you do it now.'

A muffled buzz came from somewhere and Lacey withdrew a mobile phone from her pocket, checking the screen before rapidly texting a reply. 'I gotta go,' she said, standing up.

Poppy chewed the inside of her lip nervously. Had she done the right thing? Should she have waited until she asked Jim before giving his daughter advice on sex? This was why she didn't want kids! Who needed the worry?

'Thanks for the coffee . . . and the talk.'

Lacey offered a small smile before she pushed open the screen door and looked back at Poppy. 'Don't worry, I'm not about to do anything right now. I was just curious.'

'Okay. I wasn't worried,' Poppy lied with a breezy smile.

'Yeah, right.'

That kid was too smart for her own good. She just hoped she used those brains of hers to keep herself out of trouble. She could remember the impatience of adolescence all too well, but thirteen? Poppy shook her head as she stared through the screen door at the backyard. It was a scary damn place out there these days.

Twenty-three

10th November, 1918

Today I spoke with Alex in town. It's just no use. No matter how many times I try and tell him I love him, he refuses to believe I am capable of loving him as he is. I no longer know what to say to convince him. He seems so sad, so unlike the Alex I knew before. The only time I see any spark of emotion is when he talks about the men who've returned from the war—his mates. The anger with which he speaks of the men in town who didn't go away to fight sometimes scares me. It's almost as if there's now a divide in town—those who went away and those who didn't. I'm torn in this and have had many arguments with Alex about it.

If I'd known Tom was never going to come back I would have done everything in my power to stop him leaving in the first place. I don't hold any resentment against the men who chose not to go. Alex asked me once how I couldn't be offended on Tom's behalf when he'd sacrificed his life for these men to stay at home. I dared him to ask any family in the district who'd lost a loved one if they'd have let them go away to war if they'd known then what they know now. War isn't honourable. There is nothing honourable about dying in a place so far from home.

15th November, 1918
The war is over! Officially it ended at eleven am on the 11th of November—or so the newspaper and radio tells us. I know I should be celebrating along with everyone else, but I just can't bring myself to cheer. This war has taken away so much—my beloved Tom and, I can't deny it, the Alex I fell in love with. This new Alex is not the same person.

Maggie

Maggie heard her name being called as she walked from the chook pen and headed towards the house. She placed the eggs in the bowl on the table and looked up as her mother appeared in the kitchen doorway.

'You have a visitor, love.'

She wasn't sure who she expected to see as she walked into the sitting room, but Alex Wilson was not on the list.

He looked stronger . . . almost like the old Alex she remembered. In the months since his return he'd managed to regain much of his strength and health. He rarely wore his eye patch now and she'd discovered he had a glass eye

200

that wasn't an exact match to the beautiful moss green eyes she loved so much, but it was quite close.

She was in awe of how he seemed to have adapted to life despite his injury. She'd heard that he'd taken up a job with his cousin hauling timber, determined not to become an invalid dependent on others. He'd apparently purchased his own bullock team, but Maggie saw little of him for weeks on end, and last time she had happened to see him, he'd refused to meet her eye and had crossed the street in order to avoid talking to her. Which was why it was so much of a surprise to see him turn up on her doorstep like this.

'Maggie.'

'Alex, what brings you here?'

'I thought it was time I came and paid your family a visit . . . now that I'm back on my feet.'

Her family . . . not her, she noted, biting down on her disappointment. 'Oh. Well, that's nice. Shall we go out and sit at the table?' she suggested politely, stepping back to allow him to lead the way—it wasn't as though he didn't know his way around, he'd spent half his childhood here.

Maggie held her breath as he took a seat at her parents' table on the verandah. She noticed that his skin had lost its sickly pallor; the wounds around his damaged eye were fading to a pale pink, leaving thin scars that ran across his eye socket in a jagged line, and his glass eye was hardly noticeable. Despite his injuries, he was still a handsome man . . . the man she loved.

She poured his tea and he thanked her. Maggie glanced up at his soft voice and her heart skipped a beat. He sounded so much like the old Alex that her hands began to shake and she had to quickly place the teapot back on the table.

Maggie's parents chatted politely, asking after his mother. Tom's absence was still heavy around the Abbott household, but the daily pain was beginning to ease, settling now into a weary, empty acceptance.

'I hear Frank will be home soon.'

Her mother's eyes lit up at the mention of her son's name and she nodded eagerly. Her father, she noticed, sat quietly. She knew that he wouldn't allow himself to believe his son was safe until he was back on the farm. He'd lost too much faith to trust easily any more.

When Alex rose to leave, Maggie offered to walk him out. It was the first time they had been alone in what seemed like years.

'I want to apologise to you, Maggie. I have behaved badly since my return.'

She opened her mouth to protest, but he lifted a palm to stop her. 'I can't ask for your forgiveness for the things I've said,' he said quietly. 'I can't return to the man I was. When I'm working up in the bush, things seem so much clearer and I have time to think. I've written what I can't say in a letter and I want you to have it.'

He lifted a hand to brush back a stray strand of hair from her cheek and Maggie closed her eyes, savouring his touch. Then he was gone. She watched him walk away from her, then she returned to her room and carefully opened the envelope.

My dear Maggie,
How I've missed you. I know I've treated you terribly since coming home and I have no excuse except that there

seems to be a demon inside me, a legacy of the war, which seems determined that I should not be allowed a measure of peace. I was also ashamed. I am no longer the man I once was. I saw it in your face, just as I saw it in everyone else's face the moment they saw me. I saw the pity and the repulsion. You deserve better than me, Maggie. You deserve a whole man, not some pathetic excuse of a man who has returned home a broken and bitter person.

While I want to be noble and release you to find another, I fear that I am not strong enough to do so, but I also cannot expect you to continue to put up with me as I recover, knowing all along that I may never be any better than I am now.

I am not the same man you fell in love with—that man died out on the battlefields of France, and in his place is this shell of a man who is not sure he can ever live up to your expectations.

I'm scared, Maggie. There is something dark inside me, something that wasn't there before, something I fear I cannot control. The depth of that darkness scares me more than I can tell you and I no longer trust myself to be around the people I love. I need to be alone, far from civil people and a world that doesn't understand the horror of war.

If you care for me, Maggie, I beg you to let me go and move on with your life.
Alex

Accompanying her father into town to get supplies, Maggie found herself with some spare time, a luxury she hadn't had in weeks. She went down to the river to wait for her father.

One moment she was alone, soaking up the tranquillity, and the next she'd opened her eyes and he was there before her. It had been months since she'd last seen Walter.

'I thought I must be dreaming when I saw you here,' he said, taking a step closer.

'Walter,' she said, glancing up at him nervously. Even though he had provided her with a distraction when she'd needed it, she still felt terribly guilty about her behaviour. She felt as though she had led Walter on and at the same time betrayed Alex.

'I've tried to forget you, Maggie, I have. But I miss you.'

Maggie shook her head, her emotions confusing her. 'No, Walter. I'm sorry, but everything's different now. Alex is back.'

'But you're not together.' His words felt like a kick to her stomach.

'He just needs a little time to adjust.'

'That's not what I've heard. I heard he came back not right in the head. How can you keep throwing yourself at a man who treats you like dirt, Maggie?'

Maggie bristled at the cruel words, then felt herself cringe as she realised there was some truth in Walter's observations. Alex didn't want her—his letter had been his way of telling her goodbye—and yet she honestly believed that all he needed was time. She could wait. She'd wait for as long as it took. 'He just needs . . . time,' she finished weakly.

'Are you prepared to grow old waiting for him to sort himself out?'

'It's not your concern, Walter. Go find someone else who can give you what you need,' she said wearily.

'I've missed your beautiful smile. You miss me too, don't you, Maggie? I know you do.'

She did miss him, or at least she missed the fun she had with him. She missed laughing. No sooner had she thought this than she admonished herself. It wasn't as though there was much to laugh about. The war might be over but they would all be living with the consequences for the rest of their lives.

'Meet me on Saturday night. I'll wait for you near the old stockyards down the road from your house.' Walter's words jolted her from her thoughts.

'I can't see you any more, Walter. I love Alex.' She turned and walked away. She may have weakened once and tried to dull her pain by allowing Walter to sweep her off her feet for a while . . . but she wouldn't do it again. This time, she would remain strong. She would never give Alex another reason to doubt her—even if he were trying his best to push her away.

It was hot out in the laundry as Maggie stirred the washing in the big copper pot before lifting out a sheet and dropping it into the wringer. She brushed a loose strand of hair from her face irritably as she reached down to turn the handle, passing the cumbersome sheet through the rollers in order to squeeze out the excess water before she hung it on the clothes line.

It was hot, heavy work on washing day, but thankfully this was the last of it. Maggie had been in the laundry all morning and she was more than ready for a cup of tea. This was the problem with mundane chores around the house and farm—it gave her too much time to think. At least working in the bank had kept her mind distracted from worrying about Alex and Frank.

Gordon and Dulcie had become engaged and were expecting to marry in the new year. The news had gone some way towards lifting spirits in the Abbott household. Frank was due back, hopefully in time for Christmas, and Maggie was happy that her mother had Dulcie's wedding preparations to keep her busy.

She was happy for her sister; Gordon was a decent man and clearly loved her sister, but sometimes Maggie caught herself feeling a little jealous. While Dulcie's life seemed to be moving forward, her own had come to a standstill.

Alex spent a lot of his time in the bush with his cousin and their bullock team. When he returned to town, he preferred the company of old army friends who frequented the Star Hotel. The pub had a reputation as a place for heavy drinking and there were rumours of women who worked on the premises providing company for patrons. She had heard this from Dulcie; it was never talked about in polite conversation, of course. There had also been gossip about Alex's drunken behaviour. Gordon had intervened on one occasion when he had got into a brawl with a local who hadn't been in active service. More and more since the end of the war there were fights and clashes between the men who had served and those who had not. The returned soldiers were a tight group—they had forged a bond that remained once they returned home and often alienated everyone else. Maggie understood this; after all, if you hadn't experienced the things they'd been through, how could you fully understand? But Alex seemed to be shutting himself off from everyone else and she worried about his drinking.

She wasn't the only one. Over lunch one day, Gordon was filling them in on a recent altercation involving Alex, and she felt her heart sink when her father had proclaimed his deep disappointment. 'He'll not be welcome in this house if he continues down that path,' her father had muttered. 'I expected better of the boy.'

'It's not his fault,' Maggie had said, glaring at Gordon. Why did he have to continue to bring home these stories?

'He's a grown man, Maggie. It's about time he took account of his actions. I don't know what kind of behaviour they got up to over there, but he's home now and it's time for him to settle down. I don't want you around him, my girl. Not while he continues to act like some kind of troublemaker.'

'He's made it quite clear he doesn't want anything to do with me, Dad, so you're pretty safe there,' Maggie had snapped, getting to her feet and leaving the room close to tears.

She was tired of being told what to do. Her father had made her give up her job and forbidden her to see Walter, and Alex had told her to stop loving him and move on. It hurt to know that he was pushing her away supposedly for her own good, yet at the same time was throwing his life away.

She was a woman, not a child, and she would make her own decisions. She loved Alex and she was going to show him he was wrong about their future. She would stand by him no matter what and prove that they could find happiness together. She didn't care if it took the rest of her life.

She would show him just how wrong he was. He was the same man she had fallen in love with and somehow she would prove it to him.

25th November, 1918
I've been asked to help out at the dance tonight. The last thing I feel like doing is going out in public and pretending that I'm happy. I'm not. I'm miserable. I miss Alex so badly.

For the most part, Maggie had managed to stay out in the back of the hall helping to prepare sandwiches and platters of cake that would be handed around later in the evening. The music and laughter did nothing to improve her mood. If anything it made her feel more alone and miserable. She wished she could shake this melancholy mood that hung over her.

After everything had been prepared, she decided to step outside for a moment. Two men were watching over a large pot of water they were boiling up for tea; they were swapping stories and smoking as she headed past them towards the creek at the rear of the hall. It was quiet down here, and Maggie wrapped her arms around herself as she stared down at the water gently gurgling its way downstream.

The sound of a stick snapping nearby made her jump and her breath caught in her throat as she looked up to see who was there.

'Alex,' she gasped. She hadn't even known he was at the dance.

The silence settled between them uncomfortably and Maggie wished she could step closer, place her head against his chest and feel his arms wrap around her. In the dark, lit only by the moonlight, she could see that he was watching her closely.

'You shouldn't be out here alone, Maggie,' Alex said tightly.

'It's a free country.' She didn't like the way her voice shook slightly as she spoke, but that was the effect Alex had on her.

'So they say,' he drawled, taking a long drag of his cigarette. 'I heard your father warned you to stay away from me. You should listen to him,' he said as he blew out a stream of smoke.

'I don't need his permission,' she said angrily. 'And *you* don't get to tell me what's best for me either.' Maggie saw his eyes narrow at that.

'Did you read the letter?' he asked.

'Of course I did.'

'Then I've said all there is to say on the matter.'

'Well, that's too bad. I don't have any intention of moving on. So you go ahead and do whatever it is you feel you need to do, and when you're ready, I'll still be waiting.'

'Damn it, Maggie, did you not understand a thing I said in that letter?'

'I understand that it's hard for you to be back here . . . but I'm not throwing away what we have.'

'Save your dedication for someone who's worth it, Maggie,' he said bitterly.

'Don't say that. You're the only one who believes you're not worth anything. I'm the one who never stopped believing in you,' she told him, furious that he was so deter-mined to keep pushing her away.

'But that's not entirely true, is it, Maggie?' he said in a lazy drawl.

'What are you talking about?'

Alex tossed his cigarette butt to the ground and pulled her close to his chest, his grip on her wrist like iron. 'Tell me Hicks didn't touch you while I was away. Tell me you didn't do what he said you did,' he demanded, his breath smelling of whiskey as he growled close to her ear.

'I . . .' Had Walter made up some kind of lie to provoke Alex? She knew he was angry that she'd turned him down, but she'd never thought he'd be so calculating as to tell lies to Alex behind her back.

'Tell me!' said Alex violently, making her gasp.

'I didn't do anything except go to a few dances with him,' she said, and heard her voice tremble slightly. Alex let go of her arm and thrust her away from him, standing back and breathing heavy. He put his hands to his head, his eyes squeezed tightly shut.

Maggie stared, too shocked to move. 'Alex—'

'Don't,' he said in a low tone. He opened his eyes and lowered his hands, but he still wore a fierce expression as he stared at her.

'Let me help you,' she whispered brokenly. She knew he was in pain, and all she wanted to do was to reach out somehow and help him.

'You *can't* help. No one can,' he said, turning away from her slightly and fumbling as he withdrew another cigarette from his pocket.

'I love you, Alex. I always will,' she said wiping at tears that had begun to fall. It hurt so much to see him like this.

'I can't trust myself,' he said tightly. 'These headaches . . . I don't know what happens to me, sometimes I just . . .'

'I could take care of you,' Maggie cut in. 'Let me help you, Alex. *Please*,' she begged and her voice cracked as a sob escaped.

'It's not your job to take care of me! I lost my eye, I won't stand by and lose what little is left of my self-respect.'

A silence fell between them; the muted sound of music lingered in the background.

'So you'll allow pride to keep us apart?'

He took a long draw of his cigarette but said nothing.

'Well, you know what, Alex Wilson? You can turn your back on us and forget about me, but I won't forget you,' she said with quiet conviction, and turned to head back to the hall.

'My pride is all I have left.'

His low voice made her pause but she didn't turn around.

'Then I hope it's worth it.'

The next morning Maggie sat through church barely listening to the sermon; her mind was busy going over her encounter with Alex. His anger had frightened her last night, she couldn't dismiss that. But at least he'd reacted. That proved that he still had feelings for her and this gave her hope. She was concerned about his headaches; he'd complained about them when he first came home, but last night he'd seemed to be in more pain than usual. She shivered a little as she recalled the rage she saw in his eyes.

He needed to talk to the doctor about his headaches . . . and his temper. She was sure the two were linked, and maybe if she could convince him to seek help, then perhaps he'd find a way to deal with their future.

In the afternoon Maggie helped her mother as she pinned the hem of her sister's wedding dress. Dulcie seemed distracted and Maggie had caught her more than once looking at her as though she wanted to say something. When their mother had left the room and she was helping Dulcie out of the dress, Maggie finally asked, 'Is something wrong, Dulcie?'

Dulcie bit her lip. 'Gordon heard something,' she said quickly.

Maggie let out an irritated sigh. 'If this is another tale about Alex and some fight he's been in, I don't want to hear it.'

'No, it's nothing like that,' Dulcie said. 'It's—' She paused again and Maggie straightened, placing her hands on her hips and eyeing her sister impatiently. 'Gordon over-heard that Alex has sold his share of the bullock team to his cousin,' she finished in a rush.

Maggie wasn't sure what to make of this little piece of information. 'Maybe he's got another job,' she said.

'That's the thing. Emma Bradley said she saw him in at the bank yesterday and he was closing his account.'

Closing his account? That made Maggie's heart kick up a notch. There was only one reason he'd do that . . . Alex was leaving town.

'Maybe it's for the best,' Dulcie was saying, watching her with concern.

Maggie felt her breath catch in dismay.

Alex was leaving? No. He couldn't. It was one thing that he disappeared out bush for weeks at a time, but it was something else entirely if he planned on moving away forever. She'd never see him again. No, she couldn't let that happen. She needed to stop this. She had to see him, convince him not to leave.

The dance tonight. She'd get him to meet her there. If he wouldn't listen to her and stay, then . . .

A calm settled upon her. If he wouldn't stay, then she would go with him. She'd leave. Could she really walk away from her family like that? The question was surprisingly easy to answer. Yes. She could. She had to. There was no way she could lose Alex from her life twice. If they were away from here—from her father, from people who knew them—they could start over with no prying eyes or rumours following them around.

Maggie needed to get word to Alex to meet her at the dance tonight.

26th January, 1919
I'm not sure how tonight will go. I'm both excited and terrified. If what Dulcie has said is true—if Alex is really getting ready to leave town—then I will go with him. If all goes well, I'll be writing my next entry as the start of a brand new life.

Alex and I are destined to be together, and if this is what it takes, then so be it.

Twenty-four

There was no more.

So Maggie and Alex eloped? But if that was the case, then how come no one knew about them? Was this some weird thing they did back then, ostracising family members as some kind of punishment? Or did Maggie simply never come back home after they eloped? But she loved her family; surely she would have tried to contact them. Had her parents disowned her for going against their wishes? Had they simply wiped her from the family?

Placing the diary pages on the table, Poppy tried to rationalise her disappointment. It was better than the first abrupt ending halfway through the diary. But something didn't feel right. Maggie had kept this journal religiously;

surely she would have taken it with her if she left town and, if so, there would be mention of her wedding and married life. But there was nothing save a handful of blank pages. It was almost as though she had written this entry, put the diary down, and just never come back. With a frustrated huff, Poppy went outside, needing a distraction to take her mind off the emptiness settling inside her.

She'd put off tackling the back garden but she'd discovered that gardening was something she enjoyed. It gave her a physical outlet for all her jumbled thoughts. She rubbed sunscreen on her arms and face, then began pulling the clumps of grass and farmer's friend out by the roots, working steadily from one end until she had an impressive pile of weeds and could see bare earth in the place where the vegetable garden used to be.

By the time it was finished she was exhausted, filthy and sweaty. And there was a new problem. What was she going to do with all the weeds she'd pulled out? There was no way they would all fit into the green bin for the council pick-up. They'd have to go to the tip, but she had no way of getting them out there.

Poppy headed inside for a shower to wash her hair and scrub the grime from her body then, feeling human once more, she decided to drop in on Jim with an offer he couldn't refuse.

She'd never been inside a stock agent office before, and as far as offices went it was nothing to write home about, but it was tidy and the furniture was relatively new. An empty desk sat at the front of the office and a small waiting area was set up near the front window with a water machine and paper cups.

Jim looked up when she walked in, holding up a hand in greeting and pointing to the phone to indicate that he'd be finishing soon.

Poppy took a seat in the waiting area and flipped through the latest edition of *The Land*. When she heard Jim say goodbye, she put the paper down and stood to meet him.

'Hi. This is a surprise,' he said, his hands on his hips as he waited to see what had brought her here.

Today he wore a deep blue shirt and the colour brought out the grey of his eyes. She was distracted for a moment, before shaking off her wayward thoughts. 'Yeah, well, I've come with a proposition.'

A slow grin spread across his face and Poppy gave him a dry look. 'I need some green waste taken away from the backyard and I have no way to move it. I was wondering if I plied you with steak and wine, would you be able to take it away in your ute sometime this week?'

Jim rubbed his chin, contemplating the request. 'That depends. How big a steak are we talking, and how expensive is the wine?'

'The biggest one they've got at the butcher's and now that I'm technically unemployed, it's safe to say you won't be getting Grange.'

'What happened with your job?'

'It's a long story,' she said, waving his concern off. 'I resigned. It's time for a change.' She'd blocked Gill from her emails and phone, which was one less stress in her life. 'So, do we have a deal?'

'Deal.'

'Great. So when would you like to do dinner?'

'How about tonight?'

'Tonight?' Wow, the guy didn't believe in wasting time. 'Ah, sure. Tonight will be fine. Will Lacey eat steak?'

'Lacey won't be home tonight—she's sleeping over at her friend's place,' he told her, keeping a neutral expression and watching her closely.

Did he think that just because they weren't going to have a thirteen-year-old chaperone she'd back out of the deal? Okay, so the thought had crossed her mind for a micro-second, but she wasn't going to take back her offer now. She'd look like an idiot. *Man up, Poppy. What can possibly happen over dinner?*

'Okay then. I'll go and get the steak right now. Oh, one thing, we might have to use your barbecue, unless you'd like me to try to light mine again.' She grinned when he quickly shook his head emphatically.

'I'll bring over everything, so don't do a thing until I give you the meat, and then you can do the caveman cooking thing you do so well.'

'Caveman? I take offence at that.'

'Really? Do you want me to cook the steak?'

'God no. No one touches my barbie.'

'Caveman,' she murmured, walking through the door.

'I heard that!' he called after her, but there was a smile in his voice and Poppy found herself smiling in response as she walked up the street and into the butcher's.

'So it ended? Just like that?' Jim asked as they sat across from each other out the back of his house that evening. They were eating their meal and listening to some kind of country music playing softly in the background.

'Yep. Just like that.'

'Surely you can look up records or something?'

'I gave in and did a search online for her.' Google had brought up a link to an ancestry website and listed a cemetery entry for a Margaret Abbott of Warrial.

'And?'

Poppy pushed her empty plate away from her and sighed sadly. 'She died that same year.'

'Really? How?'

'I don't know. It didn't say, it only had the date of birth and death.'

'People died young all the time back then. Maybe she got some disease. I read somewhere that after the war the soldiers brought back a lot of diseases like Spanish flu.'

'Maybe. I don't know, but I have to find out. It's driving me crazy. I'm going into the library tomorrow to see if I can find some newspaper archives or birth and death records.'

'Good idea. Hey, I've got a meeting with some clients. How about we meet for lunch and you tell me what you've found out?'

'Sure.'

The conversation stopped, but the silence between them wasn't uncomfortable, the quiet sounds of the music Jim had been playing inside floated in the air and the odd dog barked at something, somewhere down the road.

Eventually Jim said, 'So what's your story, Poppy?'

'My story?' she said, unsure what he meant.

'You've been so engrossed with Maggie and Alex's story, but what about yours? There has to be one and I've been trying to work it out for a while now.'

'I don't have a story—nothing interesting anyway.'

'I don't believe that. You're an attractive, intelligent woman at the peak of her career, and here you are hiding out in your grandmother's house in Warrial. It just doesn't add up.'

'I'm taking a break—or don't you country people believe in that kind of thing?' What was he doing calling her on the reasons for coming here? It was none of his damn business.

'Sure we do, but you've resigned from a job that you seem to really like and you're hanging around out here in the middle of nowhere. From what I know about you—well, what your grandmother told me—you loved your job, and I reckon you're used to a little more excitement than Warrial has to offer.'

Poppy shrugged. 'I guess I'm after some new challenges. Besides, I can still do my job, I'll just do it for another company. I'm taking a break to think over my options.'

'Or running away from something?'

Poppy looked up at him sharply. 'I think you're reading more into it than there really is.' He was uncomfortably close to the truth with that remark and she struggled to remain offhand.

'I don't think so.'

Poppy moved to gather their dirty plates, but Jim put his hand on top of hers and waited until she looked at him. 'Haven't you worked out by now that I want to be your friend, Poppy?'

Poppy swallowed nervously; this was not what she'd been expecting from tonight's dinner date. It was supposed to be a business transaction, pure and simple. 'I don't need friends, Jim,' she said quietly, although her voice didn't seem as confident as she'd hoped.

'Everyone needs a friend.'

Poppy was mesmerised by his soft voice and the gentle movement of his thumb across her palm.

'Dance with me,' he said, standing up suddenly and tugging at her hand.

'What?'

'I want to dance with you.'

She was still protesting as Jim pulled her against him and slipped a hand around her waist, gently moving her to the music.

At first Poppy remained stiff in his embrace, but the warm pressure of his body close to hers, and the subtle smell of his aftershave, soon filled her senses and she found herself relaxing against him, allowing him to move them slowly side to side.

His hand closed securely around her smaller one and his arm around her waist felt warm through the thin material of her top. She forced herself to unclench her hands, and felt the broad expanse of his back beneath her palms.

Closing her eyes, Poppy allowed herself to simply appreciate being in the company of a handsome man, but after a few minutes she realised somehow they'd moved closer. Then to her horror she realised her hand had been moving in slow circles against his back. Immediately she stilled and felt him pull away slightly to look down at her.

Poppy stared up at him, trapped in the bright grey intensity of his gaze, and watched as his head lowered towards hers. His kiss was as warm and strong as the man himself. She'd known it would be. Jim wasn't the kind of man who did anything by halves. Her hands moved from his back, up towards his neck, and he gave a small groan of encouragement, settling her closer against him without breaking the kiss.

What on earth she was doing? She tried to tell herself to stop thinking for once, but reality had intervened and she pulled back from Jim's kiss, catching her breath and listening to her heartbeat thundering in her ears.

'Is this what "friends" do out here?' she breathed, and she felt his quiet chuckle as it rumbled through his chest still pressed close to her own.

'I've kinda wanted to do that for a while now,' he confessed.

'It was the duck pyjamas, wasn't it? No man could possibly resist a woman dressed in duck-print pyjamas.'

'Actually it was. That and I'd never seen a woman look so damn cute while she was swearing and holding a broken toe.'

'You really do need to get out more.' Poppy was grateful he wasn't asking why she'd put a stop to their kiss, but then he wasn't letting her go, and she wasn't sure she minded that at all.

'I think we need coffee,' he said, stepping away.

'Yes, coffee would be good.' She needed something to clear her mind, to remind her why letting Jim Nash kiss her senseless was such a bad thing, because right at this very moment she couldn't recall the reasons at all.

They carried the plates inside and Poppy packed them into the dishwasher as Jim made the coffee. She loved his house. The kitchen was new—built, so he'd told her, from a flat pack with his own two hands. It was bright and roomy and clean.

'So tell me about this property of yours. What do you do with it?' She knew that he spent a great deal of time on the weekends out there, but she didn't know much else about it.

'I'm running a few head of cattle at the moment, using it for grazing. There's a house on it, it's pretty old, but I plan on renovating it, and one day—probably after Lacey finishes school—I'll move out there permanently.'

'I gather she wouldn't be too impressed if you moved away from town before then?'

Jim gave a snort of contempt. 'Hell no, that'd play havoc with her social life.'

'How are things going between you two? I haven't heard any doors slamming lately. That's gotta be a good sign.'

'Sorry about that. The downside to living in town is that everyone hears everything. Thankfully she's been all right this week, no major dramas so far.'

'It really is just a stage she's going through, you know,' Poppy tried to reassure him.

'I hope it doesn't last long. I'm not sure I can cope with it for much longer.'

She thought it wise not to tell him he could probably expect a few more years yet.

'You've done a great job of raising her. How long have you been divorced?'

'Bit over four years.'

'It must be tough being a single parent. I don't know how anyone does it.'

Jim shrugged and Poppy saw the quiet, humble side of the man she was beginning to like way too much. 'Lacey's always been a great kid. I guess that's what's made this sudden personality change so hard to adjust to. She never used to be like this.'

'Does she see her mum often?'

A hard expression she hadn't seen before came over Jim's face, and she mentally kicked herself for asking questions that were none of her business. 'Sorry, forget I asked.'

'No, it's all right. It's not as though anything around this place can stay private anyway. It's a wonder no one's told you about it.'

'I don't get out much,' she said, and smiled weakly.

'My wife left us. I guess you could say that I didn't get much of a choice in whether or not I wanted to be a single parent. The decision was made for me when I got the note she left on the kitchen table.'

Poppy flinched in sympathy. 'Wow.'

'Yeah. I didn't even see it coming.'

'Why did she leave?'

'She got a better offer, apparently.'

'Oh.'

'She ran off with my business partner,' he said after a small pause. 'It had been going on for a few months when they decided to up and leave town together.'

She watched his fist clench tightly where it rested on the benchtop. 'It fed the gossips around here for a long time. He left his wife and two kids and she left me with Lacey. His wife, Chrissie, ended up leaving town with the kids and moving back in with her parents. Lacey and I had nowhere else to go.'

'That must have been really hard.'

'If it hadn't been for your grandmother, things would have been a lot bloody harder. She was a godsend. She babysat Lacey for me after school and she'd make dinner when I had to work late or go out of town. If it weren't for her I don't think Lacey would have coped as well as she did. It was like having a grandmother right next door.'

Poppy didn't know that her grandmother had done so much for him. She'd never talked about it. Maybe because Poppy had never bothered to really ask what was going on out here. She could only imagine how much Nan would have enjoyed mothering a sad little girl who needed a good cuddle. So Jim not only lost his wife but also his business partner. What a horrible mess that must have been to sort out.

'So to answer your question, no, Lacey doesn't see her mother very often. Occasionally she might go up to see her for a week or so during the school holidays, but Lacey doesn't really like it much. Apparently their new lives don't include kids. The kids just have to fit into their lifestyle or take care of themselves.'

'That's a bit rough.' Poppy knew exactly what it was like not to feel included in a family. While her mother hadn't ever pushed her aside, she'd been too busy trying to fit into her new husband's family to consider that Poppy might be having a similar struggle.

'I've come to accept it,' Jim shrugged. 'Selfish people don't worry about anyone else. It's just sad for Lacey. I hate seeing her get hurt.'

'Maybe some of Lacey's new attitude is coming from the fact that she's suddenly missing not having a mum. Up until now she's had you and Nan to give her what a mum might give her, but now that Nan's gone and she's getting older, maybe Lacey's starting to feel a lot of resentment that her mum's not here for her. As much as she loves you, it's probably hard for her to talk to you about girl stuff.'

'Probably as hard as it is for me to listen to girl stuff,' he said dryly. 'She spends a lot of time at Tia's house. They've been friends since kindergarten. Tia's mum has told me that any time Lacey needs a mother talk, she's happy to have them with her.' He shrugged. 'We're okay, we get through it. But I can't forgive my wife and business partner for what they did. If you're married you make a commitment. And you stand by it.'

Poppy was startled by the vehemence in his voice.

'I've seen first-hand what it does when you tear a family apart. No one has the right to do that to anyone.'

And that pretty much summed up Jim Nash's opinion on that!

Twenty-five

Poppy asked the librarian where she could find the microfiche to search out old records and was directed to the rear of the library.

She hadn't known what she was looking for, but when she searched through the birth and death records she realised that something was very, *very* wrong. The date of Alex's death was a day after Maggie's.

Armed with a date, she pulled up the local newspaper articles for that time. Poppy had a feeling she'd find something, and find something she did.

It is with deep sorrow that we report today on a tragedy that has cast a dark shadow over Warrial.

At a quarter to twelve on Friday night, one of the

*town's most loved young ladies was being deliberately
and foully murdered by her jealous lover, a returned
soldier, who then committed suicide.*

*The information available shows that towards the
end of the church social in the Warrial Creek hall,
about three miles from the Warrial township, Miss
Maggie Abbott (daughter of Mr Thomas Abbott Snr of
Warrial), accompanied by Mr Walter Hicks (employed
by the London Bank, Warrial), her sister and sister's
fiancé (Mr Gordon Fellows, employed by Bruxton's
Manchester store) left the hall to walk home.*

*When crossing a little bridge over a gully on the
road, about 100 yards from the hall, Alexander
Wilson, a returned soldier who had won distinction
at the war and had paid Miss Abbott considerable
attention, stepped in front of her, pointed a revolver
at her face and fired, whereupon the unfortunate girl
fell to the ground, death being instantaneous.*

*Wilson then pointed the revolver at his head and
fired. Wilson was still breathing and was taken to his
mother's house a mile down the road where he died at
twenty minutes past six on Saturday morning.*

Poppy couldn't believe it. She slumped back in her seat
and stared mutely at the screen. No. It couldn't be true. It
had to be the wrong people. But a quick look at the names
and dates cemented the reality, and somehow, deep down,
she knew it was true.

Poppy scrolled through the next few dates until she
came to another article, which reported in detail the entire

inquest that was held three days after the shooting. It reported evidence given by the local police, the doctor who had been called to attend, and the coroner who handed down his findings.

It went into excruciating detail about the wounds and the damage done, and Poppy had to stop a few times when it got particularly graphic. The sergeant who had attended the incident told the court that he'd known both of the deceased and spoke of Alex as a quiet and intelligent man. He produced a letter that had been delivered after the incident by Alex's cousin which stated Alex had written that it was his intention to end his life and it went on to give instructions that his mother was to be his beneficiary. The coroner went on to ask questions about Alex's disposition and character and the police officer stated that he was generally sensible but that he had been known to drink heavily and would fight when intoxicated. It seemed clear that the coroner thought Alex's war injuries, particularly losing an eye and the possibility of a head injury, had played a vital role in the whole thing.

He went on to interview Gordon, who had been walking behind Poppy with Dulcie. Gordon said that they looked up to see Alex approach Maggie and Walter up ahead and moments later they heard the sound of gunshots and saw Maggie fall to the ground before Alex then shot himself.

Poppy shook her head in disbelief. Walter was with Maggie? But why? She hadn't mentioned anything about Walter. What on earth had he been doing walking home with her?

The coroner then interviewed Walter, and Poppy read through the transcription of his words, searching for some

kind of reason for him to have suddenly appeared that
night.

> *I went to a social held at the Warrial hall and saw
> Ms Abbott and her sister there. Just before midnight
> Maggie said she was leaving and I asked if I could see
> her home. I had seen Wilson that evening, and had
> spoken to him on friendly terms outside the hall. He
> appeared quite normal. I left the hall with Maggie and
> we were approached by Wilson from the left-hand side
> of the road. He said to Maggie, 'You will not walk
> home with any other man.' Then he drew one hand
> from behind his back and fired without warning.*

Poppy stopped reading and frowned. Well, that didn't seem
right; from what Maggie had written in the diary, she
found it difficult to believe Alex would be friendly towards
Walter.

Walter then went on to say he heard Gordon yell out,
'What have you done, Alex?' and that Alex then said,
'I have shot Maggie, now I'm going to shoot myself' before
turning the gun on himself and firing.

There were other witnesses who gave evidence about
Alex's character. It was the general consensus that Alex
was depressed and moody, drank a lot and could be quite
violent since his return from the war.

The coroner went on to find that Margaret Abbott died
from a pistol-shot wound wilfully and feloniously inflicted
by Alexander Wilson and that Alexander Wilson did
feloniously and maliciously murder her; and that Alexander

Wilson died from a pistol-shot wound wilfully inflicted by himself.

Poppy sat back in her chair and let out a long breath. This went way beyond anything she had ever thought of when she'd tried to imagine what could have happened to these two people. She felt gutted. Numb.

Poppy pored over more newspaper articles, searching for anything that mentioned Alex's name around the dates she now had to work with and finding quite a few. From mentions of his attendance at a farewell dance for him and another local lad when they left for the war, to snippets of letters he'd written home to his mother and relatives. There were also wounded lists, Alex among them, and Poppy noted one of the names listed along with Alex was that of the other boy who had been farewelled at the same dance when Alex had left for the war, listed as deceased. Sadness filled her heart at such a waste of a young life.

She found newspaper articles noting Alex's medal and his subsequent MIA report, and a whole piece dedicated to his return. There was a detailed account of his journey, trapped behind enemy lines before an inhuman trip across Europe where he was exchanged through the Red Cross, then taken in and operated on before being deemed well enough to survive the trip back to Australia.

Moving across to a computer at a small desk nearby, Poppy did an online search of Alex's army records and read with a lump in her throat of his bravery.

Award DCM
Sgt Alex Herbert Wilson, 14th Australian Light Trench Mortar Battery

For meritorious service and devotion to duty. Sergeant Wilson was in charge of 2 guns taken forward with the attacking infantry at POLYGON WOOD, East of YPRES, on 26th September 1917, and successfully established them in the captured line, thereby lending valuable assistance to the infantry at the time when it was very much needed. He has frequently had to perform the duties of an officer and upon all occasions his initiative, coolness and resource have been an inspiration to those under his command.

What had happened? How had this man—a hero, respected by his superiors and the men he fought beside—come home only to do such a terrible thing?

Poppy was so engrossed in her search that when her mobile vibrated on the table beside her she nearly jumped out of her skin. She answered it quickly, looking about guiltily in case the noise had disturbed anyone, but she was the only person here.

'Are you forgetting something?' Jim's voice greeted her on the other end of the line.

Stealing a look at the clock on the wall, Poppy gasped. 'Oh no! Sorry, I had no idea I'd been in here this long. I'll be right there.'

Poppy gathered together the papers she'd printed out, then left the library and drove to the café where she'd arranged to meet Jim.

She saw him seated at a table, a coffee in front of him, reading a paper, and she smiled as he looked up and spotted her.

'What's wrong?' he asked as she sat down.

She glanced up, surprised. She thought she was a master at hiding her emotions, for God's sake!

But he stared back at her, waiting patiently for her to answer him.

'I found something at the library,' she said, pulling out the papers she'd shoved into her bag. Smoothing them out, she slid them across the table and let him read through them.

'Bloody hell, I wasn't expecting this,' he said, genuinely shocked by what he was reading.

'Me either. When I realised they'd died around the same time I figured something bad must have happened, so I went to the newspaper records and searched around that date. And that's when I found those reports,' she said, nodding at the papers in Jim's hands.

'Christ! What a mess,' Jim said softly.

Poppy felt numb. It seemed so unbelievable.

'You okay?' Jim asked, his expression full of such concern that she felt tears prick her eyes.

'I just . . . I didn't think this was how it would end for them.'

Jim reached over and covered her hand. 'I don't think anyone could have imagined something this bad happening to them.'

After lunch, Poppy re-read the statements and inquest report. She tried to rationalise the information she'd found—maybe there had been a mistake—but it seemed Alex had written a suicide note and left it with his cousin, and that was pretty hard to explain away. The murder just didn't make any sense, not when Maggie's last entry suggested she and Alex were about to elope.

As she was driving home in the afternoon, Poppy suddenly changed her mind and did an abrupt U-turn. She drove until she reached a side road marked with a white signpost; she turned right and parked outside the brick gates of the cemetery.

She'd put off coming out here since her return. She didn't like cemeteries, and even more so since her grandmother's funeral. The last time she'd been here it was just before Christmas and stinking hot. Today at least it was milder, and quiet. Poppy stopped at the front of her car and closed her eyes. There was no sound of traffic, no dogs barking— just the long mournful cry of a crow somewhere nearby and the gentle whistle of the breeze high above in the branches of the trees guarding the perimeter of the cemetery.

She made her way to her grandmother's grave. A tightness in her throat was the only warning she got before warm tears started running down her cheeks. This was what she'd been fighting so long, and now it seemed there was no holding back the grief. Reading about Maggie's death and knowing that Alex of all people had been the one responsible for it had been a brutal shock, but being here, and having to face her nan's resting place, was just as upsetting. There was no more turning away from the bleak truth. Nan was gone. Forever.

For a long time she stood beside the grave, sobbing. It hurt just as much as she'd known it would and, contrary to what her mother had told her, it didn't feel good to let it all out—it felt terrible, but there was no calling it back now.

There was something calming about the silence as she stood by the gravesite, her eyes closed, and eventually her tears subsided. When she opened her eyes she found herself looking at a gravestone a few rows over that seemed to stand out from the others. Drawn towards it, Poppy made her way past the plots. Her heart constricted at the tiny gravestones that marked the resting place of small children and babies. There were so many of them. How terrifying it must have been to give birth in those early days, knowing that infant mortality was so high, as was the risk to the mother. She sniffled and wiped at her wet eyes. Being here made Poppy realise again how much we took for granted nowadays.

Coming to a stop in front of the headstone, Poppy instinctively knew whose name she'd find there, but still she caught her breath as she read the words. *Margaret Abbott. Died 26th January, 1919. Taken from us too soon.*

This was Maggie.

Poppy placed a hand on the stone and closed her eyes. She hoped somehow, in death, Maggie was released from the anguish and horror of that final meeting with Alex Wilson on a quiet summer night all those years ago.

It seemed such a waste of life.

The afternoon shadows were growing long and now that the sun had set it was getting cold. Poppy made a mental note to come back later and put some flowers on Maggie's grave when she brought some out for her nan.

She wondered where Alex was buried. A heavy sadness weighed down her heart at the thought of a man so broken he could do such a thing to the woman he loved. Maybe staying single was a good thing after all.

Twenty-six

Poppy had just put the last batch of jam drops into the oven when she heard a familiar cooee from the front door.

'Alice, hi, come on in,' said Poppy, giving the woman a warm smile.

'I hope I'm not interrupting?'

'Of course not, you're just in time for a cuppa. Come on through.' Poppy led the way back into the kitchen and took down two mugs as Alice seated herself at the kitchen table.

Poppy saw the older woman glance at the diary and bound pages sitting on the table where she'd left it earlier. 'It was you, wasn't it?'

Alice looked up at Poppy in surprise, but she didn't deny it. Instead, she let out a small sigh.

'Why didn't you tell me you knew about Maggie and

Alex when I asked you the other day? How did you come to have the missing pages?'

'I probably should have told you all about it, but I . . . it's not something I'm exactly proud of, dear.'

'How about you explain it to me then.' Poppy placed a mug of coffee before the woman and took a seat across from her, giving what she hoped was an encouraging smile.

'It was a long time ago. Your grandparents had just moved into town. One day the new owners of your grandparents' farm dropped by and gave Elizabeth a parcel. It contained that,' she said, lifting her chin in the direction of the pages from the later part of the diary. 'They'd apparently found it beneath some floorboards they were replacing and thought it might be something the family would like to keep.'

'So why didn't Nan keep it with the other half? Didn't she realise what it was?'

'She never mentioned she had the other half. We only knew what it was after we began reading through it and worked out that it was Maggie Abbott. We were sitting at this very table,' she said with a sad smile. 'We sat here and read through it right to the end.'

Poppy bit the inside of her lip. Was it was possible Nan didn't know the first part of the diary was in amongst all the old albums and documents in the cupboard? Poppy had just grabbed a few boxes with photo albums in them after the funeral to take back to the city with her.

'Did you know the story? Before you read the diary? Did you know what happened that night out at the hall?'

'It happened before my time,' Alice started, 'and I have to admit, after we read those,' she nodded down at the pages, 'I went and looked up everything I could find on it at the library. It's rather addictive once you start reading, isn't it?'

Poppy gave a faint snort of agreement. 'Just a little.'

'But I do remember hearing my mother talking about it with my aunties when I was young. It happened back in her day, but she was only a young child at the time. It was big news for a small country town like Warrial. Everyone knew each other. People would have been in shock, especially after something as awful as a murder-suicide.'

'I've read the newspaper report with the coroner's inquest. They said Maggie rejected Alex and he snapped. That's *not* what the diary says. She didn't reject him. She planned on meeting him that night. And then there's the fact Walter was there . . . I mean, it just doesn't make sense.' Poppy shook her head.

'He was obviously suffering from post-traumatic stress,' said Alice, 'and he was a heavy drinker. A lot of men came back from that war . . . and the next one, very damaged. Who knows what was going on in his head.'

Poppy knew that Alice was right, but she didn't want to believe the newspaper's version of events. 'I don't buy it . . . in the diary Maggie said her sister had told her about Alex closing his bank account and they assumed that meant he was leaving town, right?' She waited for Alice to nod in agreement. 'But what if Alex wasn't planning on leaving town . . . what if his intention had been to . . .' Poppy paused, she hated even saying it out loud. 'Kill himself. I mean, what if he couldn't take the pain and misery any more . . . but Maggie, thinking he was leaving town, wanted him to meet her at the dance that night.'

'I don't see where this is going.'

'Well, think about it. If he was planning on killing himself, he'd make sure he'd paid up all his debts and taken his money to his mother . . . he'd also have a gun with him, but maybe he couldn't resist going to the dance to see Maggie one last time . . . you know?'

Alice nodded slowly as she considered Poppy's proposal.

'And what if Maggie's plans were interrupted by Walter being there?' Poppy paused. 'It's entirely possible Alex snapped or Walter provoked him . . . and somehow Maggie ended up getting caught in the middle . . .'

'It could have happened that way,' Alice said slowly. 'Although the court didn't have the diary as evidence and the two people who knew what had happened were both dead.'

'You said the second half of the diary was discovered under floorboards? Who do you think would have put it there? Maggie?'

Alice gave a thoughtful twist of her lips. 'I don't know, it feels like Maggie wrote the last bit in a hurry. From what we know now, she went to that dance and never came home. The pages have clearly been ripped from the back of the original diary, and at a very interesting point. If someone wanted to hide the more . . . sensitive parts, I'm more inclined to think it was by someone after Maggie's death. Someone who knew Maggie well, like a sister.'

'Dulcie,' Poppy breathed, nodding in agreement.

'*If* that's what happened—and it's a *big* if—it could have been Dulcie's way of protecting her sister. It may not have been done in a vindictive way. Maybe she found the diary, read it and hid the bits that may not have sat well with her parents. If I were in the same position, I'd probably want to hold on to something as personal as my sister's diary . . . but wouldn't want to risk anything that might add to the scandal if anyone else happened to read it.'

'So how did *you* end up with this half of the diary?'

'Elizabeth decided it wasn't worth digging up the past, so she took it outside and buried it in the bottom of the garbage bin. We had a bit of a disagreement, actually. I thought it was worth keeping—I've always loved history and one day I'd love to start up a local museum; we should have had one years ago. Anyway, it was Elizabeth's decision—after all, the pages had come from her old house—but I thought about it all night and I went back before dawn and took the pages from the garbage.' She dropped her voice as though someone nearby might hear her. 'I felt a bit bad about it. It wasn't my property, after all, and your grandmother was adamant, but I couldn't help it. I just felt as though it were important that I hold on to it. When you mentioned it the other day, it was as if that was the sign I'd been waiting for, the reason I'd needed to hold on to the pages all these years.'

The two women sat in contemplative silence for a while.

Eventually Alice pushed back her chair and smiled down at Poppy sadly. 'Come on, there's no point dwelling on all this. It happened a very long time ago and they're both at peace now. It doesn't matter what we amateur sleuths think may have happened.'

Poppy moped about the house for the rest of the day. Somehow she couldn't settle. It was almost like grieving. She knew it was illogical to be depressed over an event which had happened so long ago, but she'd so wanted to believe Maggie had led a long and happy life, dying in her sleep at a ripe old age, surrounded by children and grand-children.

A soft rap at the back door roused her from the lounge where she'd been only half-listening to a program on the TV. She knew who it'd be. It had become habit for either Jim or Lacey to go straight to the back door instead of the front.

She found Jim leaning casually against the doorjamb, watching her as she made her way through the kitchen. 'Hey. I just got back from the Glenwarren sales. I wanted to check on you, see how you're doing.'

'Oh.' His thoughtfulness surprised her, though it shouldn't have because it was something she'd come to expect from Jim. He was one of those annoying good guys! And it was funny how knowing this wasn't anywhere like the turn-off it usually was. Pushing open the screen door, she let him in. 'Yeah, I'm all right. I took a trip out to the cemetery on the way home the other day. I hadn't been out there since Nan's funeral.

'Was that rough?'

Poppy led the way back into the lounge room, picking up the remote for the television to turn it down low enough to have a conversation over. 'Actually, it was kind of soothing. It's very peaceful.' She took a seat next to Jim on the lounge; their thighs rested next to each other's and Poppy found the solid presence of another human warm and comforting. 'I found Maggie's grave while I was out there.'

Jim turned slightly, resting his arm along the back of the lounge behind her as he studied her face curiously. 'I feel like I know her,' she told him, ducking her head to avoid his scrutiny. 'I know it sounds a little unstable to be obsessing over this. Logically, I know it shouldn't be this big of a deal, but there's just something about their story that gets to me, maybe that it wasn't resolved.'

'The guy shot her, Poppy. He couldn't have her so he went out there and killed her.'

'No.'

'Poppy, you read the coroner's report and they had witnesses. He wrote a suicide note and admitted he was going to do it. It was premeditated.'

'No.' Poppy shook her head and turned to face him. 'I don't think it was.'

She thought back over the conversation she'd had with Alice earlier but decided not to mention some of the theories that had arisen. Alice had been right—what good did it serve to bring up all that now and who would care? But she still held on to her original instinct that not everything was as black and white as the newspaper report had suggested.

Jim shook his head to argue with her but Poppy cut him off. 'Yes, he wrote a note to tell his cousin he was going to kill himself. But that's just it, the letter said he was going to kill *himself*. There was no mention of taking Maggie's life. If he were that intent to make sure no one else had her, if he were that ravished by hatred and revenge, he would have put something like that in the note, he would have mentioned her, but he didn't. He wasn't planning on killing Maggie, he loved her.'

'But he *did* kill Maggie,' said Jim.

'Yes,' Poppy admitted quietly. 'But it's what they said about him and the way they've portrayed him. It's not right. He didn't cold-bloodedly set out to kill Maggie. I *know* he didn't.'

'Why does it matter what his intentions were? He still killed her.'

'It matters,' said Poppy with stubborn certainty.

'Why?'

'Because they loved each other. She still loved him and even after they told her he was probably dead she believed he was alive. That's love, Jim. He didn't cold-bloodedly plot to kill her. Yes, he still committed an unspeakable act, but the war did that to him, and they send him home to deal with it all alone. If it were now he'd be offered all sorts of treatment and help. How could people expect them to just fit back in after all the things they'd seen and done? They were farmers and small-town boys. They weren't expecting that kind of horror and they sure as hell wouldn't have known how to deal with it once it was over.'

'But not everyone who returned from the war let the effects of it turn them into murders.'

'I bet there's a hell of a lot more stories like this around. Did you know about this before the diaries?' she asked pointedly.

'Well, no.'

'See! You've lived here all your life and nobody told you about it. People buried things that were too painful and hard to explain. They still do to some extent. So how were these men returning from war supposed to get any help when no one would talk about what was wrong with them?'

Jim lifted his hand that rested along the back of the lounge in a gesture of defeat. 'I don't know. Maybe you're right, but I still don't see how it makes any difference in this case. He killed Maggie. Whether he intended to or not makes no difference.'

'It makes it a crime of passion—not the way they've told it in the paper, as though he was some cold-blooded psychopath. He was a war hero. He deserved to have the truth told about that night, not the dramatised version some frustrated country-hack of a reporter decided it was going to be.'

The man who wrote those letters to Maggie couldn't have been a ruthless killer. She just couldn't bring herself to believe that. Maggie loved him and she'd known him better than anyone. Whatever happened out there—and they'd never know what it was now—it *wasn't* premeditated murder.

'I need a drink. Want one?' Poppy asked after a long sigh.

'Sure.'

Bringing the two glasses back to the lounge room, she handed one to Jim and then sat down beside him on the sofa. She looked over and saw him watching her.

'What?'

'You're one huge contradiction, you know that?' He moved his arm and touched his thumb gently to her lip. Poppy swallowed hard as his gaze fell to her mouth, almost as potent as a kiss.

'I've been called many things but no one has ever called me a contradiction before.'

A grin tilted Jim's lips. 'It's intriguing—and sexy as hell.'

She wasn't sure who moved first, but the moment Jim's lips touched hers she knew she didn't want it to end. Taking the glass from her hand, Jim placed it on the table beside him and gently leaned her back on the lounge before continuing his kiss.

Poppy felt his hand run along her rib cage, the heat from his touch burning through the fabric of her shirt.

'Tell me you want this too.'

Want it? She was on the brink of spontaneous combustion! The line set by her self-imposed embargo on involvement with decent guys like Jim had become blurred over the few weeks she'd been here. She'd changed. She didn't want to think about it any more—there'd be time for that later. Right now all she knew was there was an undeniable attraction to this man and they'd been dancing around it ever since that very first morning. 'Are you going to talk this thing to death or do something about it?' she challenged instead.

His hand crept higher but he held her gaze steadily, his grey eyes as deep and dark as a brewing storm as he waited for an answer.

'Yes. I want this.' Her stomach fluttered as the words left her mouth. She wanted this very much and felt an uncomfortable vulnerability saying it aloud.

A satisfied grin touched his lips, reigniting her desire.

'So if you're done stroking your ego, maybe you could actually do something about it now?'

'Yes, ma'am.' His grin grew wider, then his hand closed over her breast and his lips put an end to further conversation.

Taking her hands and pinning them above her head, he took his time nipping and tasting his way down her arms and neck. Poppy arched against him, desire building inside her. The combination of stubble and soft lips sent white hot sparks of longing through her and she tugged at her wrists which had been easily caught beneath one big hand.

'You need to learn patience, woman,' said Jim, before resuming his unhurried exploration of her body.

'Okay, I think I've learned my lesson now,' she said, panting, desperate to run her hands across his chest and explore his body the same way he was exploring hers.

'I don't know . . .' His voice trailed off and Poppy took advantage of his distraction to slide out from under him, tipping them both from the lounge in the process.

Jim let out a strangled grunt as they hit the floor.

'Are you okay?' Poppy asked.

'I'm getting too old for this.'

'For sex?' she asked dubiously.

'For teenage sex. Can we please find a bed and do it like grown-ups?'

Pulling Poppy close to him once they were both on their feet, he ran his hands up the naked expanse of her back beneath her shirt, sending another shiver of unfulfilled longing through her. 'You sure you're up to this, old fella?'

'That sure as hell isn't a gun you can feel in my pocket,' he murmured against her mouth.

Poppy broke from his heady kisses and led him to her bedroom. She hadn't expected the nervousness that swirled about inside her stomach. None of her previous encounters had felt this important to her. She didn't want to think about the implications of that right now. She just wanted to lose herself in the feelings.

Cupping her face in his hands, Jim stared into her eyes, searching for something she wasn't sure she wanted him to find. Slowly, almost reverently, he lowered his face towards her and kissed her. It was the gentlest of kisses, but it tugged deep down and Poppy felt something inside her begin to melt.

He ran his lips down her throat and Poppy tilted her head back to allow him better access, desire rushing through her until she couldn't stand it any longer.

Reaching down, she unclasped the button of his jeans, smiling slightly at the harsh intake of breath she felt from him against her throat. He lifted his head and quickly shuck off the remainder of his clothes and helped her out of hers. Their clothes had barely dropped to the ground when Jim brought Poppy tight up against him, a low groan escaping from deep in his chest and sending a shiver of delicious desire racing through her body.

Twenty-seven

Poppy lay quietly listening to Jim's heartbeat settle back into a steady rhythm. The sounds of the night drifted in through her open window. Crickets chirped and frogs croaked—a warning that rain was on the way.

'I should get back to Lacey. Do you want to come home with me?'

The idea of trying to explain to a thirteen-year-old what she couldn't even explain to herself was too much. 'I don't think that would be a very good idea, Jim.'

'Is it Lacey you're worried about?'

Poppy sent him a swift glance and nodded.

'I'll have a chat with her, get her used to the idea.'

'No!' She saw a flash of surprise on his face. 'It's too soon to be making a big deal about all this. I need some time to get used to the idea myself.'

She felt his gaze resting heavily upon her, but she refused to back down or to look at him. What did he honestly expect from her after one night of sex—great sex admittedly, but she was hardly about to move in with him or anything.

'Okay, I'll give you some time to get used to it,' he said. 'Let me know when you've figured it out so I know where I stand, okay?' he added with a hint of sarcasm she'd not heard from him before.

Her eyes drifted towards his bare chest, resting on the light dusting of hair she could see there, that only minutes before she'd been running her fingers through.

Snagging his T-shirt off the floor, Jim pulled it over his head and sat on the side of the bed to pull on his shoes. Poppy fought a strong desire to reach out and lay her hand on his back. He was close enough for her to touch him, but the voice of caution held her back. She'd just told him she needed time, so why did she have this urge to beg him to stay?

Jim rose from the bed, but paused as he reached the doorway. Without turning he said goodnight, hesitating as though he wanted to say something else, or maybe he was giving her one last chance to call him back. But the moment passed and he disappeared up the hallway.

Poppy stayed in bed, listening to the progress of his footsteps through the house, only finally releasing the breath she'd been holding as she heard the back door close and silence filled the old house once more.

'What the hell have you gone and done, Poppy Abbott?' she groaned into her pillow. *Made a huge mess, is what,* came the voice she was beginning to hate.

***

Poppy woke up the next morning feeling exhausted. She had hardly slept and the last thing she felt like dealing with today was having a deep and meaningful conversation with Jim about what had happened last night. Living next door to the man was most inconvenient. There was only one way to make sure she didn't accidentally run into him, and that was to leave the house.

She wasn't sure where she was headed as she backed the car out of the driveway; she just needed *not* to be home. She headed through town and turned right across a small bridge and followed a narrow country road. After a while, Poppy began to recognise where she was. It had been a long time since she'd been out this way. A *really* long time.

Thinking back, she realised she must have only been about seven or eight years old the last time she'd been out this way. Ever since finding Maggie's diary she'd toyed with the idea of taking a drive out to the old farmhouse for a look. She didn't have many memories of her grandparents' old farm as they'd sold it and moved into town when she was small. She wasn't even sure she remembered exactly where it was.

Houses had become further apart, and front yards had given way to paddocks. Soon all she could see were endless paddocks and miles of fencing. She passed a faded signpost that read *Warrial Hall*, and a few kilometres up the road drove past an old building with a verandah wrapped around the front. She slowed down to have a look. It was hard to believe this was the last place Maggie and Alex had been. She didn't stop.

A few things seemed to jog her memory as she navigated around the potholes along the narrow road. She slowed down, having a feeling it was just ahead. As she rounded a bend in the road, Poppy caught sight of an imposing stone entrance gate with a high security fence.

A frown marred her face as she pulled over to the side of the road. The elaborate entrance looked out of place here. *Millbrook* was splashed across the front of the large Hollywood-style gates, complete with intercom and security camera.

That was weird. She could have sworn the old place was just after that last big bend.

A beat-up ute appeared in her rear-view mirror, slowing down as it rolled to a stop beside her. Poppy wound down her window and lifted a hand in greeting to the old man watching her curiously.

'Are you lost? Who you looking for?'

'I think I may be. I was looking for the old Abbott farm. I thought it was around here somewhere.'

'Abbott. Well, there's a blast from the past. Hasn't been the Abbott place for a long time.'

'It was my grandparents' place. I was just out for a drive and thought I'd take a look at it.'

'You must be Elizabeth's granddaughter,' he said, narrowing his gaze slightly as he looked her over. 'Been through a few owners since your grandfather lived there.'

Poppy fought the urge to shift uncomfortably beneath his scrutiny. 'I guess my memory wasn't as great as I thought it was.'

'Well, you remembered right enough. This is the place.'

Poppy glanced at the glamorous entrance then looked doubtfully at the old man. This was not her grandparents' farm.

His chuckle startled her. 'Looks a bit different now from when you last saw it. The last owners sold it to some foreign bloke. They got rid of the old house and built some monstrosity of a mansion on it.'

Oh. Okay, so maybe he hadn't completely lost his marbles then. 'They tore down the old house?' She had vague memories of an old timber house with wide verandahs and a pretty cottage garden out the front and felt sad that someone had demolished it. Her grandparents would have been devastated if they'd known.

'They didn't tear it down. Old McPherson up the road bought it and put it on his place to rent out.'

Relief swelled inside her. 'Do you know where it is? Is it still in the area?'

'Yeah, just a few kilometres up the road. You can't miss it. Next house on the right.'

'Thanks for your help.'

'No worries.' He gave her a salute-like wave and continued on his way.

A few moments later Poppy pulled off to the side of the road. She sat in her car and stared at the old farmhouse just back from the road. There was no mistaking it this time. It was the same as she remembered.

It was strange that it had taken reading Maggie's diary to bring her out here. She felt a little disappointed that she didn't have any strong memories to connect her to this place. She would have loved to have had something that tied her to Maggie. Technically, she shared the same blood, but to have lived in the same house, to have known the farm with the same easy familiarity, would have been special.

Poppy got out and leaned against the front of the car as she surveyed the old house. She could picture Maggie sitting out on the verandah. It had probably looked a little newer back then. The paint wouldn't be quite as faded and probably the front garden would have been tended with a lot more care.

Sadness crept over her as she thought about the last time Maggie would have been inside this house. The newspaper report said that her body had been brought back here after the shooting. It was hard to imagine what that must have been like for Maggie's family. One minute they were waving their daughter off to a dance, and within hours they were laying out her body and organising her funeral.

There was no sound coming from next door when she arrived home again but she decided against venturing out the back just to be on the safe side. *Her inner coward was working overtime today,* she thought dismally as she settled in front of her computer and finished a couple of job applications. At least it would help take her mind off Jim bloody Nash.

Later that evening, having just finished dinner, Poppy was surprised by a knock at her back door.

'Lacey? What are you doing out and about at this time of the night?'

'I'm home alone. Dad's at a sale and won't be back until late. I'm bored.'

'Oh.'

'Can I stay here and watch a movie or something?'

'Well, I don't know. Your dad mightn't want you over here while he's not at home.' She saw the crestfallen expression on the girl's face and added quickly, 'How about I come over to your place and we watch a movie there?' At least that way Lacey wouldn't be breaking any rules about not leaving the house when Jim wasn't at home.

Lacey brightened and Poppy realised how much she'd grown to enjoy spending time with the teenager—something she'd never have predicted. Lacey had been dropping over in the afternoons, as she had apparently done with Nan, and Poppy had found herself looking forward to the girl's visits.

They spent the evening on the lounge, painting each other's toenails and reading through magazines. Lacey brought out her mobile phone and snapped photos of them doing pouty poses, and Poppy couldn't remember the last time she'd laughed so much.

After a while they settled down and watched a movie. 'I'm glad you came over, Poppy.'

'Thanks, kiddo, I'm glad you were so bored you came looking for me.' Poppy paused, wondering whether to bring up the subject. 'So how's Jacob?'

Lacey glanced sideways at her and screwed up her nose. 'He turned out to be a jerk.'

'Yeah, well, you'll probably find a few of them,' Poppy smiled sympathetically.

'I thought about what you said about waiting and all that stuff,' she said after a few moments. 'I don't want to end up stuck in this place. Tia's cousin had a baby a few weeks ago and she's only fifteen. I don't want to ever end up like her.'

'She's certainly got a hard road ahead of her,' Poppy said, choosing her words diplomatically. Kids having kids;

it made her sad to think so many young girls were making big decisions at such young ages.

'Besides, you were right. Claire and Teal reckon they've gone all the way with their boyfriends but they both ended up getting dumped and everyone's saying it was because the boys reckon they weren't putting out and wanted girl-friends who would.'

Poppy was silently thankful she was not back in high school. 'Well, I'm proud of you for figuring all this out. A lot of people don't work it out so young.'

'So, did you and my dad have a fight or something?'

Poppy glanced up and saw Lacey was watching her closely. 'Not really.'

'Then what happened?'

'Nothing. Why?'

'Something must have happened because one minute he was walking around whistling and all cheerful, then I woke up and he was angry and I know it's not something I've done, so it must have something to do with you.'

'We just had a difference of opinion. It's complicated, don't worry about it.'

'I'm not a kid, you know. You two think I don't have any idea what's going on around here, but I do. Dad's got the hots for you and you like him, so what's the problem?'

Hots for me? Oh for goodness sake! 'Like I said, it's complicated. Can we just watch the movie now?'

Lacey shook her head as though she was beyond trying to figure out how the adult mind worked and settled down to watch the movie in silence.

Twenty-eight

'Poppy.'

Poppy opened her eyes and blinked a few times before she registered where she was. 'Jim!'

'What are you doing here?'

'Lacey came over to my place and seemed lonely, so I offered to come back and watch a movie with her.' Looking around, she saw Lacey was nowhere in sight.

'Lacey's tucked up in her bed.'

'Oh. I must have fallen asleep before the movie ended.' *And she didn't bother to wake me. The little rat-fink.* Suddenly Poppy had the sneaking suspicion that maybe Lacey hadn't been as bored as she'd made out.

'And what were you going to do? Sneak out before I got home?'

'It was kind of a spur-of-the-moment thing. I just thought I'd keep her company for a while.'

'Nice to know you can lower yourself to associate with at least one Nash.'

'Oh for goodness sake, Jim. I wasn't ready for you to tell Lacey about us, so shoot me! I was thinking of your daughter.'

'Cut the crap, Poppy. You were using Lacey as an excuse. Admit it, you're scared out of your wits at what sleeping with me means.'

'We didn't sleep together, we had sex. It means nothing, Jim!' As soon as the words were out she wished she could take them back. 'That came out all wrong.'

'Don't hold back on account of my feelings, Poppy. You just go ahead and say what you think.'

She could see she'd hurt him with her careless words, and she was angry at herself for not thinking before she opened her mouth, but he was frustrating her with his insinuation that what had gone on between them was something signif-icant, something meaningful. 'What do you want from me, Jim? I didn't come here to start a relationship with anyone. I came here to get away from this kind of pressure.'

'Are you seeing a pattern here at all, Poppy?'

'Yes, as a matter of fact I am! Men should be outlawed.' She moved to walk past but Jim's hand shot out and caught her arm, pulling her up tight against his body. When Poppy lifted her startled gaze to meet his, she was even more surprised to find not anger but a steady, intense hunger that sent a shot of white-hot desire through her body in response.

Damn this man to hell! Why did he have this effect on her? She shouldn't be falling for him—she *couldn't* be falling for him—they were all wrong for each other! She had her life and he had his, and they were as different as two worlds could possibly be. What were they supposed to do with that? Where could this possibly lead?

'I know you, Poppy.'

'No, you don't,' she whispered, her gaze fixed on his mouth, the same mouth that could do such amazing things to her.

'Yes, I do, and that scares the hell outta you.'

'Just because we made love *once* doesn't mean you know me, Jim.'

'I thought we just had sex?' he smirked. 'But I already knew you before we slept together.'

'What do you know?' she said, and realised the snarl she intended sounded more like curiosity.

'I know that you're not as tough as you make out. I also know that you think I'm some kind of pushover because I don't treat you the way most of the other men you date do. And I know that you have feelings for me and that's what scares you more than anything else because you don't know how to deal with feelings.'

Lucky guess, that's all. 'What do you mean, the way men treat me? How do you know how men treat me?' she frowned.

'Men who are happy to sleep with you with no emotional strings, who just want a convenient woman. You don't think that's treating someone like they're unimportant?'

'Not if the woman is fine with that. Not everyone is looking for a relationship, Jim.'

Jim lowered his head and closed the gap between them.

No, this was not right! Poppy pulled away from him. 'Okay, if you know me so well, then you also know that

I'm not the type to stick around, and more fool you for thinking I might change.'

'Maybe you're right. Maybe I was a fool to think you'd realise what deep down you already know.'

'And what's that?'

'That you could be happy here.'

'Are you serious? How could you possibly have come to that conclusion?'

Jim just continued to watch her with that steady, unflappable expression she was beginning to really dislike.

'You don't know anything.' She hated the way she sounded like a spoilt child. But he was wrong about her belonging in Warrial. Wasn't he? Something stirred in the back of her mind and it unsettled her belief that she knew exactly what she wanted.

Shaking her head, she backed away from him slowly. 'Warrial is about as opposite to what I see in my future plans as you can get.'

Jim folded his arms across his chest, lazily. 'Maybe you need to re-evaluate your plans.'

Oh sure! Toss away a career she'd spent years building up, just for the privilege of living in Warrial. 'Maybe you just need to accept we're just not right for each other and that the sex was a natural conclusion to spending so much time together these last few weeks.'

'You know it's more than that,' he said, tilting his head slightly.

'I'm sorry, Jim, but it's not. Look, this is why I don't like getting involved with nice guys. They expect more than I'm willing to give.'

'Bullshit. Call it the way it really is. Stop pretending for five minutes and admit you're too scared to find someone who might actually see past your act because then you'd have admit that maybe you need to grow up.'

'Excuse me?'

'You heard me. I get that you like your independence, but you know what? Thinking you're some ice princess who doesn't allow herself to get emotionally attached to anyone just to protect herself is not only selfish, it's cowardly,' he snapped, pointed a finger towards her. 'You need to grow up and start acting like an adult, not the scared kid you once were. Deal with it, Poppy. We all get hurt sometimes but we move on.

'You think you've got it so much better than the rest of us because you can pick up and move when the whim takes you. But that's not living, and one day you're going to wake up and realise that the freedom you crave so badly won't keep you warm at night and sure as hell won't keep you company when you're old and grey.'

Poppy stared at him and felt her throat close up as she fought twin emotions of anger and shock. Who the hell did he think he was to stand there and tell her to grow up? 'No!' Poppy said loudly. 'You're wrong, and I have no idea where the hell you get off telling me about all my faults! What about yours?'

'Like what?' he said with a slight chuckle of disbelief.

'Like the fact you act like the injured party over your wife leaving you. I hate to point this out, Jim, but people don't cheat unless there's something missing from their relationship in the first place. Maybe you need to take a long hard look at your part in it all.'

She should have seen some kind of victory in the hard edge to his expression, but she didn't. She didn't want to play this point-scoring game, she just wanted to go back to a time before Jim Nash barged his way into her life and made her rethink everything she thought she knew about her future.

'You don't know anything about it,' said Jim and turned away.

Poppy heard the slight waver in his voice and instantly regretted her stupid dig. 'No. You're right. I don't. Just forget it.'

'I don't want to forget it, Poppy. That's the whole bloody point! I want you to stop fighting this and admit to yourself that you want me too.'

'It doesn't make any difference whether or not I want you. Don't you get it? There's no future for us!'

'There is if you want it bad enough.'

'Maybe I just don't want it bad enough to change my whole life.'

Jim took a step closer to her and tucked a stray strand of hair behind her ear. 'Maybe you don't have to change your whole life. Between the two of us there's got to be a way to work out a compromise. I wouldn't expect you to give up everything.'

Poppy stared at the stubble on his chin and the rugged nooks and crannies that made up his face—things she hadn't realised she'd grown to love. She loved him. It was true. She had been so consumed by Alex and Maggie that it had somehow happened without her even realising it. Poppy braced herself for the ground to give way beneath her feet. Surely the realisation of something this significant would set off a natural disaster? But nothing happened except that her stomach was doing flip-flops and she couldn't seem to get her pulse under control. She loved him.

Jim seemed to sense her silence was positive and he leaned in to kiss her. She'd never get tired of this, she thought dreamily as her body responded to the heat of Jim's searching kiss.

Maybe he was right, maybe there was some kind of simple solution to this crazy situation. And she was going to make sure she found out what it was as soon as she had her way with this annoyingly persistent country boy.

'Well, it's about time,' said Lacey with a mouth full of cereal the next morning as Poppy made her way into the kitchen. She'd woken up and found a note on the pillow from Jim telling her to sleep in and he'd meet her for lunch.

And now I'm having to face Lacey on my own, she thought with a sinking sensation. 'Ah, hi. I guess you're wondering what I'm still doing here,' she started nervously.

'Nope. Dad told me this morning before he went to work.'

'He told you?' She wasn't sure if she was appalled or relieved.

'He told me you and he were seeing each other. It's about time,' she repeated.

'Oh. Okay then.' Good. This was all very civilised. She could handle this.

'But if you two start keep me awake all night with your monkey sex I'm moving in to your place and leaving you to it.'

Monkey sex? 'I'd better go and . . . well, I'd better go. Have a good day at school, ' said Poppy, and made a hasty exit.

Twenty-nine

From her position where she sat on the top rail, Poppy smiled as she watched Jim approaching from across the dusty stockyard.

'Ahhh, okay, now I get the whole cowboy attraction thing,' she said with a smile.

'What? Only now? You didn't get it when you first laid eyes on me?'

'The closest thing I'd seen was your ute. This is far more impressive.'

'Yeah, I can see how manure, dust and sweat would be so much more appealing,' he said, wiping the perspiration from his face.

Poppy and Jim had spent the last two evenings together, sharing dinner and watching TV until Lacey went to bed. It almost felt like being part of a little family as she'd listened to him tell her about his day at work and she and Lacey ganged up on him together. It was nice, surprisingly nice. Poppy had been pushing aside the niggling feeling that she was way out of her comfort zone, determined to give whatever this was a chance. She wasn't holding any grand illusions there was a future in it. She was still too confused about her career goals to try to factor in a serious relationship with a man who lived in the middle of nowhere.

'You know you could get down here and give me a hand.'

Poppy eyed the large restless animals Jim had just herded into the stockyards.

'Down there?' Was he serious? 'Ah, I don't think I'd be that much help to you somehow.'

'Come on, the faster we get this done, the faster we can get home,' he said, wiggling his eyebrows at her suggestively.

'Is that really all you can think about?'

'Pretty much,' he said with an unrepentant grin.

'What exactly are we supposed to be doing here?'

'Drafting weaners.'

'In English please?'

Tipping his hat back on his head, he sighed dramatically as if to say, *City girls!* 'We're separating the babies from their mothers.'

'Why?'

'Because it's time. They don't need milk any more.'

'Don't they do it by themselves naturally?'

'Well yeah, they would. But by the time they weaned themselves the cows would probably be ready to have the next calf. It's better to give them a break before they start calving again.'

'Oh.'

'So, we need to separate the calves from the cows. We'll push them from the holding yard here into the drafting pound. You can work the gate.'

'Push them, what, literally?' A vision of her shouldering one of the large smelly beasts forward was enough to make her back-pedal. Poppy eyed the largest part of the stockyards where the ninety-odd head of cattle jostled restlessly on the other side of the fence. 'You want me to get in there—with *them*?' Was he crazy? She was going to get trampled!

'No. Not literally push them,' he started and then muttered something that sounded a lot like 'for the love of God' under his breath. 'We move them, a few at a time, into the drafting pound, that round bit over there,' he said, pointing. 'Then separate the calves from the cows. I just need you to open the gates when I tell you, okay?'

With a sinking sensation in the bottom of her stomach, Poppy watched as Jim climbed over the railing and dropped to his feet on the other side. 'You ready?' he called as Poppy half-heartedly pulled herself up and climbed over the railing, walking towards the drafting pound and waiting for him to let in the first of the cattle.

'Sure,' she called with as much enthusiasm as she could muster for a job she really wasn't sure she could handle.

Jim pushed the gate open and Poppy scampered out of the way as a group of ten cattle reluctantly moved into the circular yard. Jim moved confidently through the herd, stepping in and out of the cattle, cornering the calves and letting the larger ones move around him. 'Open the first gate, Poppy,' he called, and she tentatively pushed the gate open, eyeing the large animals warily as they moved past into the other yard. 'Shut it,' Jim yelled and Poppy scrambled to close it. 'I need you over the other side now,' he called, stalking back and forth in front of the four calves, which were starting to bellow loudly in confusion having been separated from their mothers. 'Okay, open the gate.'

And so it went on; Jim would let in more cattle then separate the cows from the calves, while Poppy ran from one side of the yard to the other, opening and shutting gates on demand.

'Now I know how a working dog feels,' said Poppy as she brushed past him on her way back across the yard after the fourth batch of cattle came through.

'You're a natural,' said Jim, chuckling at the unamused look she shot him over her shoulder. She'd thought it had been noisy when he'd brought the cattle into the yard earlier, but the air was now filled with the anxious bellowing of cows calling their calves from across the yard. They were down to their last batch when a calf darted around Poppy as she moved towards her position at the first gate, bellowing to its mother, clearly distressed at being separated from her. Poppy stared as a large cow broke from the mob, lunging towards her aggressively.

'Poppy, get out of the way,' Jim yelled, moments before she screamed and scrambled up the railing to safety. With her heart pounding against her chest, Poppy watched as Jim successfully managed to head off the overprotective mother, deftly opening the gate and moving her into the yard with the others before coming to Poppy's side. 'You okay?'

'I think so.'

'You climbed that fence like a pro,' he grinned up at her,

one large hand resting on her knee as she perched high on the rail, holding tight.

'It's amazing what a deranged cow out to kill you will do for your agility and speed.' Poppy tried to smile but in truth she was still trembling, even though she did feel a little ridiculous.

'She was just looking out for her calf.'

'I'm not the one taking her baby away. She should have taken her bad mood out on you.'

'Why don't you go and wait in the ute? I can finish up here.'

Tempting as it sounded, she didn't want to be scared off by a cow. She did have her pride, after all. 'No, I'm all right. There's not that many left, is there?'

The rest of the drafting finished without incident and when the gate closed behind the last of them Poppy felt a warm swell of satisfaction settle inside her. 'So now what? How are you going to keep them apart?'

'We'll move the cows back out again and leave these guys in here. I'll have to come out to feed and water them in the yards, then I'll let them out in a few days' time.'

Jim obviously took good care of his livestock. Poppy was no judge of what qualified as a good-looking cow, but the animals she'd seen today seemed healthy, solid-looking beasts. She wasn't so sure about the humps on their backs though. No cows she'd ever seen before had those.

'There's a bit riding on this mob,' Jim said, following her gaze as it rested on the cattle he'd released back out in the paddock.

'You've invested a lot of money in them?'

'Well, there's that too, I guess, but it's more my reputation on the line.'

At her raised eyebrow, Jim continued with a small grimace. 'Around here most graziers stick with your Black Angus or Hereford breeds because they're good reliable beef cattle that the buyers love. But I've got this theory that if you breed some Brahman into your cattle, you can get better results. Brahmans are suited to drier climates and hardier than most other breeds with their bigger frame. Still, most people around here think I'm crazy.'

'Other farmers around here don't approve?'

'It's not that they don't approve, it's more that they like to stay with tried and tested breeds because it's safer. That's what my granddad would have thought too. They think I'm wasting my time and money by bringing in these Brahmans.'

'So these are Brahmans?'

'The cows are. I managed to pick up a mob cheap a while back when they were passed in at auction. Never even got a starting bid. They'd come down from up north and were pretty rough. Some bloke wanted to flog them off and I saw an opportunity to fatten them and breed up a better herd by putting an Angus over them.' He pointed over at the large, impressive-looking bull that stood regal and rather aloof to one side.

'So you're creating, like, a whole new breed?'

'Well, it's not new. People do it all the time. It's just a way to create better stock. You introduce the best traits of each breed in order to create cattle better suited to the conditions you live in. Also gives the calves a bit of hybrid vigour as both breeds are totally different genetically.'

'Well, given there are this many calves, I'd say you're well on your way to success.'

'Hope so.' He nodded in agreement, then pushed away from the rail to go fill up the water trough for the calves and scatter around some feed.

Poppy looked around and could see why he loved it so much out here. For all the dust and flies and stink of cow manure, there was a harsh kind of beauty to the place. There weren't lush rolling green paddocks out here, but a gentle swell of uncleared foothills covered in olive-green bushland, which made a pretty contrast to the whiskey-coloured feed on the ground. It was now late afternoon and the shrubby wilga and tall eucalypts scattered throughout the property caught the stream of golden sunlight as the sun sank behind the hills.

A fiery golden light silhouetted Jim as he stood across from her in the yard and the image made Poppy's mouth go dry. He was beautiful. He was like no other man she'd ever known. Streaked with dust and sweat, his jeans grubby and boots worn, he was breathtaking. His long-sleeved work shirt had been rolled up to expose corded forearms. And that damn hat. Clichéd as it was, he looked like the rugged, sexy cowboy that women fantasised about the world over. All that was missing from this scene was for him to take off his shirt and tip a bucket of water over his head, just like Hugh Jackman in *Australia*.

'I think we could make a jillaroo out of you after all, city girl. Thanks for your help today,' he said, coming to a stop before her. 'You look hot.'

So do you, thought Poppy, forcing herself to concentrate on what he was saying instead of the wayward thoughts running through her head.

'How about we cool off?'

Oh, that kind of hot. 'Oh God yes, air-conditioning.' She turned towards the big four-wheel drive, eager to feel the blast of cold air against her overheated body.

'I was actually thinking of a swim.'

'A swim?' But they had air-conditioning right here.

'There's a creek just over there. Come on, I've been thinking about it all day.'

'But I don't have any swimmers.'

She watched as a grin broke out on Jim's face and she tried to ignore the rather attractive way his eyes crinkled at the corners.

'Clothes are optional. Aw, come on, Poppy, don't be a sook. You'll like it, I promise.'

'Skinnydipping? Seriously?'

'Where's your sense of adventure?'

'Swimming naked and getting caught by someone is not my idea of fun.'

'Getting caught by someone? There's no one within miles of this place. Come on, we need to wash off some of this stink.'

She'd conveniently forgotten about her own appearance, but if he was dusty and sweaty she could only imagine what a picture she made. How attractive to stink on top of it!

Pulling out a towel from behind the back seat of the four-wheel drive, Jim took her hand and led her around the stockyards and towards a thicket of trees and shrubs that ran in a crooked line down a gentle slope. As they reached the bank, Poppy bit back a disappointed sigh. She'd been envisioning a crystal-clear creek, not this muddy-looking waterhole.

'It feels better than it looks. And it's wet, which is all I care about right now.'

Glancing over at him, Poppy saw that he already had half the buttons on his shirt undone. Slowly she kicked off her boots and undid the button of her jeans.

'Need some help?'

'No, thanks. I can do it.'

Jim was already shucking off his jeans and Poppy took advantage of the fact he was struggling to get his limbs untangled from his clothing to remove her own jeans and slip her T-shirt over her head. She didn't trust the look she'd seen in his eye earlier and wanted to go into the water under her own steam, without being thrown in. Tiptoeing into the water, she bit her lip as the cool water inched its way up her calf. Although the water wasn't freezing, her hot skin made it feel colder than normal. And it didn't help that she was a wuss when it came to cold water.

She was at about knee depth when she felt her body catapulted forward as warm arms surrounded her, turning her to land on something soft as she hit the water.

Thrashing around and trying to wipe the water from her eyes, she glared at Jim with a look that should have withered him to the bone, but only had him chuckling at her as he swam on his back further out into the middle of the water.

Poppy splashed at him ineffectually, then gave up and sank back into the water with a long sigh. It really did feel divine to finally wash off the dust and sweat, and once you were in the water it didn't look as murky as it had from the bank. Poppy submerged her shoulders and tipped her head back to the sky. She didn't jump when warm arms circled her body, and a smile spread across her face as Jim's lips nuzzled her neck. 'We make a great team, Poppy Abbott.'

'Oh yeah, I can just see me trading in my calculator for an akubra.'

'You could.' Something about his tone suggested an underlying seriousness and her smile disappeared.

His chest felt warm and solid behind her and the quiet sounds of the water flowed around them. Behind them she could still hear the calves calling for their mothers.

'You do know it's way too early to be having this conversation, don't you?'

'Is it?'

Poppy pulled out of his embrace and turned to face him. 'You're serious?'

'I know what I want,' he shrugged, holding her gaze levelly.

Poppy felt a familiar panic stirring inside. This was happening too fast. It was too soon. How could they have this conversation when she didn't even know what the hell she wanted?

Despite the wide open spaces, Poppy felt as though she were being cornered. Swimming for the bank, she climbed out of the water, snatching up the towel and sitting on the grass to dry herself.

Jim seemed to sense it was best not to crowd her and he stayed in the water, watching her.

'It doesn't have to be a big scary decision, Poppy.'

'Well, it is. Everything about us is scary.'

'Hasn't seemed that scary over the last few days.'

No, it hadn't. The last few days had been great, but that was because they hadn't talked about the future.

'What on earth would I do out here, Jim? I've worked hard to get where I am. I'm hardly going to throw all that away and take up a job working down at the corner store.'

'Poppy, you've got more initials after your name than I can count. Surely to God there's something you can do freelance from here? It's not the end of the earth, and you can always head back to the city now and again if you have to.'

'I'm not ready to throw away my career, Jim. I can't believe you think it's so damn simple to rearrange my entire life. Just pick up and move here.'

It was frustrating. She'd thought about it more often than she cared to admit over the last few days—without meaning to she'd found herself wondering how she could combine her job with Warrial. The little town certainly had grown on her. Maybe it was the connection she felt with Maggie and Alex. The places in the diary, buildings she could physically still see and touch, the knowledge that they had walked these same streets so long ago. Maybe it was losing Nan and having so many of her memories around her here. Maybe it was meeting this man and his daughter who had somehow worked their way into her heart.

'Look, it's too soon to be doing any of this anyway. We barely know each other. I can't just decide to move here based on a handful of days together. That'd be madness.'

'So when you leave it's over? Is that what you're saying?'

'No.' Poppy took a deep breath and tried to gather her thoughts together. 'I'm not saying it's over, but it's barely started and I think we need more time together before we jump into anything serious. I can come back to visit now and again, see how things go.'

273

'Commute?' he said, dubious.

'I can't stay out here forever, Jim. I need to get a job! 'This—us—happened at a really bad time. I need to sort myself out before I can think about adding you and Lacey into the mix.'

'A few years ago I could have moved to the city. Lacey wouldn't have been in high school, I wouldn't have stocked this place. But I've invested too much money into it to do anything but keep going. I have to make this pay off if I want to break even.'

And that was the problem. Someone was going to have to sacrifice something important if this thing between them stood any chance of working out.

Thirty

Poppy closed the gate and climbed back into Jim's ute. Once they were back on the main road, Jim took her hand in his, resting it on his thigh as he drove back towards town. It felt so right.

Looking through the windscreen, Poppy saw the large Hollywood-style gates coming up ahead. 'I meant to ask before, is it just me or is that elaborate security system just a tad over the top for out here?'

Jim snorted. 'You haven't heard about our resident multimillionaire yet?'

'Can't say I have.'

'Aldo Gersbach. Have you heard of Gersbach Pastoral Company?'

'Vaguely.'

'He's got properties all over Australia, prime real estate overlooking Sydney Harbour. The guy's loaded.'

Poppy raised an eyebrow as she looked over at Jim. 'If he's so rich, why would he live out here in Warrial of all places?'

'He doesn't live out here, he brings his family out for a few weeks of the year; the rest of the time they live in Europe.'

'Nice for some.'

'Not wrong.'

'I know I don't remember much, but I don't recall Nan and Pop's farm being something a pastoral company would be interested in. Wasn't it only around a hundred or so acres?'

'Probably. I think they'd sold some of the original place off over the years, but Gersbach didn't just buy your grandparents' old place, he bought the two farms on either side of it as well. Now it's pretty big. The house is huge and it's built from imported sandstone. They even put in a man-made lake, fully stocked with fish and big enough to ski on.'

'Have you ever been inside the house?'

'Yeah, right! Nah, the guy's super private. He brings his own staff and keeps to himself. You rarely see them.'

'Who would have thought something like this was hidden out here.'

'Once you let go of those preconceptions, it's amazing what you can discover about this place.'

Poppy let his slight dig go; she wasn't about to get involved in a drawn-out argument over city versus country. She had to face the fact that she wasn't the same woman who came out here a few weeks ago. Something, or more to the point, she amended glancing over at Jim, someone had changed her. Change could be exciting, and she was certainly no stranger to it. She'd moved more times in her life than she could count. But when it was change she couldn't control, well, that was a whole new ball game.

Poppy looked up as Lacey knocked on the back screen door. She waved her inside as she finished up a conversation with her mother on the phone.

'Hi. I was just on my way over,' she said, pressing end as she watched Lacey making herself at home and taking a seat at the kitchen table.

'Dad was about to start on one of his lectures again, so I told him I'd come over and see if you needed any help with anything, and bring back the diary.'

Yesterday Lacey had been curious about Maggie and her diary, so Poppy had given it to her to read.

'What was the lecture in aid of this time?' Poppy asked, biting back a smile as she put the finishing touches to the cheesecake she'd made for dessert.

Lacey gave a careless shrug as she traced the pattern on the front of the diary with her finger. 'Dad answered the phone this morning and kinda met Zac.'

'Oh. Who's Zac?'

'A friend,' she emphasised with a roll of her eyes. 'He's not like Jacob, he's ... different. He's kind of geeky, actually. I don't like him in that way, he's just really cool to hang out with.'

'Oh. Well, your dad probably just needs to get used to the idea of his little girl having friends who are boys.'

'I tried to tell him but he got all weird.'

'He doesn't have a gun at home, does he?' Poppy grinned.

Lacey scoffed loudly. 'Apparently he's going to polish it up for when he meets Zac. And he thinks kids today watch too much violence on TV.'

'It'll be okay, he just needs to get used to the idea. So what did you think of Maggie's story?'

'It's kinda depressing.'

'It sure didn't have a happy ending,' Poppy conceded.

'Why do you think Alex would have done that?'

Poppy gave her cheesecake a final look before pushing it aside. 'I don't know. I think the war really affected him. He suffered through a lot during his years away.'

'But the letters he wrote to Maggie were so cool. He really loved her.'

'Yes, I think he did.'

'It just doesn't make any sense. How could he kill her?'

'I guess we'll never know.' The thought made Poppy sad.

'Maybe he meant to shoot someone else, like that Walter guy.'

It was exactly the kind of thing that could have set Alex off. It also made far more sense than the story Walter gave at the inquest, that he'd always gotten along with Alex.

Poppy sighed. 'I kinda believe that too, but I guess we'll never know for sure.'

'Well, that's what I'm going to believe. Otherwise what was the point?'

'The point?'

'Yeah. There has to be a point. Why would Maggie have risked her life by making the wrong choice? She had so much ahead of her and then she died. What was the point?'

'Sometimes there is no point, Lace,' said Poppy, taking

a seat across the kitchen table from her. 'That's life. Sometimes horrible things happen and there's just no point.'

Poppy was shocked to see tears welling in the girl's eyes. 'Oh, Lace. I'm sorry, I shouldn't have given you the diary. It's not a very nice story.'

'It's not the diary. I guess I've just been thinking about stuff lately. About my mum.'

Oh no. Poppy felt a surge of apprehension run through her. She wasn't sure how she should handle this conversation.

'I used to wonder all the time, what was the point of my mum leaving us. I mean, if she didn't want me, why did she have me in the first place?'

'Lace, I highly doubt your mum doesn't want you—'

'She left me and Dad without a backward glance.'

'Relationships are complicated. I don't really know anything about what happened between your mum and dad, but sometimes people change and—'

'She decided she didn't want to be a mother any more.'

'You need to talk to your dad about it. I don't know why their marriage didn't work out, but what I do know is that it wasn't because of you.'

'Would you ever leave your kid behind?'

What? Holy cow. 'I'm the last person you should ask about this. I don't have kids.'

'You wouldn't. Admit it, even you, a person who has a *life*, wouldn't walk out on her own child.'

Poppy was about to argue the point but was stunned to realise that she couldn't. Even though she'd never been in that position, she knew, no matter what, she'd never be able to walk out on her child.

'See.'

Lost in the confusion of where this strong emotional response had come from, it took a while for Poppy to switch her attention back to Lacey.

'Well, anyway, I haven't seen Dad this happy in a long time.'

Poppy felt her heart skid sideways in her chest. 'Lacey, your dad and I—'

'Oh, don't panic. I'm not marrying you off or anything. I'm just saying he's been really happy lately, and it's because of you.'

'Oh. Well.' Poppy fiddled with the runner in the centre of the table.

Lacey gave a snort and rolled her eyes. 'Look, whatever it is you're doing, keep doing it. While he's in a good mood, he's not on my back!'

Poppy smiled as she got up from the table to get the salad from the fridge. She handed it to Lacey. 'Here, kiddo, hold this. We better get over there before he comes looking for us. I'll just get my jacket.'

A rap at the front door brought a frown to Poppy's face. She wasn't expecting any visitors. 'You can go back over if you want, tell your father I'll be there in a minute.'

She left Lacey in the kitchen and went down the hall. She opened the front door and gasped. 'What are you doing here?'

'I came to talk you out of leaving.'

Poppy stared at Gill in disbelief. 'Talk me out of it?'

'You don't have to leave.'

Poppy looked at the man who up until a few weeks ago had been her boss, her mentor and the biggest mistake she'd ever made, and marvelled at the difference a little time and distance could bring to a situation.

'Gill, I'm not coming back to work. I've handed in my resignation. I can't believe you came all the way out here to talk to me.' Poppy shook her head and moved to close the door. 'You need to go right now, otherwise . . .'

'Otherwise what?'

'Otherwise I'll have to take action. You've tracked me down and followed me out here uninvited. That's harassment.'

'It's not harassment when you know damn well you played your part in this affair.'

'It wasn't an affair, Gill!'

'Damn it, Poppy, I've left my wife, what more do you want?'

'I never wanted you to do that! Christ, Gill, I told you we were never going to have a relationship.'

'Because I was married. Yes, I know, but now I'm not, or at least I won't be soon. It changes everything. You left before I could tell you.'

Poppy stared at Gill and felt ill. What had she done? 'I left because I knew I couldn't work with you once I realised you had feelings for me. You need to go back and fix it with your wife, Gill.'

'Fix it? *Fix it?*' he said, his voice rising a notch. 'I'm in love with you, Poppy.'

'But, Gill, I'm not in love with you. I never was. It was a stupid drunken moment that should have never happened!'

'It was more than that and you know it, Poppy.'

'Look, I made a mistake. I admit I shouldn't have flirted with you the way I did. I know I was wrong to do that when I knew you were married. But you chose to be out with me that night. You were the one who was married, not me. You need to stop laying all the blame on me and accept your part in it too.'

'I left my wife because of you, Poppy! You owe me more than a brush-off!'

Poppy set her shoulders back and looked him in the eye. 'I owe you nothing, Gill. You made a decision to leave your wife. I had nothing to do with that. And if you think coming here and trying to make me cop the blame for it is somehow going to guilt me into changing my mind about our relationship then you've made a huge mistake.'

'Poppy, please, we just need to sit down and talk calmly about all this.'

'No, Gill. We don't. You need to leave. Now.'

'Poppy—'

'I think you've been asked to leave, mate,' came a voice from behind them.

Poppy swung around to see Jim leaning against the wall behind her. Oh Christ! How long had he been standing there?

'Who are you?' said Gill.

'Someone who's not going to tell you to leave twice. Now piss off.'

'Poppy?'

'Just go, Gill. I've resigned and I won't be coming back.'

Jim reached across her and shut the door in Gill's face, then locked it. 'If he doesn't leave in a few minutes, call the police.'

'Jim, wait.' Poppy reached for his arm as he turned away from her.

He shook her off and kept walking toward the back door.

'Jim!'

'What, Poppy?' he swung around and demanded roughly. 'What can you possibly have to say to me?'

'I, I wasn't expecting him to turn up here. It's not how it sounds.'

'Oh? And how does it sound?'

'It sounds like I was having an affair with him.'

'And?'

'I wasn't!'

'Call me an idiot, but the guy just told you he'd left his wife. I'm pretty sure he wouldn't have done that if there was nothing going on.'

'It wasn't like that!' she protested. Then, at Jim's narrowed glare, she swallowed nervously and added, 'I may have flirted with him a bit at work . . . Okay, I admit, I've done things I'm not exactly proud of in the past, but I've changed since I've been here. I've realised I didn't like the person I was becoming . . . I've changed. I'm not like that any more. '

'Very noble of you, Poppy.'

'I wasn't being noble! Damn it, Jim, I'm telling you I made a mistake, but he was the one who tried to make something more of it.'

'He left his wife to come after you, Poppy.'

'I had nothing to do with that.'

'Really? You don't consider sleeping with him had anything to do with breaking up his marriage?'

Poppy squeezed her eyes shut tightly and bit back her frustration. 'If he had just gone home to his wife instead of deciding to stay out drinking, it would never have happened.'

'You're unbelievable,' he said with a harsh laugh. 'Do you hear yourself?'

Poppy swallowed angry tears. It was a mistake. Why could no one else seem to get that through their head?

Jim gave a low growl and turned away from her.

'Jim?' Poppy called. He stopped and turned back to face her and the look on his face told her that nothing she said would make him change his mind about her.

'How could you stay quiet about all this when I told you what happened with my ex-wife? And to let Lacey overhear all that. I thought even you would have had a little more consideration. Now I have a distraught daughter to deal with.'

Oh no, she hadn't realised Lacey had hung around to listen. 'I'll go over and explain—'

'No. Don't bother.'

'This is nothing like what happened to you and your wife. I did not break up Gill's family.'

'I think it would be best if you just stayed away from Lacey.'

'From Lacey? Or from you?' Poppy asked quietly.

'I can't deal with this right now.' He pushed open the back door and disappeared down the side of the house.

Poppy sank onto a kitchen chair and stared outside at the backyard, feeling numb. Everything she feared the most was happening. Her glimpse into what a happily-ever-after looked like was over. She should have listened to her gut. This was exactly what happened when you let people into your life—they went and ruined it!

Thirty-one

Taking a deep breath, Poppy marched into her grand-mother's room, armed with garbage bags. She was doing this today. No more excuses, no more second thoughts.

Opening the wardrobe, she braced herself against the familiar scent. The row of colourful dresses, or 'frocks', as Nan had always called them, were hanging neatly in the cupboard just as they had the last time Nan had been in the house.

Just do it.

Tentatively, she reached out and withdrew the first garment, sliding out the coathanger and neatly folding the dress. They were much loved and well looked after dresses—made to last—and Poppy could recall each and every one of them. She moved on to the next one and ignored the warm flow of tears that trailed down her face. It had to be done sometime.

The hours passed but Poppy ignored the clock as it made its way from morning to afternoon. She had no appetite; she hadn't slept well last night and nothing mattered now but getting this last room finished so she could move on with her life.

She'd wanted to go next door to try to talk to Jim, but she'd chickened out, unsure if she could face that cold hostility she'd seen in his face. She'd sent him a text message, though, but he hadn't replied. She wished she could at least try to explain to Lacey—apologise for what she may have overheard—but she didn't want to anger Jim any further after he'd told her to stay away from his daughter. Besides, what was there to say? She couldn't justify her actions. She accepted she'd done something wrong, but she also knew that she wasn't the same person she'd been back then. Coming back here had made her take a good hard look at herself. It was all very well to say she lived her own life, made her own choices, and no one got hurt, but the fact was, someone did get hurt. She hadn't broken up Gill's marriage, but her actions had contributed to it. She needed to acknowledge that. And the fallout wasn't confined to Gill and his wife, it had also hurt Jim and Lacey.

Well, at least she wouldn't be around to hurt them any more. She'd been offered a job interview with a Melbourne-based firm and she planned on driving down there tomorrow. She'd do the trip in a few days; the interview wasn't until next week, so she was in no great hurry to get to Melbourne, and the time alone on the road would be a welcome relief. She needed to throw herself back into work to forget about Jim and the mistakes she'd made.

Driving down to the St Vinnies depot, Poppy parked

out the front and began unloading the bags of clothes from her car.

'Hello, dear.'

She looked up at the familiar voice and smiled. 'Hello Alice. I didn't know you worked here as well.' These women were into everything.

'We all like to volunteer where we can. What have you got there?'

'I've gone through Nan's cupboards and I thought I'd drop down some clothes. I don't really know what else to do with them.'

'Well, thank you very much. I'm sure they'll be put to good use.'

'My mum will be coming down to go through some of Nan's things, but there's quite a bit of Pop's family stuff, old albums and the like, which I thought you might be interested in,' she shrugged a little awkwardly. 'I don't know what else to do with it all, but I remembered what you said about wanting to start a museum and thought maybe you could put it to use. It would be nice to think someone else might find it interesting.'

'You know, ever since our chat the other day, I haven't been able to think of anything else *but* the museum. I've been looking into it and I think I'm going to start the ball rolling and get together a committee.'

'That's great,' Poppy smiled, and she really meant it. A museum of local history would be a fantastic addition to the little town.

'So what are your plans now?'

'I'm just about finished at the house. There's not much else to do there and it's time I got back to work. I'll be leaving tomorrow. '

'So soon?' Alice frowned at her, and Poppy brushed away a strange feeling of guilt. She didn't owe these people anything. So why did she feel as though she was letting them down by leaving town?

'I'm going for an interview and if I get it, I'm taking a job in Melbourne.'

'Oh, what a shame. I thought maybe you'd change your mind about your grandmother's house.'

'That was never really an option. The work I do is with companies who are based in big cities. Bit of a commute from out here,' she smiled tightly.

'Yes, well, you know what makes you happy, I suppose,' Alice said with a polite smile. 'It was lovely to have you back for a little while. You take care of yourself.'

Poppy watched as Alice turned her back and carried the last of the garbage bags into the store. She felt as though she'd just been dismissed. *Oh for goodness sake, Poppy! Snap out of it!* she told herself sternly. *You're leaving town. What do you expect, a farewell parade?*

Slamming the car door shut, she slid her sunglasses back onto her face and headed home to her grandmother's house. She wasn't sure what was wrong with her, but she sure hoped it wore off soon.

Leaving had been harder than she'd expected, but there was very little to actually do once she'd cleaned out Nan's room, except empty out the fridge and lock up the house.

She'd bumped into Lacey while watering her grand-mother's front garden one last time. She'd put too much hard work into it 'ignore it now. She met the teen's gaze and lifted a hand to wave.

Lacey stopped on the other side of the brick wall and adjusted her backpack on her shoulder.

'Hi,' Poppy said quietly, glad she'd stopped. 'How have you been?'

'Fine.'

'Well, that's good,' Poppy said, and took a deep breath. 'Listen, Lacey, about the other day—'

'You really hurt Dad, you know,' she cut in bluntly.

'Yes, I know. It's complicated, Lace. I didn't mean to hurt him. Or you,' she added gently.

'You didn't hurt me,' Lacey said sharply.

Poppy wasn't sure what to say. She knew the kid must be torn, seeing her father so angry after he'd been so happy. But Poppy was sad that things were strained between them after they'd been getting on so well. 'I'm glad I got to see you before I left. I was worried I wouldn't.'

'You're leaving?' Lacey stared at her angrily.

'I have to start a new job . . . well, if I get it, that is.'

'Whatever. See you around.'

'Lacey,' Poppy called as the girl turned away.

'I gotta get to school,' she muttered without turning back.

'Bye,' Poppy called weakly. She felt as though a door had just been slammed on her.

The obvious distress she'd caused two people she'd grown to love hurt her deeply. She understood why Jim had reacted the way he had—she got it. He thought she was the same kind of person his ex-wife had been. But it hurt that he hadn't bothered to at least *listen* to her side of the story. She wasn't anything like his ex-wife!

Poppy closed her eyes and fought back frustrated tears. She wished her Nan was here now to hug her tightly and tell her everything would be all right. She longed for that feeling she'd had as a child, the certainty that even when it felt as though the rest of the world had turned its back on her, there was always one person who would always be there for her. Somehow she knew Nan would have forgiven her . . . given her the benefit of the doubt. Unfortunately, it seemed, she would have been the only one.

Turning off the ignition, Poppy sat for a minute and listened to the lonesome crow as it let out a noisy caw high up in the branches of a gum tree.

Reaching across to the passenger seat, she gathered the flowers she'd cut from Nan's garden this morning and walked through the rusty old gate into the cemetery.

She placed the first bunch on her grandparents' grave and felt the heavy weight of grief settle on her heart as she whispered a goodbye.

Poppy had asked everyone she thought might be able to help her, but she hadn't been able to find out where Alex had been buried. She knew from the newspaper accounts that he had been buried on the same day as Maggie, that men from his army regiment had been the only people in attendance other than his mother. There had been a public outcry that he'd been buried in consecrated ground, given he was not only a murderer but also had committed suicide, and it was suggested that his body might have been removed from the cemetery and buried elsewhere. One thing was sure, Poppy had searched the cemetery records and found nothing. All trace of Alexander Wilson had vanished. Her heart ached that she couldn't find his resting place, to be able to place a flower on his grave. She would have liked to have shown him that not everyone had forgotten him.

She laid the flowers at the base of Maggie's headstone and smiled softly. It was almost like visiting an old friend. How many people got the opportunity to *really* know an ancestor who had been dead almost a hundred years? She'd been given a gift and Poppy's heart swelled in gratitude.

Maggie had never given up on Alex—or love. She'd made mistakes, and had been far from perfect, but she'd never given up on love the way Poppy had. Their story showed Poppy that even though life could be cruel, and there were no guarantees that you wouldn't get hurt, *not* risking your heart was not living. Maggie's passion, all of it, from the giddy heights of infatuation to the depressing and heart-wrenching lows, had been *living*. A life, no matter how short, filled with love had to be better than a long one filled with mediocre. At least Maggie had experienced real, honest love in her young life.

Poppy refused to look back in the mirror as she passed the *Goodbye from Warrial* sign. She would *not* look back. What was the point? She hadn't seen Jim again, and she couldn't bring herself to confront him. The hurt and bitterness on his face that last night was not something she wanted to experience again.

She'd slipped a note into his mailbox letting him know that she'd be back once she got herself sorted out and that she'd arranged to have the lawn mowed once a fortnight. She couldn't in good conscience allow him to continue the upkeep on Nan's house and she knew he'd never accept payment for it. Her note was polite and impersonal. No one reading it would suspect he'd managed to chisel out a piece of her heart. No one would know she'd fallen in love with not only Jim Nash but the whole package—his daughter, the town and even his stinking cattle, only to have it all ripped away.

Thirty-two

Paddocks flashed by her window as she drove. The highway stretched out before her and the radio station belted out a string of country-music hits. After a few minutes she turned the volume down and frowned as she tried to locate a strange knocking noise which seemed to be growing louder with each passing mile. She tried to ignore it, determined to make it into Glenwarren and find someone to check it out, but then the oil light came on and she knew she was in trouble.

Poppy pulled over onto the side of the road; the knocking was louder now and something told her pushing on was not a good idea. She turned off the engine and pulled out her mobile, giving her details to the roadside assistance operator, then she sat and waited.

After an hour or so she saw the orange lights of the NRMA truck coming over the rise. The mechanic listened to the noise, shaking his head slowly. 'You're lucky you stopped when you did or you would have seized the engine. I'll have to tow it back to the workshop.'

'How bad is it?'

'Sounds like a big end knock.'

'A what?'

'You've got a knock in ya big end. When was the last time you checked your oil?'

Poppy was still trying to work out if the guy had just insulted her. 'My oil?' When *was* the last time she'd checked her oil?

'Hmm, just as I suspected. Well, there's not a lot I can do out here. I'll have to get it back to the workshop.'

'Is it easy to fix?'

'Depends. Might be just a matter of cleaning out the sludge in the sump, or you might need a new engine. Depends on how much damage you've already done,' he said, scratching his head.

A new engine? Fantastic! 'How long will that take?'

'Gotta wait and see if that's what the problem is first. Climb in and I'll give you a lift into town.'

Poppy pulled herself up into the cabin of the large tow truck and stared dismally out through the front windscreen. So much for her big escape—she'd made it as far as Glenwarren.

There was no way the problem was going to be fixed today, so after leaving her car in the mechanic's capable hands, she caught a taxi and booked into a motel for the night.

The motel had a restaurant, so Poppy made her way to the bar to wait for an acceptable time to order dinner. No matter how hungry she was, she refused to sit down and order dinner at six pm only to be finished an hour later and back in her room staring at the TV for the remainder of the long lonely night.

Poppy ordered a glass of wine and took a look at her surroundings. As far as country motels went, it was pretty nice, but there was a slightly dated feel to the décor.

Accepting her wine from the same man who had booked her into her room earlier, she smiled her thanks and sighed as she took her first sip.

'Looks like you needed that.'

Poppy's glance slid sideways to a man seated two bar stools down from her. 'It's been a long day.'

'I hear ya.'

Poppy took another sip and hoped the man wouldn't try any awkward pickup lines. He was nearly old enough to be her father.

'Trevor Mackalvie.'

With a resigned sigh Poppy gave a nod and introduced herself. Dealing with her grandmother's bedroom, a broken heart, her job interview up the air and now her car broken down, the last thing Poppy needed was this middle-aged, balding George Clooney wannabe trying to chat her up. How bad could one day get?

'So, you just passing through?' Trevor pushed on, seemingly oblivious to her desire to be left alone.

'Yes.'

'Me too. Well, kind of. I'm on the road a fair bit with work.'

Biting back another sigh of frustration, Poppy fought to be civil. The guy was obviously a 'talker'. 'What line of work are you in?' she asked politely, because it seemed Trev wasn't taking the hint that she wasn't in a chatty mood.

'I manage a few properties for an investment company. Part of my job is trying to juggle the bookkeeping for the various properties my boss owns around the country.'

Poppy's curiosity was piqued, despite her irritation. That sounded interesting.

'So what's your day been like?' Trevor asked.

'Car trouble. I was on my way to a job interview.' That would obviously not be happening now—at least not by car. She'd have to organise a flight and deal with the hassle of retrieving her car later. Maybe after she got a taste of city life again this strange compulsion to feel miserable about leaving Warrial would ease. Maybe she'd just forgotten how much she liked the hustle and bustle of city life. It had caught her unawares, how much she liked living in a small town, but surely she would eventually have grown bored with it.

'What about you? What kind of work do you do?'

'I'm an accountant.' It was too complicated after the day she'd had to go into detail.

'Who you interviewing for? Someone local?'

'No, I'm supposed to be on my way to Melbourne.' Trevor whistled after Poppy told him the name of the company. She supposed she shouldn't have been surprised, it was a global company, but she hadn't expected a farm manager to know who they were. She really needed to work on her assumptions.

It was refreshing to be able to have a conversation with someone in a similar line of work, and before long they were discussing their respective jobs.

'I used to work for Abernathy and Sons,' he said, taking a sip of his beer.

Poppy raised an eyebrow. Abernathys had one of the best reputations in the business. And its operations were a world away from Glenwarren.

'You're wondering why I left?' he asked with a dry chuckle. She gave him a guilty smile. 'I guess that old saying is true about being able to take the boy outta the country. I got sick of the city and the stress. I also had a divorce hanging over my head that didn't help matters any. I wanted to get back to where I grew up and so here I am.'

'You don't miss your old way of life?'

'Sometimes, but then that was a long time ago. I'm happy doing what I'm doing now. I'm a bit of a jack-of-all-trades nowadays. I get to drive between the New South Wales properties and then fly up north when I need to touch base with the bigger properties we have up there. Beats fighting with peak-hour traffic each day.'

'That's a lot of travel, though.'

'Yep. It's getting to the stage where I need to be everywhere at once and can't quite divide myself in that many ways. Mind you, if I were only doing the book work I could do my job just fine sitting behind a desk somewhere. Hell, I could even do it in my pyjamas at home if I wanted to. These days everything can be done online, but I need to be out in the field to keep on top of everything.'

'Our restaurant is open now, thought you might like a menu,' said the bartender.

Poppy read through the dishes and realised she was starving. By mutual agreement, she and Trevor decided to eat at the bar together. Poppy was feeling a bit silly at her rash assumption that Trevor had been trying to hit on her. He was only after some conversation and company. Who could blame the guy? He spent all day on the road driving hundreds of kilometres between farms. Poppy asked him more about his boss and the properties he managed and was surprised to discover one of them was out around Warrial.

'It wouldn't be Millbrook by any chance, would it?'

'Yeah. That's one of them.'

Poppy chuckled. 'My grandmother used to live on that property, or at least one of the properties that became Millbrook.'

'Small world, huh,' he said, tipping his beer glass against hers in a toast.

'So how many properties do you handle?'

'We've got five down here. I've just come from Millbrook actually. And then we've got another three up north. One in Far North Queensland and two in the Northern Territory. They've been our problem children. Everything up there is done on a much bigger scale, including the stuff-ups!' he said, grinning. 'I just don't get the time to concentrate on our smaller properties around here like I used to.'

Later, after they'd finished eating, Poppy said, 'I just hope I can still make the interview. I doubt the car will be fixed in time to drive, so I'll have to fly.'

Trevor considered her silently for a few moments. 'You know, I wasn't kidding about this job getting too big for me. The boss and I have been talking for a while about dividing up my job, keeping the accounting and paperwork for the properties down here separate from the bigger ones up north. Mind you, neither of us has actually sat down and done anything about putting the plan into action, but maybe it's time we did. Maybe you should have a chat with him before you rush off to Melbourne.'

'I don't know anything about farms.'

'That's not essential, and you'll learn. Your forensic background would come in very handy. We need someone used to paying very close attention to detail. My boss is a foreign exchange dealer by trade, and you've got experience dealing with overseas bank accounts and whatnot. You'd actually be perfect. These properties are only a small part of his business dealings. We've got to outsource a lot of the stuff I'm not familiar with, not to mention the things I don't have time for. In fact the more I think about it, the more I think this would be the perfect solution. Too much time is wasted when we have to outsource. If we had someone with your experience, we'd alleviate that problem altogether.'

Poppy was surprised by his offer, but she couldn't really see herself driving hundreds of kilometres each week like he did.

'If you were based around here somewhere, the properties aren't too far away. An easy day's drive, but often the job can be done over the computer and phone. There'd be no need for you to be on site all the time.'

Poppy chewed the inside of her lip thoughtfully as a bubble of excitement began to rise inside her. Hadn't Jim suggested this very kind of job? In her old line of work it hadn't really been an option—at least not with a new employer. This would be a career change. She'd no longer be working in forensic accounting. She mulled this over for a while and waited for a burst of indignation at the possibility of sacrificing her career, but it didn't come. The thought of leaving her career really didn't sting as much as she had anticipated.

If she had work out here she and Jim might stand a chance. She would be able to give him time to calm down and maybe then she could approach him again, show him she wasn't the kind of person who would intentionally break up a marriage. There was a part of her that refused to give up hope. There was also a part of her that didn't want to leave. Maybe her relationship with Jim wouldn't go anywhere—that was a possibility she had to face—but that didn't change the fact she liked living out here. Would that change if she knew for certain Jim would never forgive her? Could she live out here if she didn't have Jim and Lacey in her life? She honestly didn't know, but she thought she might be prepared to give it a go.

A new start.

Not only a new career but a new life.

Poppy did her best to concentrate on the rest of the evening's conversation, but the truth was she could barely recall a single word of it later that night, alone in her motel room. She turned Trevor's business card around in her fingers as she sat on the edge of her bed staring at the phone. All she had to do was make one phone call. She put the card on the bedside table and crawled under the blankets. She'd sleep on it tonight, give Trevor a chance to talk to his boss, and then see how she felt about it tomorrow.

Thirty-three

The knock on the back door startled Poppy as she looked up from the cup of coffee she'd been stirring. For a moment she felt like Maggie with her *insides jumping about like a cage of butterflies*. She walked around the bench and opened the door.

'Hello, Jim.'

'Hi, Poppy.'

She'd arrived home yesterday afternoon. Poppy thought she'd give him one more day before she went over and knocked on his door; he'd beaten her to it.

She'd grieved. And while it still hurt to think about Nan no longer being here, she was able to accept the sadness that came with it. She no longer had to push it away, frightened to feel the loss.

Poppy stared at Jim, drinking in his appearance as

though he were some figment of her imagination and might disappear at any moment. But had that been the case, he'd be wearing a smile and throwing his arms around her, not standing here with an almost unreadable expression as he searched her face.

'I saw your car in the driveway,' he said, shoving his hands in the front pockets of his jeans. 'I thought you were heading for Melbourne.'

She looked at him, striving for a calm she wasn't feeling. 'So did I. My car had other plans.'

'Alice filled me in on your job in Glenwarren,' he said tightly.

Alice hadn't wasted any time. Poppy had only spoken to her about a half hour ago.

'You took a job, just like that?' he asked.

Poppy heard the anger in his voice and frowned. 'I wasn't planning on it. It just happened.'

'So let me get this straight. I beg you to get a job in Warrial and all I get is the I'm-not-giving-up-my-career-for-you speech. And yet here you are, accepting the first job some stranger offers you in Glenwarren.'

'I wasn't looking for a job there, Jim, it just happened! And it's not like it's just *any job*, it's a career path I hadn't thought of before, and not one that was available in Warrial. Anyway,' she said feeling defensive, 'why do you care? You refused to even speak to me before I left.'

'You *lied* to me. I had a right to be pissed off.'

'You didn't even give me a chance to tell my side of the story!'

'You left before I had a chance to ask.'

'How much time did you need? Excuse me if I didn't

want to hang around just to get the cold shoulder from you.'

'I didn't expect you to leave so soon!'

'Yeah, well, I didn't expect you to take Gill's word over mine.'

'It took me by surprise, and you *did* lie to me.'

'I did not lie to you! I just didn't tell you about it because it happened before I even met you. It was in the past, and all right, I get why it upset you—maybe I should have told you about it once I found out what happened with your wife, but I didn't. I was ashamed of what happened and maybe I knew you'd freak out and refuse to have anything to do with me. I really liked you, Jim. I wasn't expecting to . . . fall in love with you.'

There was a silence and Poppy held her breath as she waited for him to say something.

'It caught me off guard, brought back some painful memories,' Jim said, lowering his gaze to the floor.

Poppy closed her eyes briefly. 'I get that. But you should have at least listened to my side of the story instead of turning your back on me.'

She watched as he rubbed a hand across the back of his neck, a sure sign he was frustrated, and her heart tugged at the familiar gesture.

'You're right. I should have at least let you explain. I'm sorry.'

His apology took her by surprise and she let out a shaky breath.

'Look,' Poppy explained, 'I was the kind of woman who kept things simple. I was into casual relationships—sometimes one-night stands—and before you make a judgement call on that, I'll point out that I didn't go out on the prowl every weekend to pick up stray men. I was too wrapped up in my job for that. But if it looked as though the relationship could get serious, I ended it. I pushed people away before they could get too close . . . before they could *matter*. I'm sorry if that offends you, but it's the way it was,' she said with a shrug.

'I'm not offended. We just come from two different backgrounds where relationships are concerned. I married young and thought it was going to be forever. Lacey's mother and I met at university and I'd never had any other serious girlfriends before her. If I'd chosen a different path, maybe I'd have been like most of my mates and played the field a bit before I settled down. But I didn't. I don't judge you for not wanting a serious relationship. It was never about your lifestyle, Poppy.'

'Lifestyle? You make it sound as though I was a swinger or something.'

He ignored her outburst and continued. 'It was hearing your boss was leaving his wife for you. It felt like you'd slapped me across the face.'

Poppy gave a tired sigh. 'I guess it would have been a bit of a shock to walk in and find a man swearing his undying love on my doorstep.'

'To say the least.'

Poppy noticed his hand was rubbing the back of his neck again and she reached over, pulling it down gently. 'It's okay. I probably would have reacted exactly the same way if I were you.'

Jim stared at her, his gaze searching. 'You were right, you know,' he said quietly. 'I guess I spent so long being angry that the two people I trusted the most in my life had betrayed me that I didn't really consider what I might have done to stop it happening in the first place. When I first took over my granddad's business I felt as though I had a lot to prove. Even though I'd been born and raised here, people were used to dealing with him and suddenly this young upstart takes over and starts trying to implement different ideas . . . it took a long time to gain their respect and I was terrified of losing the business Granddad had spent so long building. I probably didn't pay the kind of attention to a young wife that I should have. I lived and breathed the business and I should have picked up on how miserable she was out here.'

Poppy listened, knowing how hard it was to have to look deep inside and take responsibility for your life.

'I should have stopped you leaving.'

'I would have had to leave eventually. It was weird how it all happened. I'd have been in Melbourne by now if my car hadn't broken down.'

'I would have followed you.'

Poppy swallowed over a lump in her throat at his words.

'So tell me what this big career change is then.'

'I'm the new accounts manager for Gersbach Pastoral Company.'

Jim lifted an eyebrow in surprise. 'Yeah?'

'Yep. I'm overseeing all their New South Wales properties, including Millbrook. It's pretty huge, but I like a challenge. I think it'll be good for me.'

'So you'll be based in Glenwarren?' Jim asked. 'Well, I guess it's a lot bloody closer than Melbourne.'

'Actually, that's the reason I came back this weekend,' she said, smiling slightly. 'I have to make up my mind by Monday if I want to sign a lease on a flat in Glenwarren.'

'I don't understand. What's stopping you?'

'I wanted to see if there was anything worth sticking around Warrial for first. I can pretty much do this job from anywhere with an internet service. Glenwarren is an option, but so is staying here. I've kinda got used to this place.'

Jim didn't say anything and Poppy felt the first twinge of disappointment.

Then he broke the silence, saying softly, 'I'd made up my mind to follow you to Melbourne. I wanted to tell you I'd do anything I had to do to be with you.'

Poppy could only stare. He'd been willing to give up everything to be with her?

'I'm not sure Lacey would have been too happy about that.'

'Are you kidding? *Melbourne?* She's probably already packed. You can be the one who tells her that's no longer on the cards,' he said with a small grimace.

Hope welled up inside her as they looked at each other. *He still loves me,* she thought with a surge of relief.

'I'm so sorry, Jim. I never meant to hurt you or Lacey,' she said, taking a step closer to him.

Jim pulled her into his arms and kissed her, washing the last of the doubt from her mind.

'Stay.'

'Okay.' *Okay? Seriously? After all that . . . just okay?* Poppy's inner feminist rolled her eyes and threw her hands in the air, giving up. Poppy ignored her; this was where she wanted to be more than anywhere else in the world and she couldn't be happier.

Epilogue

It seemed only fitting that when Poppy and Jim had their engagement party it should be held here, in the little hall on the outskirts of Warrial.

Jim had proposed two months after she'd moved back into her nan's house and started work for Gersbach Pastoral. She'd accepted—how could she not? She fell more in love with the man with every passing day.

They'd had some pretty big decisions to make, not least of all where they'd live, and Jim had put forward a plan that had moved her to tears.

'Here's what I was thinking,' he'd said, handing her a glass of wine and sliding across the property section of the local newspaper.

Poppy glanced down at the paper as she took a sip of wine and almost spluttered it across the table when she saw the large red circle Jim had made on the page.

'I think we should sell both our houses and buy the McPherson's place,' Jim explained, watching her closely for a response.

Poppy could only stare at the photo of the old house in shock. Maggie's house . . . the Abbott farmhouse that had been moved to the McPherson property when Gersbach had brought her grandparents' farm.

'What do you think?'

'But what about your plans to move out to your place . . . You've been doing up the house out there,' she said faintly.

Jim shrugged. 'I've only done the basics . . . we could rent it out. I'll still use it for grazing . . . But when I saw this, well, it kind of seemed like fate,' he smiled.

Maggie's house . . .

Poppy's smile had been quickly followed by a flood of happy tears. 'Yes!' she'd nodded, reaching for Jim and pulling him close. 'I can't imagine anything I'd like more.'

Poppy left the CWA ladies to finish setting up the hall for the party and walked outside.

It was quiet. Peaceful, like the cemetery had been.

It was strange to be here on such a happy day, in the place where the whole unspeakable tragedy had unfolded that night.

At one time, back in the early 1900s, this narrow little country road had been the main highway. The coroner's report had said Maggie had been walking along the old highway, but seeing the road today, it was hard to imagine it ever being much more than a country track.

The moment I see him I get the most dreadful attack of nerves and I can't, for the life of me, string together a complete sentence!

*All I know now is that when I reach the point where
I think I can no longer go on. I remember your face,
your smile, the way your eyes light up when you're
happy . . .*

*I know he still loves me. In my heart, I believe he will
find the peace he needs and maybe then we'll finally
be together . . .*

Poppy heard the words from Maggie's diary and Alex's
letters echo around her. She stepped onto the small wooden
bridge, placed her hand on the railing and breathed deeply.
This was where it all ended. Right here, she thought sadly.
She stood there a few more moments; she wasn't sure she
believed in ghosts, but she could understand how tragic
moments in time might leave behind a lasting imprint.

Poppy closed her eyes and pictured the scene as it had
been described in the newspaper accounts. Even though it
had been late at night, the reports had said the moon had
been very bright. Around her it was almost as though she
could hear the chatter from inside the hall spilling out into
the darkness. The yelling and laughter of farewells being
called out as people began to trickle out into the night to
make their way home.

Maggie

It was not turning out the way she'd planned. All night she'd
been waiting for Alex, but she feared he wasn't going to show.
He couldn't leave her . . . She wasn't sure how she would
cope if he left and never came back. She couldn't let him.

To add to her distress, Walter had shown up.

With a heavy heart, Maggie left the hall when the dance ended with no option but to go home. She felt close to tears. Walter was determined to walk her home, and Maggie was too miserable to bother protesting. All she could think of was that Alex had already left and she would never see him again.

As they approached the bridge Maggie saw a figure materialise from the shadows.

'Wilson, I already told you—she doesn't want to see you,' Walter said in a low voice as he stepped in front of Maggie.

'What?' She pushed Walter aside and stood between the two men, searching for answers even as her heart leapt at seeing Alex. *He'd come.* 'What are you talking about, Walter?'

'I saw him hanging around here earlier—I was trying to spare you a confrontation.'

'That was none of your concern, Walter,' Maggie snapped. She turned her gaze onto Alex and her breath caught at the sadness she saw in his eyes.

'Alex . . . please don't go. Dulcie said you were leaving town . . . I'll do anything, Alex . . . I'll stay away from you—whatever you want—but please don't leave. I couldn't bear it if you weren't here.'

Alex didn't say anything, but stood looking into her face, his eyes dark pools of sadness. 'I can't do this any more, Maggie,' he finally whispered.

'Then take me with you,' she said quickly, her hands grabbing at his arm. 'Please, Alex. I love you.'

Alex shook his head slightly. 'I can't take you with me, Maggie. Not where I'm going. You need to find a man who can love you the way you need to be loved. Who can give you the life you deserve. I can't do that.'

'Alex, please.'

'Just leave her, Wilson. Haven't you done enough damage?' Walter intervened.

'Shut up, Hicks. This is none of your concern,' Alex growled dangerously.

'I'm making it my concern,' Walter said, taking Maggie's arm and trying to pull her away.

'Let her go!' Alex demanded, taking a step forward.

Maggie struggled to pull her arm out of Walter's hold. 'Walter, let me go right now,' she demanded.

She was sure that it happened fast, too fast, and yet in her mind it seemed as though it were in slow motion. From behind his back Alex pulled out a pistol and aimed it at Walter, who was pulling frantically on her arm. He dragged her towards him, just as a loud explosion sounded and the world went dark. She felt herself falling, so slowly, and she heard Alex crying her name. She wanted to go to him . . . reach for him . . . but he sounded so far away . . . and then there was only silence.

Poppy

Opening her eyes, Poppy wiped away the tears that had begun to fall. *Oh Alex,* she thought sadly, *I know in my heart you never meant to hurt Maggie that night. No one will ever be able to prove it, but I know it. You're not a murderer or a monster.* She wasn't sure why it was Alex

311

she thought of straightaway, but somehow she knew that whatever had happened, Maggie would have forgiven him.

Somewhere nearby she could hear a farmer on a slasher; the smell of freshly cut hay floated in on the breeze.

She didn't want to remember them here, on that night so long ago. She wanted to remember them during happier times. She wanted to remember their love.

Poppy took one final look at the road leading to the bridge. She hoped that the Alex Maggie loved had come back to her after that night and he had finally found some peace.

Poppy heard her name being called and turned to see Lacey and Jim waiting for her. Her heart lifted at the sight and she raised her arm to wave back. If Maggie had taught her anything, it was that love was worth fighting for, and there was no guarantee how long you may have it for. Poppy didn't intend to waste a single minute. Straightening her shoulders, she headed towards the hall where her new family stood ready to celebrate the beginning of their life together, and she couldn't wait to get started.

Author's Note

This story is based on real events that happened in my home town at the Warrell Creek hall back in 1920. I was given a newspaper clipping which reported the murder-suicide, and the moment I read it I was hooked.

One bright moonlit evening a young girl and her friend walked home after a dance. A man approached her, took out a gun and shot her before turning the gun on himself. That man was Alick McLean, a returned veteran, and the young woman was Gertie Trisley, a much loved and kind-hearted nineteen-year-old who was respected throughout the district.

I had so many questions and the writer in me just couldn't let the story go.

While researching the story, I came across a website with a series of letters written by a soldier during the First

World War and, much to my delight, I discovered this soldier was Alick McLean.

Through these letters I discovered a young man who loved his sister and his mother, who wrote to them often and spoke of his pride and admiration for his fellow soldiers fighting alongside him in a faraway country. He was full of that famous Aussie larrikin humour and strength that came to define our nation after this terrible war.

He received a Distinguished Conduct Medal for bravery but his war ended on 4 September 1918 when he was wounded in action, losing his right eye. He returned home and went to work with his cousin as a timber getter, hauling logs from the bush with bullock teams.

It was hard to imagine this Alick as the same man who, on the night of 25 November 1920, shot and killed a young woman with no apparent provocation and then turned the gun upon himself.

Following the shooting the local newspaper was filled with reports from the funerals and the coroner's inquest; I have copies of these transcripts on my web page if you'd like to read them (http://karlylane.com).They certainly make fascinating reading. However, take note, the language used back then was somewhat confronting compared to newspapers of today.

My heart went out to Gertie and her family, but I was drawn to Alick and felt compelled to give him a voice. I felt a need to delve into the background of this horrible tragedy to try to make sense of a seemingly senseless act.

There could never be an excuse for what Alick did, and it wasn't my intention to make one. However, behind the scenes in this era there was unrest and upheaval. There *were things that needed to be brought to the foreground in order to better understand some of the influencing factors behind this tragedy. How so many of our young men left home excited by the prospect of adventure overseas, to fight for their country only to return home and discover they no longer seemed to fit into their old lives.*

The characters of Maggie and Alex are fictional, as is Alex's war history. There was an Operation Michael, as mentioned in the story, and I tried to place it in the time line as closely as possible, but if there are any errors relating to some of the timing, it was entirely my fault, and I hope you'll forgive the bending of some minor points for the good of the story.

The Granny Barton and Tobias Brown incidents described in Maggie's diary entries were based on real events. Granny Sutton, who was Alick McLean's aunty, was a staunch supporter of recruiting. Tobias Brown is based on a man named Edward Searle, who was, in fact, a relative of mine. He did indeed goosestep along behind the parade with a pot on his head in protest at the war and was subsequently thrown into the Nambucca River. I loved being able to entwine real local history and colourful characters into this book.

I had no idea when I first started writing this book that I would be discovering so much about my own family history in the process, or that I would have such a strong connection to these two people I wasn't even related to. To be able to walk down the main street of Macksville and know that many of the buildings standing here today were there when Alick and Gertie had been alive makes me feel as though, despite the distance of time, we're all very much still connected and that it's important we never forget our past.

This novel is more than the tragic story of two lives destroyed. It's about a nation who sent their sons, brothers, fathers and husbands to a war that changed not only their generation but generations to follow.

Karly Lane

Acknowledgements

Trevor Lynch—without you this book would never have been written. Thank you so much for telling me the story of Alick McLean, I can't imagine life without knowing this man.

To Michelle Ennis and the Trisley families of Macksville—thank you for all your help and sharing your family stories, photos and that amazing re-enactment video with me. Although Maggie was never intended to be Gertie, I hope she did a good job representing her nonetheless and that Gertie would have approved.

Fran Farrall and Professor John Mcquilton, for your academic assistance with all things related to rural Australia and the First World War.

Thank you to Barry Stride and Geoff Minett for your local knowledge.

The Country Women's Association of Australia for being the magnificent organisation that you are and for all the fantastic work you've done in the past right through to the present day.

Graeme Henderson—I thank you from the bottom of my heart. I can't tell you enough how much your generosity has meant to me.

Judy and Chris, thank you so much for your stockyard help. Brenton Miller, as usual you were my go-to man for all things related to stock agents; thank you so much for your help. And Susan Howle, a big thank you for coming up with the details of Poppy's new career.

As usual, a huge thank you to Julia, my amazing editor, for all her wonderful suggestions, and to the staff at Allen & Unwin for bringing you my books.

A huge thank you to my husband and children for their patience and support, and to my parents, Greg and Elaine, for all they do.

And lastly to all our ANZACs past and present; thank you for doing our nation proud.

ALSO BY KARLY LANE

NORTH STAR
Karly Lane

Since her divorce a year ago, Kate Thurston feels like she's lurched from one disaster to another. Her teenage daughter, Georgia, seems to have morphed into a monster overnight, and her son Liam breaks her heart with his sad brown eyes.

When Kate receives news that her grandfather has bequeathed her North Star, the vast property that has been in her family for generations, it feels like the perfect opportunity to flee the hectic pace of city life for a calmer rural existence.

As soon as she arrives at North Star, however, Kate realises she's going to need every ounce of determination to restore the rundown homestead to its former glory and fulfil her dream of turning it into a bush retreat. And as for the farm, well it's in utter disarray.

As she starts to make headway with the homestead's restoration, and falls for a local bloke, Kate finally feels like life is going right for her. Then her ex-husband comes to town and triggers a series of events that will change her life forever . . .

With dollops of mystery and lashings of suspense, *North Star* will have you reading through the night.

ISBN 978 1 74331 009 0

MORGAN'S LAW
Karly Lane

When Sarah Murphy returns to Australia she desperately needs a break from her high-powered London life. And though mystified by her grandmother's dying wish for her ashes to be scattered under 'the wishing tree' on the banks of the Negallan River, she sets out to do just that.

While searching for the wishing tree, Sarah stays in the small township of Negallan. It's there that she finally has some time to relax and unwind, there that she finds herself drawn to a handsome local farmer, and there that she discovers her enquiries about her grandmother are causing disquiet within the powerful local Morgan family.

Will the Morgans prevent Sarah from discovering the truth about her grandmother? And should she risk her glittering career in the UK for a simpler existence in the country, and the possibility of true love?

Morgan's Law takes you on a compelling journey into a young woman's hopes and dreams.

ISBN 978 1 74331 423 4

BRIDIE'S CHOICE
Karly Lane

Bridie Farrell and Shaun Broderick come from opposite sides of the tracks. But unlike Bridie's family, who are perennial strugglers, the Brodericks are the wealthy owners of Jinjulu—one of the most prestigious properties in the district.

All her life Bridie has longed to leave the small town she grew up in. But time after time family responsibilities have kept her anchored there. Meanwhile, Shaun's dream of taking over the management of Jinjulu is dashed by his dictatorial father who tries to rule Shaun's life both on and off the farm.

The Brodericks are dismayed when Shaun falls in love with 'that Farrell girl', whom they deem unsuitable. And they don't just make their feelings clear to Shaun but to Bridie as well.

Faced with a choice, Bridie must decide whether to turn her back on her heart or her dreams in order to make the biggest decision of her life . . .

From the author of the bestselling rural sagas *North Star* and *Morgan's Law*, this absorbing novel is about alternative destinies and the power of love.

ISBN 978 1 74331 757 0